Praise for *Belonging*

'*Belonging* conjures flesh-and-blood characters caught up in the horrors of the Indian Cawnpore Massacre of 1857 and of the First World War. In perfectly judged, luminous prose which sings off the page like the sharpest poetry, Umi Sinha stitches together the stories of three generations with the precision, skill and artistry reminiscent of exquisite needlework. This is a big-hearted book from an author who can write with luminous delicacy and unflinching, visceral immediacy.'
                                                    Catherine Smith

'I am overflowing with admiration for Umi Sinha's *Belonging*. What makes this such a captivating book to read? It enriches you. The carefully reconstructed histories of the First World War remember Indian soldiers who gave their lives and those who were betrayed, massacred, and – just as tragically – those who survived. Sinha quickly and effortlessly makes her characters come alive. She has precision timing when it comes to hooking the reader with a moment or a half-revealed situation. You have to keep reading. She is simply one of the best storytellers I've come across in a very long time.'
                                                    Kadija Sesay

'*Belonging* is a mature, measured and relentlessly unfolding novel about friendship, alienation, betrayal, loss, self-discovery and unfulfilled love. It is also about secrets: the unspoken and unspeakable stories that shape the actions and relationships of humans. The book achieves a larger, darker resonance with the layering of English ideas of race and class on India's caste system. Here, the betrayals, the silences and atrocities we discern in the relat̶͟ wider
context of ͟ ͟ ͟ ͟ ͟ ͟ ͟ ͟ ͟ ͟ ͟ ͟ ͟ ͟ ͟ ͟ ͟ ͟ ͟ l, told
beautifully ͟ ͟ ͟ ͟ ͟ ͟ ͟ ͟ ͟ ͟ ͟ ͟ ͟ ͟ ͟ ͟ ͟ ͟ ͟ Ross

BELONGING

umi sinha

First published in 2015 by

Myriad Editions
59 Lansdowne Place
Brighton BN3 1FL

www.myriadeditions.com

3 5 7 9 10 8 6 4 2

A CIP catalogue record for this book is available
from the British Library

ISBN (pbk): 978-1-908434-74-6
ISBN (ebk): 978-1-908434-75-3

Designed and typeset in Baskerville
by Linda McQueen, London

Printed by CPI Group (UK) Ltd
Croydon CR0 4YY

To the memory of
CLAIRE H. SANSOM,
SOE code-breaker, and one of those
teachers one never forgets,
who encouraged me to believe I could write

And for ANN CHALK,
because I promised

'It is interesting that Hindus, when they speak of the creation of the universe, do not call it the work of God, they call it the play of God, the Vishnu lila, lila meaning play. And they look upon the whole manifestation of all the universes as a play, as a sport, as a kind of dance…'

Alan Watt, *Zen and the Beat Way*

'The past is never dead. It is not even past.'

William Faulkner

FAMILY TREE

Narrators' names in capital letters

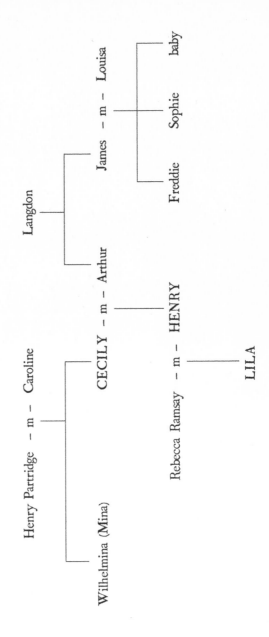

Lila

The child climbed up the shelves of the almirah, placing her bare feet between the folded piles of embroidered linen. She knelt on the top, leant down and closed the heavy carved doors, then pulled herself on to the wide shelf that ran above door height along the back corridor of the bungalow. The shelf, used to store old luggage, was covered in dust, and she looked regretfully at the marks it left on her nightdress. Her ayah would be cross, but it was too late to think of that now.

There was room to stand upright on the shelf. Balancing like a tightrope walker, she picked her way through the bags and cases until she reached the fanlight above the dining room doors. The panes of glass were fly-spotted and covered in cobwebs. She knelt and brushed the cobwebs aside, wiping the stickiness off on to a nearby carpet bag, then licked a finger and rubbed a small clean circle into the glass. Now she could see.

In front of her the frill of the punkah hung motionless; the punkahwallah would still be on the front verandah, fanning the guests in the drawing room. She looked down at the table.

The silver, which tarnished quickly at this time of year, was freshly polished, and the cut glass sparkled in the candlelight. She peered at the tablecloth but its elaborate embroidery was obscured under the weight of crockery, glass and silver; all she could see was the border on her side, which seemed to consist of a repeating Tree of Life motif with brightly coloured flowers and fruit. Her mother had been working on it for months, shut away in her room. It was a surprise for her father's birthday – her mother had laid the table herself so that even the servants would not see.

Rain rattled on the corrugated roof and humidity wrapped around her like a blanket. She knew she should not be up there but she was eager to see her father's face when the tablecloth was revealed in all its glory. She had been planning it all day, and slipped away as soon as he had finished reading to her, while her ayah was helping her mother to dress.

She hoped they would not be long. It was uncomfortable kneeling on the shelf. Bits of grit were digging into her knees and she pinched her nose to stop herself sneezing. She shifted to ease her legs and one foot slipped off the shelf behind her.

'Oho! What are you doing up there, baby? Are you up to mischief again?'

She jumped as Afzal Khan's deep voice boomed out. He reached up and grasped her foot, pulling her back towards the edge.

'Sssshh,' she whispered, trying to wriggle free. 'Let go!'

He lowered his voice. 'Come down, Missie Baba. Memsahib will be angry if she sees you up there. And you will get very dirty.'

'Ssssshh!' she said again. 'I want to see the tablecloth!'

'Where is Ayah?'

'In Mother's room. She thinks I'm in bed. Please don't call her!'

He laughed. 'Don't make such big-big eyes at me! Who would believe you are twelve years old? My daughter is the same age as you and she is soon to be betrothed. Now be quiet. I'm going to open the door. Do I look smart?'

She turned and peered at him. He was wearing a white starched tunic with polished brass buttons and his saffron turban and cummerbund.

'Your turban isn't straight.' She reached down and adjusted it for him. 'Now you look very handsome.'

He laughed and tickled her foot and she jerked it away, stifling a giggle. 'Stop it!'

He took a deep breath, stood up tall and pushed open the doors, emerging into the dining room below her. The stiffly pleated fan on his turban fluttered as he crossed the room to open the doors that led into the drawing room. He bowed. 'Dinner is served, memsahib.' Then he came back through the dining room and out the doors beneath her, closing them behind him.

She leant over and snatched at the fan of his turban. He grabbed at it, settling it back on his head, then turned and shook his finger. 'You behave, or I'll call Ayah.'

'Will you save me some birthday cake?'

'If you behave like a jungli, no – climbing up like a monkey to spy on people!'

'Oh, please, Afzal Khan!'

'Then stop eating my head. I have work to do.' He walked to the door that led out to the compound and called to the bearer to be ready to bring in the dishes.

She turned back to the fanlight. The punkahwallah must have moved round from the drawing room, because the cloth frill of the punkah was moving now, stirring the candle flames in the silver candelabra so that the leaping tigers and rearing elephants on their bases moved in the shifting light and the open mouths of the mahouts on the elephants' backs seemed to quiver in terror.

The drawing room doors opened and her father came through with a pregnant lady on his arm. He looked tired and preoccupied, as he had for some days now. As he approached the table he glanced up and for a moment she thought he had seen her, but he pulled out the lady's chair before seating himself in his usual place, directly opposite her vantage point. Her mother came in next, on the arm of an older man with a brush moustache and military bearing. She was wearing her green silk with the emerald brooch and earrings that matched her eyes. The other guests followed. Uncle Roland was there with a pretty lady friend with blonde curls, but Uncle Gavin was missing.

A procession of dishes flowed in from the kitchen, the rich smells of meat and saffron-flavoured sauces rising to where she was sitting and making her mouth water. The guests' own bearers served their masters and mistresses and lined up behind them, ready to step forward when needed. She waited, absorbed in watching them, lulled by the low murmur of voices and occasional laughter.

Most of the faces were turned towards her mother, who was sitting with her back to the fanlight, so all the child could see were her animated hand gestures and her ringlets swaying as she turned her head. Her father, sitting opposite, seemed abstracted, and barely spoke or touched his food.

She noticed the blonde lady pick up the edge of the tablecloth and examine it, then say something to Uncle Roland. He looked down at it and then sharply up at her mother, then glanced towards her father, who didn't seem to notice.

At long last dinner was over and Afzal Khan emerged from the compound with the cake. He paused as he passed below her and she felt the heat of the candles on her face as she bent towards it. It was a giant confection of meringue topped with mango and orange cream, with the words 'Happy 50th Birthday, Henry' inscribed on it in chocolate in her mother's flowing hand. The guests exclaimed as Afzal Khan placed it in the centre of the table and poured champagne from the ice bucket on the sideboard, then cheered and laughed as her father took three breaths to blow out the candles. There were toasts and more conversation as the cake was eaten. Her legs had gone to sleep and she had almost joined them by the time the bearers moved to clear the table.

As the plates, place mats and large silver platters were lifted away, voices rose in admiration, then faltered. A hush fell as everyone stared at the cloth. The servants, puzzled by the silence, turned to look, the dishes poised in their hands. It was like the scene from *Sleeping Beauty* when everyone in the palace was turned to stone.

She knelt up and rubbed at the smeary window, trying to see the cloth more clearly, but all she could make out was a mass of swirling colours and shapes. Then everything was noise and motion: there were shouts of anger and disgust as people jumped to their feet; chairs fell to the floor but no one stopped to pick them up as they jostled to get out the doors to the drawing room. The lady in pink looked faint; the pregnant lady snatched up a napkin and was sick into it; the elderly man put his arm around her and glared at her mother.

Alarmed, she turned to get down but servants were spilling out of the doors below her so they could run round to see to

5

their masters and mistresses. From the front of the bungalow she heard Afzal Khan shouting for the syces to bring the carriages up.

She looked back into the room and saw the old soldier stop and squeeze her father's shoulder as he passed, but her father did not look up. His eyes were fixed on the table in front of him and his face was expressionless, as though he was listening to a voice only he could hear. Uncle Roland appeared in the doorway and hesitated. He stepped towards the table as though to speak, but stopped, his eyes fixed on the tablecloth in front of her father; then he turned and walked from the room, brushing past Afzal Khan, who was handing out hats, shawls and sticks to the departing guests. When the last one had gone, Afzal Khan pulled the double doors closed from the other side. She waited for him to come back so she could ask him what had happened but he must have forgotten her, because no one came.

The rain had stopped now, and everything was silent except for the steady creaking of the punkah; only the two of them remained in the dining room, her father staring at the cloth, her mother at the sideboard. It wasn't until her father moved that she realised she had been holding her breath. He pushed back his chair, got heavily to his feet and walked past his wife without looking at her.

As he passed below the shelf, she turned. There was a moment when she might have reached down, when she might have touched the top of his head where the scalp showed through the thinning hair. But he had already moved on, down the corridor towards his study.

Her first impulse was to jump down, to follow him, but curiosity held her still. She shifted and rubbed her legs, gasping at the agonising pins and needles, as she watched her mother dreamily stroking the cloth, her head tilted, as though she too was listening to some faraway sound.

But when the sound came it was not far away at all but very near, and so loud that for a few moments afterwards the child's ears rang.

She threw herself backwards off the shelf, and as her feet hit the ground she heard Afzal Khan shout something from the compound and the scrape of a dining chair. She would never remember getting to the study, just the feel of the cool brass knob under her hand and the sight that met her eyes as she fell in the door.

Inside the study, a fountain of red – a pure, beautiful red – had spouted up the wall behind the desk and spattered over the ceiling. The smell of cordite and something sharper, metallic, caught in her throat. On the shelf behind the desk the bronze statue of Shiva was dancing in the lamplight, his shadowy limbs undulating against the wall in his circle of flames. She stared at it, trying not to look at the thing slumped over the desk. There was a strange vibration, a silent drumbeat; the air quivered in time to it and the shadows moved faster, the god's limbs a blur. She shivered and looked down at the fine red mist settling on her bare arms.

Blind and dizzy, she turned towards the door and collided with someone coming in. Sharp nails sank into her shoulders. She bit back a cry of pain and looked up. Her mother was standing in front of her, looking not at her but at the wall behind her. In the soft lamplight her face was as composed as the picture of the Madonna that hung above her bed. Her eyes followed the fountain up and back down to the desk, as the child waited for her expression to change. She heard her mother's breath release and felt a shudder run through her as her fingers released their grip. She took a step back and then, as the girl watched, her eyes widened and her lips curled into a smile.

PART ONE

Lila

It's strange how a whole life can be changed in an instant. A dozen years later, I'm still haunted by that moment when I might have reached down and touched Father's head as he passed below me. If he'd known I was there, or if I'd jumped down then, instead of staying to see the tablecloth, and followed him to his study, I believe he would not have done what he did.

That night, Afzal Khan took me to a neighbour's house and left me there. I had never spent a night apart from Ayah before and cried and begged for her to be sent to me, but she didn't come.

I stayed there for a few days until it was arranged that I would be sent to England to live with my great-aunt Wilhelmina. A Mrs Twomey, who was travelling to Tilbury with her daughter, would take me with her. Afzal Khan and Ayah both came to say goodbye. Out of his uniform and starched turban Afzal Khan looked smaller and older; he wept and repeated, '*Khuda hafiz, khuda hafiz*,' invoking Allah's protection. Ayah looked older too, her eyes red and swollen from weeping; she kissed my hands and cheeks and held my

11

face and called me her sweet baby. I pleaded with her to come with me but she shook her head. Even before I asked I knew she would never leave Mother, but as the carriage drove away I looked back and saw her wailing and throwing dust over her head.

At Karachi I stood on the ship beside Mrs. Twomey and Jane and watched the crowds of people who had come to see their loved ones depart. The Indians screamed and wept; the English, including Mr. Twomey in his solar topee, waved their handkerchiefs. Streamers of marigolds and gardenias stretched from hands on deck down to the quay. As the boat pulled away, Indian passengers threw garlands from the deck into the triangle of water between the ship and the dock. I watched as they were caught up in the wake and bobbed away.

For the first week I ate and slept in a daze, convinced that I would wake to find myself back in our bungalow with Father calling, 'Hurry up, slowcoach! Ram Das is waiting with the pony,' and I would know it had all been a nightmare. I was sharing a cabin with Mrs. Twomey's daughter Jane, who was seven, and one morning I opened my eyes to find her already up and playing with her doll, Jemima. As I lay listening to her, the cabin solidified around me: the sun through the porthole was lying in a band across the panelling, illuminating the lines and colours of the wood grain; I could hear Jane singing to her doll, and feel the ship rolling under me, and I knew it was true. It had really happened: Father was gone and I would never, ever see him again. My life stretched out ahead of me, an endless succession of empty days, and I leant out of my bunk and was sick on the floor.

When I felt well enough I went out on deck to the point of the bow. It was a rough stormy day with lashing winds, mountainous waves and spray blowing horizontally across the deck. There was no one else about. I stood there and screamed until my throat and stomach hurt and my eyes and nose were raw from the tears and the wind, and when I finally stopped screaming I found I had lost my voice and I was glad because there was no one I wanted to speak to and nothing I wanted to say.

Everyone on board knew about Father; Mrs. Twomey had told them. I had seen her standing in groups of people talking in her high-pitched excitable way. I saw the looks of pity and curiosity directed at me and I hated them all. They sat at table dressed in their finery amidst the mirrors and chandeliers and polished wood and gleaming brass; their mouths opened and closed, food went in and words came out, and their laughter was mocking and ugly.

The only place I felt comfortable was standing at the bow, alone with the blue sea and sky that stretched all the way to the horizon. The emptiness came right into me. I stood there hour after hour watching the bow slice through the smooth skin of water, peeling it back to curl away behind us in a froth of foam. The wash of the wake swept my head as clean as the inside of an eggshell. I wanted it to go on forever.

The first thing my great-aunt Wilhemina said when she met me off the boat was, 'You may call me Aunt Mina and I shall call you Lilian. As for India and the past, we shall never speak of either again.'

I had opened my mouth to greet her but I looked up into her cloudy brown eyes and closed it again.

I stared out the window as we drove to her house. It was the middle of August and everything was unfamiliar: the sun was a hazy glow behind a pale grey sky, there were drab people walking along empty streets, and no colours or smells. Even the sounds were tinny and unreal. And I was cold – colder than I had ever been, although they told me it was summer.

High Elms, Aunt Mina's square white Georgian house, lies in a small Sussex village in a fold of the South Downs. Behind the house the land slopes sharply up to the top of Devil's Dyke, from where it is said one can see four counties and, on a clear day, the shadowy hump of the Isle of Wight. In front of the house, stretching as far as the rolling North Downs that ring the horizon, lies the shadowy blue Weald with its patchwork of fields and woods that Constable called the 'grandest view in the world'. But I was in no mood to appreciate it then.

Inside the large house I felt stifled by the thick muffling curtains and soft carpets, the heavy dark furniture and brooding silence. In India, my window had always stood open at night, and the voices of the servants, their laughter and quarrels, and the smell of their cooking, drifted in on the warm night air. Here, my room was on the first floor at one end of a long corridor and the rest of the floor was empty except for Aunt Mina's room at the other end. My window looked north over the Weald, though the view was blocked by the elms that gave the house its name. In the day I stood at my window listening to the silence and sometimes, if I listened carefully, I could hear a distant vibration – always the same, a soundless voice repeating the same phrase over and over, but no matter how hard I strained I could not make out the words. At night no sounds came up from below and the silence was so profound that I imagined that everyone had died and that I would wake up in the morning and find myself alone.

Night after night I had the same dream, which I still have sometimes. It is dark and I am back in Peshawar, walking up the drive to our bungalow. It lies quiet, its whitewashed walls glimmering in the moonlight, punctuated by the shadowy rectangles of its windows and the open front door. I go inside and walk through the empty rooms. All the furniture is gone and I can feel sand, blown in from the desert, gritty under my feet. In my bedroom the windows stand open. The muslin curtains float upwards and the strong sweet smell of raat-ki-rani drifts into the room on the night air.

Hindus believe that when you cross the ocean – which they call the kala pani or black water – you lose your caste, and your caste defines your place in the world: where you belong and, ultimately, who you are. You become an outcast. My own experience, even though I am not a Hindu, tells me that this is true.

Henry

Today we went to the Club for lunch to celebrate my eleventh birthday. I was surprised because Father is nearly always sick on my birthday. When his native officers come to ask after him, Kishan Lal tells them he has malaria. Last year I asked Kishan Lal why it always happens and he said it's because Father is thinking about 'that time', but he won't say any more. He says it is better forgotten. Father must think so too, because he never talks about it, but I know that my mother died when I was born and that's why Father hates my birthday and never speaks of her. I hate it too because I think about my mother dying and wonder if it was my fault, and the bad dream comes, and I don't have a party because there are no other English boys my age here because they've all gone away to school in England. Mohan and Ali don't care about birthdays anyway. They don't even know when theirs are.

Mohan and Ali are my friends and their fathers are in my father's regiment. Sometimes the regiment goes on manoeuvres and I go too. We sleep in tents and in the daytime Father marches and drills his men and they have mock battles and ambushes. This year Mohan's father made us wooden

16

rifles and we practised crawling on our bellies and ambushing each other. We've decided we're all going to be soldiers when we grow up, even though Mr. Mukherjee says I am too clever, but Father is clever and he's a soldier. When we get bored with that we go fishing and hunting. In the evenings we watch the wrestling and then the sepoys sing songs and tell stories round the campfire. Father can still beat almost everyone at wrestling except Jemadar Dhubraj Ram, who is very big and strong, like Bhima in the *Mahabharat*. Mr. Mukherjee is telling me the story. He gave me this diary and says I must write in it every day.

While we were having lunch, Colonel Hewitt's wife came up and wished me happy birthday and Father asked her to sit down, even though I know he doesn't like her. She looked at me in that way that mems always do and asked Father if he didn't think, now that I was eleven, that it was time for me to go to school in England. Father asked me what I thought and I said I wanted to stay here. I like Mr. Mukherjee and I like living with Father and Kishan Lal and being friends with Mohan and Ali. Then Mrs. Hewitt sniffed and made that camel face that Kishan Lal says mems make when they disapprove of something and said she and the other ladies had been talking and thought that my mother would have wished me to have a proper English education.

I thought Father would be angry but he just said he was grateful for her concern and he was quite satisfied with the arrangements he had made for my education. He told her that Mr. Mukherjee is one of the cleverest men he has ever met, that he speaks six languages, and that if I am going to live and work in India what I learn from him will be far more useful than anything I could learn at an English public school. Mrs. Hewitt went red and I hoped that she would go away,

17

but she said that she was surprised that Father should have such confidence in a native; surely he knew they could not be trusted, especially the clever ones. And then she leant over and said quietly, '*Remember Cawnpore!*'

I didn't know what she meant so I looked at Father. His face had gone white and his scar was twitching, as it does when he's angry, so that it jerks the corner of his eye and mouth together, but all he said was, 'I suspect I have more reason to remember it than you have, Mrs. Hewitt.' Mrs. Hewitt did look frightened then. She got up and said, 'I beg your pardon, Colonel Langdon. I never meant... I am so sorry... I had forgotten... Of course I know...' Then she looked at me and stopped talking and went away.

I asked Kishan Lal what happened at Cawnpore but all he did was shake his head and mutter something about the Devil's wind.

21st July 1868

I haven't written in my diary for a week. As soon as we got home after my birthday lunch Father went to his room and Kishan Lal took him his medicine tray, and the next day he did not get up and Kishan Lal had to send to the Lines to say he was ill. I heard him tell Allahyar that he was expecting it. Father stayed in his room and I heard him shouting for more medicine, and when he did come out his eyes were red and he smelt of whisky. I know Kishan Lal worries but he doesn't say anything except to tell me not to disturb Father, as though I don't know that. On the night of my birthday I had that dream again in which I was shut in a dark hot place and couldn't breathe, and I woke screaming but Father didn't come.

I told Mr. Mukherjee today that I have written in my diary. I was afraid he would ask to see it because I don't want him to see what I wrote about Father, and that I haven't been writing every day, but he said a diary is private and that I don't have to show it to anyone.

Today he told me more of the story of the *Mahabharat*. It was a great war between the Kauravas and the Pandavas, who were cousins. There were a hundred Kauravas and only five Pandavas and I said that was silly because obviously the Kauravas would win. But he said the Pandavas were cleverer than the Kauravas, and anyway there are millions of Indians and only a few British and yet we still manage to rule the whole country. I asked how we do and he said it was like when the Romans ruled Britain. In those days Britain was made up of small, separate tribal kingdoms and the people were disunited, but the Romans were disciplined and had good government and administration and built roads, just like we build railways. He said that one day Indians would want their country back and then we would all have to go home, as the Romans did. I said India was my home and I didn't want to go back to England. He said if all the English felt like me then we would fight. I said I would never fight with Ali and Mohan and he said that one could never tell − the Pandavas thought that too and then they had to fight their own cousins. I asked him why they did and so he told me the story and read me the bit where Arjuna, who was one of the five Pandava brothers, saw his teacher, and his cousins, and their uncle, the kind old blind king who had raised him and his brothers, facing him on the battlefield. Then Arjuna started crying and asked his charioteer, who was really the god Krishna in disguise, how he could fight and kill his own relatives and teacher, to whom he owed so much. And Krishna said this:

Thy tears are for those beyond tears; and are thy words
words of wisdom? The wise grieve not for those who live;
and they grieve not for those who die – for life and death
shall pass away,
because we have all been for all time: I, and thou,
and those kings of men. And we shall be for all time,
we all for ever and ever.
If any man thinks he slays, and if another thinks he is slain,
neither knows the ways of truth. The eternal in man cannot
kill;
the eternal in man cannot die.
For the death of what cannot die, cease thou to sorrow.
Think also of thy duty and do not waver.
There is no greater good for a warrior than to fight in a
righteous war.
In death thy glory in heaven, in victory thy glory on earth.
Arise therefore, Arjuna, with thy soul ready to fight.

I recited it to Father last night when he got home from
the Lines. I wanted to ask him if he ever had to fight and kill
people he liked, and if that's why he gets so sad, or whether
it's just about Mother, but I didn't dare.

13th September 1868

It has rained heavily nearly every day for the last two months
and there has been nothing to do except lessons and reading,
and nothing to write about. Mr. Mukherjee made me write a
précis of all the Scott novels that I've read, which took ages,
because I've nearly read them all, so I didn't want to write any
more. My favourite one is *Ivanhoe* because I like the fighting
but if I were Ivanhoe I would marry Rebecca, not Rowena.
He seems to like her better, but Mr. Mukherjee says he can't

marry her because she's a Jewess, and when I asked why he said I am too young to understand. We are reading *Great Expectations* now and I like it, though I don't like Estella at all because she's so mean to Pip.

15th September 1868

Yesterday something peculiar happened. Father called me into his study. I don't usually go in his study because he doesn't like to be disturbed, so I knew it must be important. I like it in there; it's dark and cool and smells of leather. There are shelves and shelves of books, and bronze and marble statues of the Indian gods. My favourite is Shiva, dancing in a ring of fire.

Mr. Mukherjee says Shiva danced the world into being. Before that there was nothing, but when he danced his energy started everything moving and time began and matter was created. It's the movement that makes everything look solid but really it isn't. It's an illusion, which means it looks real but it isn't. The Sanskrit word for it is 'lila', which means 'sport' or 'play'. It's a girl's name too. Shiva is the Creator, but also the Destroyer, and when he opens his third eye the illusion will dissolve and the world will end. Mr. Mukherjee says Hindus believe that this is the last age of our earth – the Kali Yuga – when the world will be destroyed and everything will be burned to ashes.

I asked Father about it but he wasn't listening. He told me that he has been thinking about what Mrs. Hewitt and the mems said: that I am growing up and that it's time for me to get to know my English relatives, although there is only one – my aunt Wilhelmina. He said that her father has died and she is all alone and he has written to ask her if she would like to come and live with us.

21

I asked him if Aunt Wilhelmina was his sister and he looked at me as though I was stupid and said, 'Mina is your mother's sister. Her twin sister. Surely you knew that?' I was so surprised when he mentioned my mother that I couldn't think of anything to say, even though there were lots of things I wanted to know. He said that Aunt Mina is a sensible woman who will be able to teach me about manners and clothes and how to behave in polite company, which he is not able to teach me, being just a rough soldier. I thought she sounded like a mem, but then I remembered that she and my mother were twins.

I was afraid he'd be angry but I really wanted to know so I asked if she looks like my mother but he just said he hasn't seen her for many years. He still didn't seem upset so I asked him what my mother's name was. He looked shocked and said, 'Surely you must know that! Her name was Cecily.' I wanted to say, 'How could I know when you never told me?' but his scar twitched and I didn't dare.

I thought about my mother in bed last night. I couldn't really think about her before because I didn't know anything about her, but now I can imagine her. Father was fair when he was younger, Kishan Lal says, and he has very blue eyes, but my hair and eyes are dark. She must have been dark, then, like Rebecca in *Ivanhoe*, and like me. I am like her – like my mother. Cecily is a pretty name. I wonder if it's my fault that she died and whether Father blames me. All I have of hers is a small pebble with a hole through it that I wear on a cord around my neck. Kishan Lal told me once that it had belonged to her and was some kind of magic charm. He said it kept me safe and that it was God's will that I survived. I asked what he meant but he wouldn't tell me.

Cecily

Dearest Mina,

It has only been a few days and already I miss you more than I can express. It was not until the boat pulled away from the quay and I saw the distance growing between us that I realised what I have done. I had forgot that we have never spent a night apart before, and I feel as though I have been cut in two, and have left the wisest, cleverest and best part of myself behind! I know that you and Mama think I am too young to marry a man so much older than myself, and travel so far from home, but, in all the excitement of shopping for my trousseau and planning my journey, I scarcely had time to consider the future. It is strange to imagine being married to Arthur – even writing his name, rather than 'Major Langdon', feels peculiar! – and I cannot imagine us ever being as easy together as James and Louisa. Of course they are closer in age than Arthur and I are, whereas I always feel like a child when I am with him. I know they were surprised when they met me at Southampton and learnt I was only nineteen.

When I told James that I was in awe of Arthur he said he had always regarded Arthur as a sort of god, because he was ten years older and seemed so much wiser, and then of course Arthur went out to India when James was still just a boy, so they did not see each other for many years. I told James I found the prospect of marrying a god alarming. I hope Arthur is endowed with more patience than the Greek gods in our school books or you will shortly be corresponding with a linden tree! The more I learn about him, the more I am in trepidation of meeting him again.

Darling Mina, I miss Home so much already! For the first two nights aboard I lay in my bunk and wept with loneliness, but on the third day (as *you* were not here to do it) I gave myself a proper lecture, and after I had recovered from its severity (and the sulks that followed it) I decided to make myself useful to poor Louisa. Her condition makes her susceptible to *mal de mer*, and Luxmibai, the children's ayah, is also suffering, so I have become not just nursemaid but fellow pirate to Freddie and Sophie. I have made Freddie an eye patch so he can pretend to be Admiral Nelson, which fancy he indulges me in, although he says he would rather be the Duke of Wellington as he intends to be a soldier when he grows up, like his uncle Arthur. Little Sophie, on the other hand, is very ladylike, even at three. She is so gentle and sweet, yet has such dignity. She is very like Louisa. If any of the gentlemen tease her she looks at them so gravely they are quite discomfited. Freddie finds the rough seas wonderfully exciting and I share his pleasure in them, so we romp about on deck playing hide-and-seek and admiring the great waves lashing the side while Sophie sits and watches us.

Everyone has been very kind and James is taking good care of me. There is a rigid order of precedence aboard the ship, which Louisa tells me I must get used to. She says that, in India, preceding someone of higher status into a room can cause mortal offence! So, as an unmarried lady, affianced to a

24

mere major in the Indian Army, I should be seated at a lower table; but, as I am also the future sister-in-law of a collector and magistrate, I have been placed beside James at the table of the 'Heaven-Born'.

Mina, you cannot imagine how alarming it is to find oneself surrounded by these Olympians. They argue and bicker about how India should be ruled and the best way of dealing with the natives, quite as the Greek gods used to fight amongst themselves about the tricks they planned to play upon poor mortals. The talk at table is all of politics. I feel very foolish and stupid, but they are all perfect gentlemen and, having realised the extent of my ignorance, have taken it upon themselves to educate me. At every meal, therefore, I sink under the weight of words such as 'annexation' and 'abdication' (I am still on the letter A!). Apparently Lord Dalhousie has been annexing native rulers' kingdoms like a governess confiscating sweets from naughty boys, and there are fears the natives may rebel. Some of the Great and Good, like Mr. Weston, say the natives should prefer to be ruled by us for we are just and impartial; others, like James, feel the natives do not necessarily appreciate what is good for them but would rather be ruled by their own kings, however corrupt and dissolute these may be. Fortunately, when I begin to drown, James diverts their attention with some observation about 'growing unrest among the Zamindars' or some such exotic phrase (he has reached Z).

After an evening of such talk I retire to my bed with my head spinning. I am so worried that when Arthur meets me again he will realise how empty-headed I am and regret his proposal.

You are naturally wondering why I do not talk to the ladies, but they are even more alarming than their husbands.

I spend much of my time at table trying to avoid Mrs. Weston's scrutiny. She is the wife of a judge and her eyes bear a remarkable resemblance to those of the poached pike we used to have on Fridays. The life of a memsahib seems so dull! They talk of nothing but their servants – their laziness, dishonesty and stupidity – and warn me how I must guard against diluted milk, falsified accounts and tailors who cut garments too small in order to steal the extra cloth. They have not a good word to say about anyone. One of them complains that her khansamah, ordered to serve jugged hare for a dinner party, served it with its fur still on, having singed only its ears! Another tells of how her 'boy' informed them, in front of their dinner guests, that the pudding had been burnt, but in trying to dodge her husband's attempts to box his ears for his impertinence he dislodged his turban, and the pudding, which he had concealed there, fell to the floor. When I laughed they looked quite shocked, but it seems to me that such antics must provide some diversion in what otherwise seems a very dull life.

I almost feel sorry for the poor natives, and wonder if they feel themselves to be as fortunate to be ruled by us as we consider them to be. If I were a native I should much rather be at the mercy of an oriental despot than Mrs. Weston! At lunch today she told us how she once suspected her children's ayah of stealing their sweetmeats, so she poisoned the sweets with emetic of tartar and turned the woman off when she became ill. In future I shall take the precaution of arriving at the table before she does!

Please tell Cook I have her lucky stone safe. I wear it around my neck under my dress, but at dinner yesterday it slipped out when I leant forward and Mrs. Weston saw it and asked me what it was. I explained that it is believed to ward off witches, and that it also serves as a talisman against drowning. She gave me her poached pike stare, muttered something about superstition and has not spoken to me since. So please tell Cook it is fulfilling *both* its purposes!

But really, Mina, despite my complaints I know I am fortunate, for if I were not travelling with James and Louisa I should be confined to the lower deck with the other unaccompanied ladies. For the sins of being unmarried and travelling alone, they are segregated from the rest of the passengers and must even eat separately. As many of them are going to friends in India in the hope of catching a husband there, they are nicknamed 'the Fishing Fleet', and those who return unwed are called 'Returned Empties'. How very humiliating that must be!

I must stop now as I must write to Arthur and to Mama and Papa. We shall be at Gibraltar tomorrow and I can post my letters there. I shall write again from Malta. How I wish you were with me, but you must come and visit as soon as we're settled!

Your loving sister, Cecily

Malta, 23rd September 1855

My precious Mina,

Your letters were waiting when we got here and it was so good to have news of everyone at home. I received a letter from Peter too. He says his heart is broken and he will never care for anyone again. I am sorry to have disappointed his hopes, but I never led him to think I cared for him. I could never do so, knowing him as we have since we were babies. I know you will be kind to him, Mina.

27

Since we entered the Mediterranean, the sea has been much calmer and Louisa has been able to get up and move around. She says she is so thankful to me for caring for the children, but I need no thanks, for I have not enjoyed myself so much since I put my hair up and was no longer permitted to climb trees.

There is a Mrs. Burton at our table who is returning to India after leaving her children in England. She eats hardly anything, drinks only water and seems always on the verge of tears. The other ladies hardly address a word to her. Her husband, who is a magistrate, seems very solicitous. He told James the Indian climate did not suit her and she came Home a year ago with the children to recuperate. She is now returning to India with him, and the children have been left with relatives.

Louisa says she dreads the thought of parting with hers when it is time for them to go to school, as neither she nor James has any family living and they will have to go to strangers. They have found a respectable couple in Bognor Regis who are willing to take them, but she says they are so dull and humourless that she cannot bear the thought of the children growing up like them.

The more I become acquainted with Louisa, the more I admire her. It is too bad you and Mama did not have time to get to know her. She grew up in India – her father was in the Army and her mother died when she was very young so she managed his household and acted as his hostess. She knows much about the natives and their customs, as well as Anglo-Indian life, so she is a great help to James. I know Arthur likes her very much, for he told me so, but I hope he does not expect me to be like her.

It is almost suppertime so I had better close this letter. We stopped at Gibraltar, which is a large rock in the sea, where

I wrestled with a monkey for possession of my hat, but I was laughing so much I let go and it put on the hat and followed me up the rock, mimicking the airs and graces of a coquettish lady! Today we spent a lovely day at Valletta, driving to the Città Vecchia and visiting the catacombs and St John's Armoury. I have enclosed some watercolour sketches of both places with Mama and Papa's letter. Our next stop will be Alexandria, where we will leave the *Candia* and travel by boat to Cairo and then cross the desert by camel or horse carriage to Suez, where we shall take another ship to India. I shall write to you from Cairo.

Goodnight, dearest Mina, from your Cecily

P.S. Mrs. Weston took Louisa aside before dinner and told her that Mrs. Burton is not a respectable person and had to return to England, not to recuperate from an illness as she says, but because she was *addicted to gin*! She said that is why none of the other ladies speaks to her, and warned Louisa against her. So at dinner we both made a particular point of addressing her as much as possible, though I fear it only alarmed her, poor thing.

Lila

Poor Aunt Mina! When I look back I can see how difficult I must have been, but I could not see her side of things then. It seemed to me that she wished to annihilate everything that made me me – my name, my memories of India, even my character. She was trying to turn me into someone else, someone who would fit into this new life – but I did not wish to be anyone but myself and I fought her with all the weapons at my disposal. I know she found our life together as hard as I did. She was doing what she thought was best for me, but I was too much for her, and try as I might – and I did not try very hard – I could not like her.

During the first few weeks I lived with her she took me to various doctors, all of whom said the same thing: that there was nothing wrong with my vocal cords. They suggested that the cause of my silence was shock (Aunt Mina told them, as she told everyone, that both my parents had died of the cholera) and that all I needed was time. Apart from my morning lessons, which she took herself, I was left to my own ˡevices. On the whole I did not mind those lessons, though it ˙ed me when I wrote 'Lila Langdon' on my schoolbooks ˙ossed out 'Lila' and put 'Lilian'. 'Lila is a native ˙d, 'and you have a perfectly good English

30

name.' I wished I could have the satisfaction of telling her that 'Mina' is also a native name. But, if I could not talk about the things that meant most to me, then I would not speak at all.

I spent most afternoons hidden away in my great-grandfather's study, picking out books at random from his bookshelves. I was used to entertaining myself. When Mother was unwell, Ayah would sit with her, placing handkerchiefs soaked in cologne on her brow and massaging her temples, and I would be ordered to go away and be quiet.

Most of my great-grandfather's books were dry and difficult to understand but one day I came across Robert Louis Stevenson's story 'The House of Eld', about Jack, who was born into a land where everyone wore a fetter, fixed upon each child's ankle as soon as he or she could walk. These fetters were regarded as a mark of superiority, even though they raised ulcers, and unfettered strangers who could move about freely and painlessly were looked down upon. But Jack questioned what everyone else accepted, even though his uncle, the catechist, warned him against it, and one day he decided to take a sword and seek freedom from his fetter. The story ended with him accomplishing his mission, but at a savage cost: the loss of everything he loved.

It was a parable intended for grown-ups, not for children, and I did not understand it then. Reading that cruel ending always made me weep, but still I found comfort in it, for in some strange way Jack's story seemed also to be mine, and made me feel less alone. I too had lost everyone and everything that I loved: Father, Ayah, Afzal Khan and all my other friends. I missed the sun-warmth that, even in an Indian winter, greeted me as I emerged on to the verandah each morning to sit basking in its golden glow, its red-gold light behind my sleepy eyelids; the sound of monsoon rain rattling on the roof. I missed Afzal Khan's teasing when he brought me breakfast, the syce's broad smile as I emerged for my ride; I missed my picnics with Father, sitting on a hilltop looking out at the great orange sun changing shape and colour, slowly turning purple as it sank towards the dusty plain. I missed the colours and the sounds and the smells, but most of all I missed the feeling of being loved. And yet I did not give anyone a chance to love me; I held myself apart through my silence, and slipped away as soon as visitors came, retiring to the study to hide myself in books.

Aunt Mina did not approve of my spending all my time reading. She was a woman of her generation and thought I should learn some more practical accomplishments. She tried to teach me embroidery, but I resisted all her efforts until eventually she gave up in irritation, saying crossly, 'You are just like Cecily: stubborn and wilful.'

I knew that Cecily was Aunt Mina's twin sister and my grandmother, and that the room I was given must once have been theirs, for on the wall opposite my bed were two cross-stitch samplers. The first was a neatly embroidered picture of a square three-storey Georgian house like High Elms, with a border of tall trees and a text that read:

REGARD THE WORLD WITH CAUTIOUS EYE
NOR RAISE YOUR EXPECTATIONS HIGH.
SEE THAT THE BALANCED SCALE BE SUCH
YOU NEITHER HOPE NOR FEAR TOO MUCH.

Wilhelmina Emily Partridge, aged 9 years, 1845

The other contained just lettering formed in large clumsy red and black stitches and read:

CECILY DID THIS AND
SHE HATED EVERY STITCH!

Cecily Alice Partridge, aged 9, 1845

I decided that I liked Cecily and wished I knew more about her; all I did know was that she had died shortly after Father was born. But there were traces of her all over the house: there was music with her name on it in the compartment of the piano stool, and in the schoolroom I found some old exercise books in the drawer of the table at which I did my lessons. They were full of sums and Latin and French vocabulary. Mina's notebooks were neat and tidy but Cecily's seemed to have been filled hurriedly in an untidy scrawl disfigured with blots, and there were pages and pages of lines: *I must not be hasty and impatient. I must guard my tongue in the presence of my elders and betters. I must study patience and perseverance.* But along the bottom of each page was scrawled, *I don't care, I don't care, I don't care.*

I liked her more than ever.

One afternoon when Aunt Mina was out I went down to the morning room, where she wrote letters and paid bills, to drop off my homework. On the corner of her writing bureau stood a photograph of two girls. They looked almost identical and yet I knew at once which was Aunt Mina. She was seated, wearing a dark dress, her hair neatly arranged and her mouth unsmiling. Standing behind her, with a hand lightly resting on her shoulder, was a girl in a pale dress; her hair was coming loose from its pins, creating a soft halo around her face, which was in three-quarter profile and slightly blurred, as though she had turned to smile at someone standing outside the frame.

As I placed the picture back on the bureau I noticed, lying on the top of a pile of letters and notebooks, a small knobbly pebble on a leather thong – one of those 'lucky stones' with holes pierced through them that one finds on Sussex beaches and which hang outside almost every cottage in the village to ward off witches and evil spirits. I recognised it at once: Father used to let me play with it as he told me stories about his adventures across the Northwest Frontier with Uncle Gavin. Then he would bend to kiss me and I would put the cord back over his head, as I had that night of his birthday party when he finished reading to me. He told me his mother had placed it around his neck when he was born to keep him safe. It was his 'lucky talisman' and he promised me that one day it would be mine – so I did not feel guilty for taking it.

I unbuttoned my collar and slipped the cord over my head, tucking the pebble into my blouse, where the lump hardly showed beneath my serge pinafore dress. Later I wondered about those letters and notebooks and went back to see, but they had disappeared and the bureau drawers were locked.

The weather improved towards the end of the month and Aunt Mina kept urging me to get some fresh air, so after our lessons were over each day I began to explore the Downs behind the house. I made a hideout for myself in a hollow thicket of gorse and on my way up the hill I buried under a bush the packed lunch that Cook had carefully prepared and wrapped in waxed paper.

On windy days the hill sheltered me, and I huddled, wrapped in a blanket I had taken from the chest in my room, waiting for the day to pass. If it was sunny I sat looking over the Weald, imagining Father was sitting beside me. He had told me he used to play on the Downs when he stayed with

Aunt Mina in his holidays from school, and imagining him there made me feel closer to him.

Simon appeared, one afternoon, poking his head into my hideout as I was rehearsing the names of our household in Peshawar, scratching them into the moist earth in order not to forget them. He looked like a pixie from one of my old storybooks, very pale-skinned, with white-blond hair and silvery-grey eyes. I had never seen anyone so pale and, perhaps because he looked so different from anyone I had ever known, I immediately took a dislike to him. He peered curiously at me and then around my hideout and said, 'May I come in?'

I shrugged.

When he stepped in I saw that he was dressed in a Norfolk jacket, tweed knickerbockers, long socks and muddy boots.

He stood for a moment looking around my shelter. 'What are you doing?'

I kept scratching names in the dirt.

He held his hand out. 'I'm Simon. Simon Beauchamp. It's pronounced Beecham but it's spelt B-e-a-u-c-h-a-m-p. What's your name?'

I picked up my stick and scratched 'LILA' into the mud next to the other names.

'LIE-la,' he read.

I shook my head and wrote 'LEE-LA'.

He looked at my other scratchings. 'Are they names too?'

I nodded.

'But they're not real names, are they? They're just made up.'

I shook my head again and wrote 'INDIAN'.

'Oh! *You're* that girl who lives at High Elms. The funny one who can't talk.'

I stared at him.

'Sorry.' His eyes shifted down, then up to meet mine. 'Are you really an orphan? Mother says your parents died of... choler... choleric... or something.'

I maintained my stare as a tide of colour washed up into his face. He shuffled his feet and his eyes wandered the shelter in search of inspiration. At last he blurted, 'Do you know we're nearly related? It's true! My great-uncle Peter wanted to marry your grandmother, but she married your grandfather, so he got engaged to your aunt Mina instead.' I frowned while I tried to work that out. 'They were twins so I s'pose it didn't make much difference. But then he went out to India to fight the treacherous natives and died there of the... the same thing...' He trailed off. 'His name was Peter Markham, and he was my mother's uncle. So we are nearly related, aren't we?'

I could tell that he was babbling because he was uncomfortable. That silence gave power was an unexpected and welcome discovery.

He looked around again and his face brightened. 'Do you want to play a game?'

I shrugged.

'Do you know "I'm thinking of something"?'

I nodded. It was a game I played with Father sometimes.

His eyes flicked to my stick. 'I'm thinking of something beginning with S.'

I wrote 'STICK'.

He looked disappointed. 'Your turn.'

I won easily.

Simon should have been at school with other boys his age but he was considered delicate, so a tutor gave him lessons in the morning. The boys in the village were too rough for him to play with; he told me they taunted him and called him a sissy and a girl. He was going to be fourteen that autumn, around the time I was to turn thirteen myself, and would soon be going away to boarding school, once he was considered strong enough. But until then we saw each other every day and became companions of a sort. It helped that I thought myself superior to him – he was so childish that I felt like the older, wiser one.

Dry days we spent on the Downs where we played hide-and-seek and I taught him to play Fivestones and Seven Tiles; rainy days were spent in the old schoolroom where we played chess and Parcheesi. He soon got used to my silence and began to frame his questions as Aunt Mina and the servants had learnt to – so that I only had to nod or shake my head to reply. Aunt Mina seemed relieved that I had found a friend. I wonder now if his discovery of my hiding place was as accidental as it seemed, or whether Aunt Mina and Mrs. Beauchamp had put their heads together.

I did not have much in common with Simon, but I tolerated him because I knew that he was lonely, and I understood loneliness. In India, Father and the servants had been my only real companions. All the other children my age were at school in England and Mother did not like me to play with Indian children. She had pressed Father to send me away too, but he refused; he had hated being sent away when he was a boy.

Simon's tutor had been giving him extra lessons all summer to prepare him for school but on the day before he was due to leave he developed a fever. His departure was put off to give him time to recover, and over the next month I went over to visit him every day. Mrs. Beauchamp sent the dogcart for me each morning and I was driven to their house in the next village, which lay less than a mile away along the foot of the Downs.

I could tell that Simon's complaint was more one of nerves than health. He was perfectly happy playing games or talking when we were alone, but, as soon as one of his parents entered the room and asked how he was feeling, his temperature soared. He was made to rest in the afternoons, and so I often ended up joining the grown-ups downstairs. Right from the start, the Beauchamps treated me as one of the family. Like Simon, his mother was small and fair, but her hair was a deeper gold and her eyes a warm blue. She dressed in the latest fashions, in beautifully cut patterned long coats over narrow ankle-length skirts in vivid peacock colours, unlike Aunt Mina, who wore old-fashioned dresses with a small bustle, in grey or muddy mauves and lilacs. They were unlikely friends, because Aunt Mina was deeply conservative and Mrs. Beauchamp supported women's suffrage, but the two families had known each other for years.

I came to know Mrs. Beauchamp quite well because she took an interest in me. Simon told me she'd always wanted a daughter and added, rather bitterly, 'I think she'd like me better if I was a girl,' though she seemed to me to like him well enough – certainly more than my mother had liked me. I knew Mr. Beauchamp less well because he was a Labour Member of Parliament and stayed up in London during the week. He was small too, like Simon, but dark, with shiny nut-brown eyes, and he was always very kind to me.

The Beauchamps had lots of visitors: Mrs. Beauchamp's suffragette friends met there and Mr. Beauchamp often brought friends and fellow M.P.s home from London at weekends and in the parliamentary recesses. I enjoyed being there – the constant flow of people and the preparations for visitors brought the house alive and made me feel connected to the bigger world. But my mornings at their house came to an end when Simon went off to school. After that Aunt Mina arranged for his tutor to come to me.

I was surprised to find that I missed Simon, and he obviously missed me, because I received a letter from him after the first week. I could tell that he wasn't happy. Most of his fellow pupils would have been there for a year already, and even the new ones had had a month to form friendships. As his letters continued I noticed that he never mentioned any of the other boys; then, towards the end of the first term, he mentioned having made a friend – 'a boy in the year above me, a frightfully decent chap, but the rest is a surprise…' And then the letters stopped. I told myself I didn't care and when he wrote to say he was bringing his friend home, and that I was bound to like him – 'Everybody does!' – I was determined that I wouldn't.

Henry

Aunt Wilhelmina is nothing like I imagined. She is not pretty
at all. Her hair is not dark but greyish, and she wears dull
colours because she is in half-mourning for her father. He
was my grandfather and his name was Henry too, Henry
Partridge. I was named after him. Partridge is a funny name
because it is a kind of bird and Father and I sometimes go
shooting for them. He must have been very old when he died
because Aunt Mina looks old, though Father says she's only
thirty-two. Kishan Lal is worried because he says she should
be married by now and she must be looking for a husband.
I said Father was too old to get married but Kishan Lal says
a man is never too old. He says Father is a fine man and any
woman would be lucky to catch him, even now. Father is
fifty-eight so that means he was twenty-six years older than
Mother. That's a lot.

I wondered if Aunt Mina would cry when she saw me,
because the mems always cry when relatives visit them, but
she didn't. She shook my hand and looked me up and down
like Father's subhedar-major does when he inspects the sepoys,
and then she told Father that I was dreadfully sunburnt and

that my clothes were quite unsuitable. She said, 'One could almost take him for a native.' I saw Father's scar twitch a little, but he just said, 'That's why we need you, Mina. I trust I can leave his transformation into a well-brought-up English boy in your capable hands.' I wondered if she could tell he was being sarcastic, but she just said that she would do her best but she knew she could never hope to replace my own dear mother, and then her eyes filled with tears and Father said he had to see to his men and went to the Lines and left me with her.

After he had gone, she inspected the house and I could tell she didn't like it because her mouth puckered up as if she were sucking a green tamarind. Kishan Lal saw too and looked even sulkier. He was already cross because Father had asked Mrs. Hewitt and some of the other mems to help to get the house ready and they had made new curtains for her room and stood vases of flowers all over the house. They also told Allahyar to prepare only English food for Aunt Mina, so for lunch today we had boiled mutton and potatoes. It was like lumps of gristle in peppery water and when Father asked Allahyar what it was he said proudly that it was called 'harish stoo' and that the memsahibs had shown him how to make it. Father told Aunt Mina it was supposed to be Irish stew and in his opinion Allahyar's Indian cooking was preferable, but that she must, of course, do as she thinks fit.

When Father got back from the Lines this evening he took her round the cantonment to leave her cards on all the other ladies.

15th December 1868

Today, as soon as Father had gone to the Lines, Aunt Mina said she would blush to entertain anyone in the house in its present state, and she told Kishan Lal to call all the staff and to tell them that the house needed a thorough clean and that the bathrooms were a disgrace. She ordered each of them to start scrubbing a different room and sent them off to fetch cleaning water and soap. None of them, except the sweeper, came back, so Aunt Mina sent me to find them but they were all hiding and the compound was empty. When Father came home for lunch Kishan Lal told him the servants were all threatening to leave. Father explained to Aunt Mina that each servant has work according to his caste and religion and cannot be expected to do another's work. He told her if she wants anything done she must tell Kishan Lal, who will manage the other servants. Aunt Mina went red and said that she had never heard anything so ridiculous, but Kishan Lal was pleased.

We both hope she will go home soon.

19th December 1868

This afternoon Aunt Mina asked me to read to her from my school books, so I read her my favourite passage from the *Mahabharat*. Mr. Mukherjee says it's a very fine description but he wasn't here because he doesn't come on Saturdays.

'In the midst of the great battle, surrounded by the clash of arms, the pounding of hooves, the rattle of trappings, the shouts of warriors and the screams of wounded men and beasts, where the dust churned up by the horses dimmed the sun and blood turned the earth to mud, Krishna suddenly stopped the chariot and sprang to the ground. Raising the wheel of a disabled chariot over His head, the Lord raced towards the great general Bhishmadeva like a lion charging an elephant. Just moments before, wave after wave of lethal arrows from Bhishmadeva's bow had crashed down upon Arjuna's chariot. In amazement, the other warriors had seen the figures of Arjuna and his driver Sri Krishna disappear behind the curtains of the general's arrows. It had been certain that Arjuna was about to fall before the fury of the attack.

'And then Bhishmadeva's bow was still. It dropped to the ground, and the invincible general stood unarmed and stared with widening eyes at the Lord charging furiously toward him. In intense concentration he noted every detail of Krishna's appearance: he saw how the beautiful flowing black hair of the Lord had turned ashen from the dust of battle; he saw how beads of sweat adorned His face like dew on a blue lotus flower; he saw how red smears of blood from wounds made by his own arrows enhanced the beauty of the transcendental body of the Lord. Bhishmadeva watched the Lord rushing towards him, preparing to kill him with a hurl of the wheel, and he was filled with ecstasy.'

But Aunt Mina didn't like it. She said she had never heard such nonsense and that she hoped Mr. Mukherjee was not filling my head with superstitious native ideas. Then she asked to see my scripture book and was cross when I said I didn't have one and asked what I learnt at Sunday school. I said I didn't go to Sunday school. She asked me what I did do on Sundays and I said that I played with my friends Mohan and Ali. She asked whether I had been confirmed yet and when I said no she was shocked and she said she would have to speak to the chaplain. I didn't tell her that the last time the chaplain was at our house was when he came to argue with Father about not taking me to church. I don't know what Father said to him but he seemed very cross when he left. Afterwards

Father asked me if I would like to go to church and I said no. But today, when Aunt Mina asked Father whether we would be attending Sunday service with her tomorrow, he said yes. Afterwards Kishan Lal told me this was the first sign. 'First sign of what?' I asked, but he just shook his head. Why will no one ever tell me anything?

26th December 1868

I haven't seen Mohan and Ali once since Aunt Mina arrived. She is always finding something to keep me occupied. She says prayers every morning and evening and we have been to church three times since she has been here – once on Sunday, to midnight mass on Christmas Eve, and again yesterday morning. When she first came she wanted the whole household to be present for morning and evening prayers, as she says they are at Home, but Father said the servants are not Christians, and he has no intention of trying to convert them, and he forbade her to try do so. I could tell she didn't like it but she didn't say anything, so I asked him to speak to her about Mohan and Ali, but he just smiled and said, 'Softly, softly, catchee monkey, Henry.' I asked Mr. Mukherjee what it means but he doesn't know.

Church is not as I imagined it. I knew it would not be like the pujas that the sepoys do on feast days, but I did not know there would be so much talking and singing. It's quite boring but Mr. Mukherjee says I should try to listen as it will help my Latin.

Father is being very nice to Aunt Mina, so he must like her. He has called on all the important mems in the cantonment with her and even takes tea with them when they come here if he is not at the Lines. He has told Kishan Lal that Aunt Mina is now the mem and must be obeyed. Kishan Lal calls her 'the Great She-Elephant' and mutters under his breath whenever she asks him to do something. She has changed our food to chops, pies and cutlets, like the other English families eat, and tea is now served with lemon, instead of with milk and sugar and spices as Father and I like it.

For Christmas we had roast chicken and roast potatoes and red cabbage. Aunt Mina supervised the cooking and Allahyar sulked, but I thought it was nice to spend Christmas at home like other people and not at the Club. Afterwards we played cards and I wondered if this was how it would be if Mother were alive.

6th January 1869

It's very late now and I have lots to write before I forget. Something queer happened tonight. Father and Aunt Mina were invited to an Epiphany dinner at the chaplain's house to celebrate the arrival of the three kings. I thought at first they meant three real kings till Father explained. Kishan Lal was very gloomy when he heard they were going together because Father never accepts invitations. He said that soon Father will be completely under her spell and that we need to keep an eye on them. And he was right, because when Father came in to say goodnight he brought Aunt Mina too. He was wearing his evening clothes and looked very smart and Aunt Mina was wearing a shiny mauve dress and jewellery. As they left I heard him warn her not to expect too much as it would be an indifferent dinner, followed by maudlin songs performed by members of the Fishing Fleet hoping to ensnare a husband.

After they had gone I got dressed and followed them. I got past our chowkidar easily – I knew once the trap was out of sight he would go and collect his dinner from the kitchen and the gate would be unguarded. I wasn't sure how I'd get past the chaplain's chowkidar but when I arrived he was standing outside the gate talking to our syce, so I slipped past without them noticing. By the time I reached an open sitting room window the guests had already gone in to dinner so I hid in the flowerbed behind a raat-ki-rani bush and waited. They took ages to eat dinner and I was almost asleep when I heard the ladies coming back. Aunt Mina and Mrs. Hewitt sat down right next to the window and I could hear them talking about Father. Mrs. Hewitt was congratulating Aunt Mina on working wonders with him and said they had all been convinced he was going native because he sat on the verandah in his pyjamas and seemed to prefer arranging nautches and wrestling matches for his sepoys to mixing with his fellow Europeans.

Then the gentlemen came in and the chaplain's wife called for everyone to gather round the piano and a lady called Miss Pole was invited to sing. Miss Pole looked just like her name – she was very tall and thin, with a pointed nose – and she clasped her hands under her chin and began to sing in a reedy voice about someone who had falsely sworn a vow and broken it, and how his lover had pined away with grief and died blessing him. I could see that Father was trying not to laugh. Then they all begged Aunt Mina to sing and she said no and they said yes and in the end she agreed, as she obviously meant to all along. She went to the piano and Father stood to turn the pages for her.

I was surprised when she started because she sang beautifully. The song was called 'What Voice Is This?' and it was about someone who had died and how her voice was carried on the evening breeze. It made me sad, but Father didn't seem to be listening. He was just staring at the floor and forgot to turn the page so the chaplain had to jump up and do it. And then she got to the end and her voice went high and sweet. She was singing: 'The dead shall seem to live again, the dead shall seem to live again, to live again… to live again…' and then Father turned and knocked the music off the stand and almost ran out of the room. Everyone looked surprised and Aunt Mina stopped. The chaplain picked up the music and she started again, and then Father came out of the front door on to the verandah and I had to duck back behind the bush.

He stood still for a moment, breathing loudly and making a funny choking sort of noise, and then he plunged off the verandah and rushed straight past our carriage and down the road with the syce staring after him in amazement. He looked even more confused to see me come out of the flowerbed. 'You wait here for Memsahib,' I said, and followed Father, but by the time I got home he was already in his room. I came straight here to mine, which is next to his, and listened at the wall, but there was silence. Not long after, Aunt Mina came home in the trap. I heard her thanking the syce before she came into the house and went to her room.

Cecily

SS Madras, 10th October 1855

Dearest Mina,

You must have wondered what had become of me after such a long silence! I am penning this on the ship to India, for it was impossible to find the smallest opportunity to write when we were ashore. The steam-barge from Alexandria to Cairo was so crowded that all except the most elderly members of the party were without berths and had to forage for armchairs or a space on the floor. Shepheard's Hotel, where we were supposed to stay, was already full of passengers coming from India, and even the older members could not obtain a bed. They slept upon couches in the public rooms, but some of us younger ones decided to pay a visit to the public baths, which are open all night.

It was the most romantic evening; I wish you could have seen it, Mina. Men in burnooses carrying flaming torches escorted us through the streets, and in the bath-house women with huge arms pummelled us black and blue and then anointed us with oils and perfumes. Mrs. Weston, who accompanied us as a self-appointed chaperone, protested vigorously at having to disrobe in public but even she was no match for two brawny Turkish women who held her down and rubbed and scrubbed, laughing and making faces of disgust at one another. We were all quite mortified when they showed us the rolls of dirt that rubbed off us, though I was so sore for the next few days that I suspect it was not dirt at all but skin! Afterwards, feeling wide awake (as one is bound to do when one has been flayed alive!) we kept a vigil on the hotel steps till dawn, watching the donkey boys gather in the streets and people in colourful costumes going about their business. I am enclosing a watercolour I made of the scene but you will have to imagine the delightful warmth of the night air and the scent of jasmine, woodsmoke and spices.

The next day we set out for Suez. Because of Louisa's condition, she and the children's ayah travelled in a van pulled by horses, but James and I rode camels. Freddie rode with James and Sophie with me. It was romantic, as I had imagined, but the motion of a camel is quite different from that of a horse and I am still unable to sit down without a cushion! However, anything was better than being confined in one of those tiny crowded vans. Poor Louisa and Luxmibai were very thrown about and bruised.

Aden looked quite sinister, when we arrived in the dark, with strange shadows standing against the sky. A guide told us it is Cain's burial place and lies under a curse. The hotel was full of rats, which kept jumping over our beds, so you can imagine we did not sleep well! I was quite relieved when our steamer finally arrived. The cabin arrangements are rather primitive compared to the *Candia*, but everyone seems pleased to be approaching our journey's end. It is all so exciting!

I can't wait to see India but as we get closer I find myself feeling less and less brave about meeting Arthur again. If only we had met at the beginning of his long leave and had time to know each other better. But I can hear you and Mama saying that I have made my bed and must lie in it, and I shall. I know I am young and silly and have a lot to learn, but I cannot imagine having a better teacher than Arthur.

I send you all my dearest love and will write again from Calcutta.

Your loving Cecily

Garden Reach, Calcutta, 3rd November 1855

Dear Mina,

It was so lovely to find all your letters waiting for me when we reached Calcutta yesterday. The ship arrived late as the sea has been quite stormy and I was shocked to find our wedding has been arranged for the ninth – in six days' time! – and we leave for Cuttack on the fourteenth. We are to be married in the cathedral. Arthur organised for the banns to be read and has made all the arrangements. I must confess to being nervous about marrying so soon after arriving, but it seems there is no alternative, as Arthur has used up all his short leave and is due back with his regiment in three weeks.

Everything is so different here that I wonder if I shall ever get used to it. My first experience of India was quite startling – near Madras some natives rowed out to meet us in canoes, offering fresh fruit and curious trinkets, but as they got closer it was apparent that they had wholly forgotten to put on any clothes! You should have heard the screams and giggles from the Fishing Fleet on the deck below, but Louisa did not bat an eyelash. I overheard Mrs. Weston telling one of the ladies that the secret to managing natives was not to think of them as men at all!

The sea was very rough around the coast and poor Louisa was quite ill, but she improved when we entered the more sheltered waters of the Bay of Bengal. On the way up the east coast we passed a place called Puri. At dinner Mrs. Weston said there is a famous temple there where each year a procession of great wooden chariots filled with idols is pulled through the streets and the natives used to lie down in front of them to be crushed, in order to gain merit in future lives. She says it is an example of how superstitious the natives are, but James says it is all nonsense.

Before Calcutta we had to take on a pilot near the mouth of the Hoogly (is that not a divine name for a river?), for the shifting sandbanks are very treacherous. The captain pointed to some masts sticking out of the water, which is all that is left of the ships swallowed up by them. There were great bats swooping about at evening, and all night one could hear the wail of jackals, but that was not the worst! The day we arrived I was woken early by a knocking on the wall of my cabin. I rose and dressed and made my way on to the deck and when I looked over the railing I saw two corpses floating beside the ship with their heads banging against the side. One of the sailors on a lower deck was trying to push them away with a pole. The captain told us that the natives use the river to dispose of bodies, as it is their holy river. Most of the dead are cremated, but those who die of the small-pox or in childbirth are placed in the river unburnt. We saw a lot more bodies as we made our way upriver, and everywhere we looked there were vultures and crows making a hearty meal. The water looks like soup, and the banks are lined with crocodiles that look just like logs. It is quite sinister to see them slip silently into the water.

But Calcutta is a grand city, with fine buildings and gardens, and seems almost European. I am staying with the

51

Wellings, who are friends of Arthur's, and he is putting up at his club. The Wellings live in Garden Reach, in a charming Indian-style house with a long garden that extends down to the river. I had a surprise when we arrived, for we were greeted by a genie, over six feet tall and almost as broad, with a long black beard parted in the middle and tucked behind his ears. He was wearing a costume of purple and white with gold buttons, and a saffron turban. I thought him a maharajah at the very least and almost curtsied, but Arthur informed me just in time that he was merely the khitmutgar – the major domo. Colonel Welling addresses him as 'boy'!

It was strange seeing Arthur again at the port. He was accompanied by Col. Welling and another friend in uniform and from a distance I could not tell which of them he was. I was so afraid I would not recognise him, but of course I did when they came forward. He looks so important and distinguished in uniform that I feel quite in awe of him and whenever he asks me a question, even how I take my tea, my mind goes perfectly blank! I fear he must think he has become engaged to an imbecile! Fortunately James and Louisa are remaining in Calcutta as guests of the local magistrate until the wedding, and their presence makes everything easier. Afterwards they go on to Lucknow, where James is to take up the post of collector and magistrate.

6th November 1855

The Wellings have been really very kind. Last night they held a party in our honour. I wore my light green taffeta with the silver sash and received a great many compliments on my singing, though it felt odd to sing without you. Officers are not encouraged to marry until they reach the rank of major, so there are many unattached young officers starved of feminine company, and some are such terrible flirts that it quite turns one's head. When I told one of them I was engaged to Major Langdon he groaned and said bitterly that no junior officer stood a chance against the 'liver-decayed old Anglo-Indian with his parchment face and treasure', which I thought rather impolite. As you know, my 'liver-decayed old Anglo-Indian' does not care to stand up, and I was engaged for every dance, so we barely spoke. I am sure Arthur regretted that Papa, Mama and you were not here to sit with him and have one of those discussions that you all so enjoyed.

Today we saw the sights of Calcutta and tomorrow Mrs. Welling is taking me shopping for Christmas presents, as it takes seven weeks for the mail to reach England. I am also to buy material for some new dresses, for she tells me the ones we had made will not do for this climate. I forgot to tell you that we were asked to remove our crinolines on board ship to avoid blocking the gangways, and Arthur tells me he has never seen the point of them and considers them absurd, especially in this heat. He even suggested – in front of the Wellings! – that I should leave off my corsets. I did not know where to look, but it is true that I am finding it hard to breathe, although this is supposed to be the cool season.

I must stop now for the khitmutgar is waiting to take the letters and packages to the post and he looks so imposing that I dare not keep him waiting. It is hard to believe that by the time I receive your reply it will be nearly spring in England and I shall have been married for over three months! Mrs. Arthur Langdon – it sounds so grown-up, I shall hardly believe it is me! This is the last time I shall sign myself,

Your ever-loving sister, Cecily Partridge

Garden Reach, Calcutta, 10th November 1855

Mina darling,

I do not know how to say this – I am sure I should not but there is no one else I can talk to and I feel so alone. *I do not know how I shall bear married life!!*

I never imagined it would be like this! How could Mama not have told me? Did you know, Mina, and yet not warn me? Arthur tells me it is what all married couples do, but I cannot believe it. Surely Mama and Papa would never do such things – and as for the thought of Mr. and Mrs. Weston behaving in such a way, it is just too absurd! All Mama said was that I should leave everything to Arthur, and that when a man and a woman love each other everything seems perfectly natural. But it does not seem at all natural to me. It is so unromantic – surely *this* cannot be what all the fuss is about in books?

Oh, Mina, I cannot think how I shall face Arthur again! This morning, when the maid came in to change the sheets, she grinned at me horribly and I felt so humiliated that everyone might know, that I could hardly bear to face the Wellings at breakfast. Fortunately Mrs. Welling kept up such a chatter that no one had time to think of anything else. Then, after church, Arthur went to make arrangements for our journey to Cuttack, and when he had gone she must have seen I was not myself because she said I would soon become accustomed to marriage, and even grow to like it, but I do not believe it. I keep thinking that I shall be married for years and years and years. How ever shall I bear it?

Your wretched sister, Cecily

13th November 1855

Dear Mina,

Please forgive my letter of last week. As soon as I had sent it I regretted it, but it was too late to recall it and as the mail only goes once a week you will have had a whole seven days to reflect on my stupidity! Oh, Mina, I am sorry to be such a goose, but it has all been such a rush, and I miss you all so much, and it is so hard knowing that I shall not see you for another four years until Arthur gets his next long leave.

Louisa and James are leaving for Lucknow tomorrow and I shall miss them and the children dreadfully too, especially little Sophie. But I know that none of this is any excuse and that Mama would say that Arthur is now my family. And, indeed, he has been very good. When he came home and saw that I had been crying he said I needed time to get used to married life and he hoped that when we got to know each other better I would come to enjoy it. In the meantime, he has promised not to trouble me until I am ready and has moved into the dressing room next door. I was worried what the Wellings might think, but Arthur says I should not care what others think but do what is right and comfortable for me. He is so straight and honest that I know he must be right about what a man and wife do in private, but I cannot get used to the idea. I mean Mama and Papa! The Wellings! Mrs. Weston! Surely it cannot be! It seems so undignified. But if it is so I must pray for the strength to learn to endure it, for I am determined to be a good wife to Arthur. But before you accept an offer from anyone, Mina, make sure that Mother explains everything to you properly.

We leave for Cuttack in the morning. Give my dearest love to everyone at Home.

Your loving sister, Cecily

Lila

Simon was right: I did like Jagjit from the start, despite my resolution not to. He was tall – as tall as Simon was small – and very thin, with fuzzy black down growing in odd tufts on his cheeks and under his chin. His high-bridged nose looked too big for his face, and his mouth tilted up on one side when he smiled, forming a dimple in one cheek.

His hand engulfed mine as he looked into my eyes with his earnest dark brown ones. 'Hello, Lila, I'm Jagjit. I've been looking forward to meeting you. Simon says you grew up in India, so we already have something in common.'

Ever since I had arrived in England I had noticed how different people were. Their eyes never held yours but were always shifting about, as though they were afraid of letting you see who they really were. And no one ever seemed to say what they really meant. But Jagjit's brown eyes settled on me with liking, his voice warmed when he spoke to me, his lopsided smile did not seem to find me wanting. For the first time since I arrived in England I regretted my decision not to speak.

What was it about Jagjit that disarmed everyone who met him? The servants took to him at once, and even the villagers, who were usually suspicious of strangers and still looked at me out of the corners of their eyes, liked him and invited him to play in their Sunday cricket matches. Everyone, that is, except Aunt Mina. She was polite, of course, but she never met his gaze and never spoke to him unless he addressed her first. Thinking about it now, I realise that she must have seen Jagjit as a threat to her efforts to banish my memories of India and turn me into an ordinary English girl. But, perhaps because he was the Beauchamps' house guest, she tolerated him.

Although Jagjit was a year older than Simon and almost two years older than me, he did not seem to find us dull, as I had feared he would. The two of them helped with the Christmas decorations at High Elms. Being tall, Jagjit could reach places we could not, so he hung the ivy from the tops of doorways and pictures, and placed the decorations high up on the Christmas tree, while Simon and I did the banisters, the mantel shelves and the lower branches. Jagjit liked Christmas because he said the preparations and smell of cooking reminded him of the festivals they celebrated at home.

And it was true that it did feel special. The smell of spices and dried fruit filled the house and as Christmas came closer even the servants seemed excited. I heard Cook say to Ellen, 'It's like old times, with a child in the house. Such a pity the poor little thing is dumb.'

'She's peculiar if you ask me,' Ellen said, and giggled. 'And no wonder. I heard the mistress tell that Mrs. B. that her father topped hisself and her mam was doolally.'

I had no idea what 'doolally' meant, but I could guess. So Aunt Mina did know what had really happened. No wonder the people in the village thought I was queer.

On Christmas Eve we went to church for midnight mass. Jagjit came too. Usually he stayed behind at Simon's while we were at church, but he said he was curious. At school assembly, he told me, before prayers began, the headmaster would give the order: 'Jews, Hindus and Muslims fall out,' and all non-Christians would leave the hall.

I had always found Sunday services a bore but in the dark, with all the candles lit, the church seemed like a magical cave, decorated with great arrangements of berried branches and flowers, and fragrant with incense. We were invited to the Beauchamps' for Christmas lunch the next day, and there were piles of presents under the tree, with mince pies and mulled wine for the adults and warm spiced apple juice for us. Aunt Mina's gifts to us were practical: warm clothing for me, and a leather writing case for Simon. She had bought a fountain pen for Jagjit, but did not look at him when he thanked her. The three biggest presents were from the Beauchamps, and when we opened them we found that they had given us matching sleds. 'Rats! Why can't it snow?' Simon burst out, and Jagjit and I exchanged smiles, like the parents of a small, eager child.

Two days before New Year, I woke with an uneasy feeling that something was different. It took me a few moments to notice the silence: the absence of birdsong, of trees rustling, of the clattering of the milkman's cart as he did his rounds. And there was an odd light – a white glare – coming into the room round the edges of the curtains. I waited, and listened, but nothing changed, so I got out of bed and nervously pulled the curtains back.

At first all I could see was white. The world had disappeared! I felt a thrill of fear. Then, gradually, I made out shades of grey in the whiteness. It covered everything, smoothing out angles, curving gently up the hillside, balancing on top of trees and bushes, forming white pompoms at the ends of branches. White crystals were piled up round the windowpanes and I became aware that I was freezing. It was early, not yet time for Ellen to wake me, so I got dressed and went outside. The snow came halfway up my Wellington boots and I stamped around, enjoying the crunch under my feet. I bent and scooped some up. Wetness seeped through my glove and my fingers went numb. I had read about snow and seen pictures of it in books so I knew it was cold, but had always imagined it dry and fluffy, like cotton wool.

Simon and Jagjit came over and we went up the slope behind the house. Half the village children were out, struggling through the drifts with their sledges made from wooden boxes and trays. We had never mixed with them and I didn't care much for them because they stared at me and whispered. Jagjit's arrival triggered another bout of wide-eyed silence, just as it had done in church when he followed Simon in to midnight mass. The children nudged each other and giggled, but by the end of that afternoon he was giving the smaller ones rides on his sledge and tumbling them, screaming with laughter, into the snow.

That evening we played charades with the adults and when it was our turn we chose the wedding scene from *Jane Eyre*. Simon, who was the smallest and fairest, took the part of Jane, dressed in one of my white petticoats with a lace curtain for a veil. I was Mr. Rochester because Simon said I was the best at scowling; I wore his blue velvet suit, which was a bit tight. Jagjit played the mad wife, with a cloud of tangled black hair and white powder caked into the fuzz on his cheeks and chin. He wore one of Mrs. Beauchamp's nightdresses, which barely reached his knees; his hairy legs and big feet stuck out comically underneath. We wrestled with each other as he pretended to bite me, while Simon stood by wringing his hands.

For the next few days, while the snow lasted, we raced around the garden, hiding behind bushes then leaping out and pelting each other with snowballs. Simon ran up to me and thrust a handful of snow down the neck of my coat. I squealed and he stopped and stared at me, then turned to Jagjit. 'She made a noise! She did – she made a noise!' Jagjit looked at me and I turned away. 'I'll show you,' Simon said to him, and picked up another handful of snow, but as he reached for me Jagjit tackled him, knocking him into a snowdrift. In the scuffle that followed, my squeal was forgotten, but later that evening, as we sat by the fire in the schoolroom groaning while our fingers thawed out, I saw Jagjit watching me thoughtfully.

The next morning, to my surprise, Jagjit came over on his own. Aunt Mina called me down from my room where I was reading.

'It's that Indian boy,' she said. I could tell from the set of her lips that she wasn't happy. 'I've put him in the library and I'd like you to stay in the house. I want you within earshot.' She gave me a meaningful look that annoyed me – what did she think he was going to do to me? But I went into the library feeling surprisingly anxious, wondering how I could entertain him. I was used to being in the background while he and Simon talked.

He was standing looking at the books and turned as I came in. 'I hope you don't mind, Lila. Simon's gone into Brighton with his mother to buy school shoes, so I thought I'd come over.'

I noticed that although he had almost lost his accent he said 'i-school' instead of 'school', just as Afzal Khan used to. For some reason it made me feel easier with him. I smiled and shook my head.

'Your aunt didn't seem very happy to see me.'

I rolled my eyes.

He laughed. 'What shall we do? Do you want to go out?'

I shook my head again and cast about for something. My eyes fell on the Parcheesi board and I pointed at it.

'Ah, but I'm a champion,' he said. 'Are you sure you want to risk it?'

It was restful being with him. He didn't talk all the time like Simon, and didn't seem disturbed by my silence. When I took one of his pieces, instead of getting cross or sulking he smiled that funny lopsided smile.

'I think you're a hustler, Lila. I can tell you've played this before? Was it in India?'

I nodded, remembering the games with Afzal Khan, and Father when he was home.

Jagjit was watching me. 'Do you miss India? Mrs. Beauchamp said you lived in Peshawar, not so far from us. You know what it would be like there at this time of year… those winter evenings, when everyone is coming home from their day's work…'

He paused as though visualising it and I could see it too: the band of white mist rising from the warm earth as the evening air cooled, leaving the tree tops floating like dark clouds on a white sea; the great orange ball of sun flattening over the horizon; the wooden wheels of hay carts creaking along the dusty paths, the bullocks' white coats tinted pale violet in the slanting golden rays; the smell of woodsmoke, and the graceful women in bright saris – peacock-blue, emerald and pink – supporting their water pots with one hand, their elongated shadows stretching across the sun-baked earth as they returned to their Untouchable village.

My eyes filled with tears.

He reached out and rested his hand on mine, warm and consoling. I looked into his dark eyes and for the first time since leaving India I felt comforted.

Henry

Aunt Mina went to Father's room in the night. I had just
finished writing down what happened at the chaplain's, which
took ages, so it must have been very late. I was getting ready
for bed when I heard her knocking on Father's door. I went
to my own and opened it a crack. Aunt Mina was standing
there with a candle, but she looked so much younger that at
first I didn't recognise her. Her hair was loose and she had a
colourful shawl wrapped around her.

Father opened his door. He said 'Cecily?' very loud as
though he was shocked and she said, 'It's Mina, Arthur. I'm
sorry – I didn't mean to startle you.' Even her voice sounded
different, softer. She said she couldn't sleep and wanted to talk
to him.

Father didn't say anything for ages. I could hear him
breathing hard, and then he apologised for leaving the
chaplain's house like that and said, 'It was just that you
sounded so... so like her.' Aunt Mina said she was sorry too,
and that she'd forgotten Cecily used to sing that song. She
asked if she could come in, just for a minute, and he let her
in and closed the door.

I went out on to the verandah and slid along the wall between my door and his. I know it was wrong but I thought they would talk about Mother and I wanted to hear. I pressed myself flat against the wall by his door. I heard Father say that he still misses her, and dreams about her. He said he sometimes finds himself fantasising that she was taken, that she is alive and living in a bazaar somewhere, and that he still looks at the hands of women in burkhas, hoping to recognise hers. Aunt Mina said surely he could not wish such a wicked thing, and even death would be preferable to *that*, but I don't know what she meant.

She told him everyone was saying that he cared more for the natives than his own people and asked how he could forgive them after what they had done. Father said he did not think there was so much difference between them and us, and that we were just as guilty – he more than most, for he had betrayed the trust of a better man than he would ever be.

Aunt Mina said surely they deserved everything that was done to them and Father said the thing he always says to me when I complain about anyone: 'When you start pointing the finger of blame it goes all the way back to Adam.' Then he said it was late and they were both tired and why didn't they talk tomorrow?

Aunt Mina began to cry and said she had waited eleven years to talk, and in all that time he had hardly written to her even though when they first met she was the one who had talked to him most, and everyone had been surprised when he chose Cecily. She said Cecily had always charmed everyone and got her own way, that she was indulged and spoilt, and how did he think she'd felt when he'd asked Cecily to marry him when everyone had expected him to ask *her*. Father said he was sorry if he had disappointed her but it was all water under the bridge now. And then Aunt Mina said there was still me to think of and didn't he think that I needed a mother? I almost stopped breathing but Father said surely she must know by now that he wasn't good husband material and, anyway, he suspected that she was not cut out for Indian life and would be happier at home.

She didn't say anything for ages, and I could hear her crying, and then she said, 'You've put her on a pedestal but she didn't deserve it. She never could bear anyone else to have something she didn't, and as soon as she got it she changed her mind. She never loved you.'

I didn't want to listen any more then, but I didn't dare to move in case they heard me, and then Aunt Mina said she was sorry and Father said, 'No, don't apologise. You're right, Mina. She didn't love me. She deserved someone young, like that boy Peter. I should have known better, because India is full of foolish old men who've married silly young girls and it never ends well.'

I heard Aunt Mina leave and I wanted to go to him and say that whatever had happened I knew it wasn't his fault, and that I was sure my mother had loved him, but I knew he wouldn't like me to have heard. I had just starting sliding back along the wall towards my room when he walked out on to the verandah and over to the top of the steps leading down to the compound. I pressed myself against the wall, hardly daring to breathe. He rested his hands on the pillars on either side of the steps and bowed his head, and from the back he looked just like the figure above the altar in church.

I heard him say 'Cecily' and then he called out 'Ram! Ram!' and his shoulders began to shake and I knew he was crying. I don't understand why, because Ram is the name of a Hindu god.

8th January 1869

Last night I had the dream again. It's always the same: I am in a small hot space, with something covering my face so I can't breathe. My eyes, nose and mouth are filled with darkness and in my ears there is a terrible screeching and I open my mouth to call for help, but no sound comes.

Then Father was there, holding me in his arms and rocking me. 'Wake up, Henry. It's all right. You're safe now. It's just a dream.' My heart was pounding so hard I thought it would leap out of my chest, and then I heard Aunt Mina's voice, sounding shaky and frightened, outside the door. 'Is everything all right, Arthur? I heard someone screaming.' And Father said, 'It's all right, Mina. It's just Henry, having a nightmare.' And I said, 'You won't send me away, Father? Promise you won't send me away.' And he said, 'I promise, Henry. Go back to sleep now. You're not going anywhere.'

Cecily

Cuttack, 3rd December 1855

Dear Mina,

There is so much to tell you, I don't know where to begin!
I am writing to you from our new home in Cuttack. The
journey took just over a fortnight by pony cart, and palanquin
in the places where there were no metalled roads. I do not
know why people complain about travelling in India for to me
it seems quite delightful, like an extended picnic. We spent the
night in pretty little rest houses, called 'dak bungalows', which
provided everything we needed – a simple meal of an omelette
or chupatties, and a curry of meat or lentils. Afterwards we
would sit on the verandah talking until it got dark.

We arrived in Cuttack just as the sun was setting. There
is no dusk here – night falls suddenly, like someone blowing
out a lamp. And then, out of the darkness, we saw pinpricks
of light, like fireflies floating towards us and growing brighter
and brighter. Then drums started up and there was shouting
and cheering and a crowd of men in colourful uniforms and
turbans appeared out of the dark, bearing torches. They were
Arthur's men, come to greet us. They garlanded us both with
gardenias and marigolds and tied a gold turban on his head.

Then they lifted him on to a white horse and led him ahead of us through the streets with the band playing, and people threw rice at us as we passed. It was so romantic – like being in a story from the *Arabian Nights*!

But I have told you nothing of Cuttack and the house. Briefly, then, Cuttack is a pretty town strung out along a river, with a church, a mosque and a temple, and the cantonment is full of little white bungalows with small gardens bursting with flowers. It all looks quite English and very clean, with straight roads and neat white fences.

Our house is the same as all the others. The drawing and dining rooms are connected by double doors, and there are two bedrooms with their own dressing rooms and primitive bathrooms. Arthur has a study at the back, and a verandah runs all the way round the house. The rooms are high, with cloth ceilings, which are removed in the hot season to allow the heat to rise and punkahs to be hung. The kitchen and servants' quarters are behind the house in the compound. It is so strange to see things that I have only heard talked of, or read about in books. It is all very bare but Arthur says I can order anything I want from the catalogues and make it just as I want it, for he knows 'women like their fripperies'. He has ordered me a piano as my Christmas gift. He is so very kind and thoughtful and I am determined to love him, and I know I shall when we know each other better.

Give my love to Mama and Papa and tell them I will write to them soon.

Your loving Cecily

P.S. I almost forgot to say Merry Christmas (although I know you will not receive this till nearly February).

1st January 1856

Darling, darling Mina,

Thank you so much for the beautiful shawl, which is perfect for these cooler mornings. I could hardly believe my eyes when I saw it. How ever did you find the time to embroider it all? Whenever I feel homesick I shall wrap myself in it and feel comforted.

I wore it to church on Christmas Day but I am afraid I heard nothing of the service for all my thoughts were with you at Home. I kept picturing Mama and Papa and you in our little church. Do you remember the time Peter put burrs down the back of my dress and Mama sent me out of church for fidgeting? And now you are engaged! Oh, Mina, I am so happy for you both. Please do give him my love and my congratulations on his commission. I am sure you will miss him when he goes away but, as you say, it is important for him to establish his career before he marries.

I am afraid I am not managing my household tasks very well – with so many servants it is hard to remember who does what, so I am forever getting it wrong. It is all so complicated. You can imagine how nervous I am at the thought of having to oversee them all. Arthur says I should leave it all to the khitmutgar, but the other ladies tell me I must not or we shall be shamefully cheated and taken advantage of. I wonder if I shall ever learn to be a good 'mem'. Arthur says if I do he will divorce me!

Your loving Cecily

5th March 1856

Dear Mina,

I have just received your reply to my foolish letter from Calcutta and, although I know I deserved it, I thought it very unkind. It is true that you and Mama warned me I was too young to marry and travel so far from home, but it is never nice to hear someone say 'I told you so'!

I know I should not have written to you about such private matters, but we have always told each other everything, and there is no one here that I can confide in. But, as you rightly say, matters between a husband and wife should remain between them, so you need not worry about my involving you in my troubles again.

Your chastened sister, Cecily

23rd April 1856

Dear Mina,

I am so sorry for not writing to you for over a month. Arthur has been ill with malaria and I have been so afraid. I had no idea what a terrible illness it is. The doctor says there is nothing to be done except to keep him cool and quiet and dose him with quinine.

I don't know how I would manage without his native officers. His subhedar and jemadar have been coming daily to visit him and give him news of the men. They even take it in turns to sit with him through the night so I can rest. It is such a comfort. His subhedar is called Durga Prasad, which means 'gift of the Goddess Durga' (she is the goddess of war, appropriately enough), though he does not look at all fierce but the very image of the old Indian with a turban and white beard on the box of that old wooden puzzle in our nursery! The jemadar, Ram Buksh, is quite young, with flashing white teeth and a handlebar moustache, like a pirate. He speaks English quite well and tells me that Arthur has had malaria before. They have told me many stories of his bravery and it is clear that they both respect and admire him. How I wish I had known him when he was young!

The doctor has told me that I am to take him to the hills, where it is cooler, as soon as he is strong enough to travel. I will write again from there.

Your affectionate Cecily

P.S. I am learning some Hindustani now, for Ram Buksh has been giving me lessons. I know Arthur will be pleased.

Lila

I thought of Jagjit often in the three and a half months between Christmas and his next visit at Easter. I felt closer to him than anyone I had met since coming to England, because I knew that he, like me, was missing his home. He had told us how strange things seemed to him when he first arrived in England – all the things I too found odd: the grey skies and fogs, the bland food and the lack of sounds and smells. But he said the queerest thing of all was arriving at Tilbury and seeing white men on the dock acting as porters, dockers and sweepers. He couldn't believe it when he got into a taxi to the station and the driver called him 'sir'.

I would have liked to know more about his home and family, but Simon wasn't interested enough to ask and, although the Beauchamps always enquired politely after his parents and brother, they left it at that. The main subject at their lunch table was politics. Keir Hardie, who had just resigned as leader of the Labour Party, was a frequent visitor. He supported free education, women's suffrage and home rule for India and Ireland, and was a close friend of Mrs. Pankhurst. Her sister, Mrs. Clarke, lived in Brighton and was often there too, so the talk was usually of matters that had been raised in the House: as well as the causes close to his heart, they talked of Germany's growing militarisation and the fear that the situation in Bosnia and Servia would lead to a European war. I was surprised by Jagjit's grasp of history and politics. The adults treated him like an equal and he often joined in the discussions, especially when the subject of India arose.

Aunt Mina stayed silent on these occasions. She disapproved of both the Labour Party and the Votes for Women movement and would have preferred to keep me away, but she did not want to offend the Beauchamps.

One Easter Sunday, we went over for lunch after the service. There were no other visitors that day, and during the course of lunch Mr. Beauchamp asked Jagjit what he planned to do when his schooling was finished. Jagjit told him that his father wished him to go to university and study law, with a view to joining the I.C.S.

Mrs. Beauchamp laughed. 'So you're going to be a civil servant! Do you know, I was in the village yesterday and the baker's wife asked me if it was true that you were a prince! Actually,' she went on, 'an Indian prince did come here once, before I was born. I remember my grandmother mentioning it. She said he was very cultured and quite charming. I believe he even stayed at the Devil's Dyke Hotel. You might remember that, Miss Partridge,' she said, turning to Aunt Mina.

For a moment Aunt Mina did not reply. Then she said quietly, 'Yes, I do remember him. He was charming. And a snake, and treacherous – as they all are.'

Mrs. Beauchamp's eyes widened.

'Ah, yes,' Mr. Beauchamp said, glancing at Jagjit, 'but he wasn't a real prince, was he? As I recall he was called something Khan... began with an A? Azim? Wasn't he from Cawnpore, something to do with...'

He trailed off as Mrs. Beauchamp caught his eye. She said quickly, 'I think to the villagers every Indian is a prince. They think of Ranji, of course, who played for Sussex. You play cricket, don't you, Jagjit?'

'No, I don't, Mrs. B., although I've been unable to convince the games master, who seems to think just because I'm an Indian I should be good at it. But Mr. Beauchamp, do you perhaps mean *Azimullah* Khan, who was – '

'Perhaps we should all take a turn in the garden,' Mrs. Beauchamp said, cutting across him.

There was a silence while Jagjit looked around the table, puzzled. Aunt Mina's face looked as though someone had laid it on the ironing board and pressed it. 'I'm sorry,' Jagjit said. 'Have I said something I shouldn't?'

'It *is* a lovely afternoon,' Mrs. Beauchamp said into the silence.

Once outside, the Beauchamps and Aunt Mina walked around the lawn while the three of us wandered over towards the orchards, where the buds on the apple trees were still tightly furled. April had been cold, and the day was chill and damp.

'Did I do something wrong, Lila? I always get the feeling your aunt dislikes me, but I never know why.'

'Perhaps it's because you're Indian,' Simon said. 'She was engaged to my Uncle Peter and he died, out in India. But that was a long time ago, so she shouldn't *still* be upset.'

I thought of Aunt Mina young, as she had been in the photograph, and wondered if I would remember Father when I was as old as she was. Part of me shrank at the thought of the long, lonely years she must have spent in that big empty house, brooding on the past, but I felt pleased at the thought that I would never forget him, as Aunt Mina had not forgotten Peter.

I think, now, how sad it is that we lived in the same house for so many years, both locked into our pasts, unable to speak of the things that mattered most to us.

A few days after that lunch, we cycled out to Shaves Wood. The following week would bring unseasonal blizzards and deep snowdrifts, but that day was sunny and seemed to hold the promise of spring. We sat under the green-gold canopy of unfurling leaves; the bluebells were just beginning to open around us, scenting the air with their delicate fragrance, as we ate our cucumber sandwiches and drank our lemonade.

Because of the inclement weather I had not seen much of the boys that week and I felt shy and separate. I sat listening, trying to look interested, while they talked easily of school, and masters, and other boys. Jagjit made an effort to include me, as he always did, but I could tell it was making Simon impatient so I wandered off to collect some bluebells and wood anemones and wove them round with wild honeysuckle to make three crowns and some bracelets. I placed mine around my head and wrists and wandered back.

As I approached the clearing where the boys were sitting I heard Simon say, 'Why does *she* have to do everything with us? It's so boring.'

I stepped behind the trunk of a beech and waited for Jagjit's reply.

'Come on, Simon. She's hasn't got anyone else.'

'Do you always have to be so dashed kind to every lame dog?'

'Isn't that why we're friends? Have you forgotten what a bad time *you* were having at school before I intervened?'

There was a silence, and I imagined Simon's face flaming

as he struggled for words. He stammered out, 'I th-thought you *l-liked* coming home with me. You could always stay at the b-beastly school if you prefer.'

I heard him stamp off.

Jagjit sighed and stretched out on the rug in a patch of sunlight.

I crept silently into the clearing but as I approached him he opened his eyes. His mouth pulled up, creasing his cheek. 'You look like a peri – a fairy – in that crown. Are those wings you're hiding behind your back?'

I showed him the two other crowns.

He smiled. 'Is one of them for me?'

I nodded.

'Why don't you put it on for me?'

He reached up and lifted his turban off, preserving its stiff pleated shape, then untied the white handkerchief securing his topknot and shook his hair out. The long black rope of it uncoiled as far as his waist. He sat up and I knelt in front of him and placed it on his head.

'You heard us, didn't you?' His eyes searched mine.

I hesitated, then nodded.

'I thought so. He didn't mean it, you know. It's just that he's a bit nervy. He had a bad time at school when he first arrived. New boys do, especially those who're young for their age, and it doesn't help if you look like him. You get the wrong sort of attention from the older boys.'

I wondered what he meant.

'What are you thinking, Lila?' He dipped his head until his eyes were so close to mine that they blurred into one giant Cyclops eye. 'You notice everything, don't you? What do you really think of us all? That we're a lot of fools with our yak-yak-yakking?'

I shook my head, but he'd already turned away. 'I'd better go and find Simon or he'll sulk for the rest of the day.'

That evening, alone in my room, I tried to make myself speak aloud, but it was harder than I'd imagined. I had always thought that when I was ready I would open my mouth and speech would come, but it felt ugly, unnatural, as though there were two tongues in my mouth, tangling round each other. The words slid away as I fumbled for them, and the sounds that emerged were more like frogs than pearls. The thought of talking in public filled me with dread: I imagined the attention that would be focused on me, the fuss that would be made. And once I started there would be no turning back; I would have to speak to everyone, not just to Jagjit and Simon and the Beauchamps and Aunt Mina, but to Cook and the maids, and to people at church and in the village and to people I had not even met yet. And by now everyone was so used to my silence that no one ever asked what I thought, or left a gap in the conversation for me to fill. I should have to force my way in and I shrank from that. No, I was not ready. And then the blizzard came unexpectedly, bringing deep snow, and, by the time the path was passable again in May, the boys had gone back to school.

A month later, the suffragettes held a huge demonstration in London and for weeks beforehand the Beauchamps' house was full of women sewing banners and tabards in the W.S.P.U. colours of purple, white and green. I went over after lessons to help. I did not sew, but I could cut and shape and pin. It was fun and I was looking forward to accompanying Mrs. Beauchamp, but Aunt Mina refused to allow it. The papers were full of it the next day – they said it was the greatest demonstration ever held in Britain. I was deeply disappointed at not being able to go, and it made me resent Aunt Mina even more.

Henry

17th February 1869

A woman has come to live in the bibighar. Father brought her home with him soon after Aunt Mina left. When I asked him who she was he told me she is someone he used to know a long time ago.

The bibighar is just an outhouse in the compound – one room with a small bathroom at the back. It used to be full of old furniture but before the woman came Father ordered Kishan Lal to get it cleared out and whitewashed, and had some rugs, a string bed, a low table and a lamp put in. There is a curtain at the door and window.

Kishan Lal says the woman arrived in a covered litter, which was carried right to the door, and he only caught a glimpse of her, but I heard him say to Allahyar, 'Judging by her dress she's a Muslim, but then that's hardly a surprise.' Then Allahyar got cross and told Kishan Lal he was the son of a raandi who plied her trade in the bazaar, and Kishan Lal called Allahyar a bhenchod, and Allahyar picked up the kitchen knife, so I stepped in and asked what raandi and bhenchod meant. I know they're rude words because Ali told me, and I knew that would stop them fighting.

They both looked at me and Allahyar said, 'Get out of here with your notebook, you little spy,' and Kishan Lal told him not to speak to me like that and then he told me to keep out of other people's business and that my notebook would get me into trouble one of these days. I said Mr. Mukherjee had told me to write it and then they both agreed you could never trust a Bengali and said I'd better not show him anything I'd written about them.

20th February 1869

This afternoon I took my books into the compound to work. When Kishan Lal asked what I was doing I said it was cold in the house and I wanted to sit in the sun.

'You'd better make sure your father doesn't catch you hanging around her,' he said. 'He won't like it.'

'Why not?' I asked, but he wouldn't tell me.

The woman did not come out all afternoon. I saw the mali's wife taking her a tray of food just before we had dinner, so she can't be a servant. She doesn't seem to have a name either. Kishan Lal and Allahyar always say 'her' if they have to speak of her. 'Take *her* her dinner.'

28th February 1869

I have heard the woman going to Father's room at night. She plays an instrument that has a strange twangy sound, and sings. Sometimes they talk and sometimes they're quiet. Once I heard her crying. I have decided not to listen any more.

I still spend most evenings and weekends at the Lines with Father, watching tent-pegging or wrestling. Mohan, Ali and I have started to wrestle too, but Ali is the strongest, even though he is younger than Mohan and I. He says it's because he's a Pathan, but Mohan asked how it is that Dhubraj Ram can beat his father, then, and then they fought and Ali won and Mohan went off sulking. I told Ali about the woman. He said he had heard his father talking about it with the other men. The woman is Father's bibi. A bibi is a bad woman who lives with a man when they aren't married. He says lots of Englishmen used to keep bibis before the memsahibs came and that's why the outhouse is called a 'bibighar', which means 'bibi's house'. I feel sorry for her. It can't be nice living alone in that tiny room and no one speaking to her and never seeing anyone except Father.

7th April 1869

The weather is hotter now and the bibi has started leaving her door open with just the curtain hanging and sometimes when there is a breeze I can see in a little bit. Yesterday I was practising playing ball against the side of her house when Kishan Lal came out and told me off. He said Father wouldn't like me disturbing her. I said she hadn't complained but he said he would tell Father if I didn't come away at once. Everyone seems to be cross since she came.

This morning, after Mr. Mukherjee had gone, I went out with my Urdu poetry book and began to practise the poem I am supposed to learn by heart, marching round the compound. Mr. Mukherjee told me that walking helps when you are trying to learn poetry because you can stamp out the rhythm. I don't really understand the poem, which makes it hard to remember. I kept forgetting the last two lines, and then a voice said them for me. It was a beautiful voice, like honey, and I turned round but she was behind the curtain.

'Why don't you come out?' I said, and she opened the curtain and looked at me.

She is quite old, older even than Aunt Mina, and tall, with a pock-marked face and a long silver plait that reaches almost to her knees. She smiled at me and I smiled back. She asked me if I understood the poem and I said no and she said it was about the pain of love and I was too young to understand it. And then she asked me some questions and I told her about Mr. Mukherjee and my lessons and she said I sounded very clever, like my Father. I don't know why no one likes her because I think she's nice.

14th May 1869

The bibi and I are friends now. Every day after lessons I read my poetry or my Urdu homework to her and sometimes she helps me with it and sometimes she plays her dilruba and sings. Mir is her favourite poet and her favourite song is this one. I wrote it down and Mr. Mukherjee translated it into English for me.

> My friendless heart's a city reduced to ruin,
> The great world has shrunk to a patch of rubble.
> In this place, where love was martyred,
> What now survives but memories and regret?

I asked her why her songs are always so sad. She says ghazals are like that. The loved one is always unobtainable, the lover has no hope, the mistress is cruel – her eyebrows are as sharp as daggers; her eyes shoot arrows. Mr. Mukherjee says in England in the Middle Ages they had 'courtly love' and the lover was always tested, sometimes to death, to prove his love, a bit like in *Ivanhoe*. It seems silly to me. She told me she used to be a singer and perform at mushairas. They are competitions where each singer takes it in turns to sing a couplet, and at the end of the night the one whose couplets are the cleverest is the winner. I asked if she ever won and she said she did. Then she told me that was how she met Father. He used to come and listen to her sing. Then she said, 'That was a long time ago, when we were both young.' She sounded sad. I wanted to ask more but I didn't like to. I wonder if Father knew her before he knew Mother.

She lent me the book and that night Father picked it up off my bedside table and looked at the poem, which I had marked with a slip of paper. I thought he would ask me about it but he seemed to think Mr. Mukherjee had given it to me. When I asked him about the poem he told me it was written after parts of Delhi were razed to the ground and some of Mir's relatives were killed. I asked him who did that and why. He sighed and said, 'I wish I could answer that, Henry.'

Cecily

28th May 1856

Dear Mina,

We are back from the hills early because there has been some trouble with the sepoys. Arthur says it is nothing to worry about, but he insisted upon returning at once although he is still quite weak. He wished me to remain there until it gets cooler but I could not let him travel alone, although I have hardly seen him since we returned as he spends even more of his time at the Lines.

You cannot begin to imagine the heat, Mina! The sun blazes down from a white sky that hurts one's eyes and the only time one can go out is in the very early morning. Except for my rides then, I am confined to the house. The dust is dreadful and almost chokes one, and the tattie blinds have to be soaked each morning to trap the dust and cool the breeze passing through them. They are kept drawn all day and we live in the dark like moles. Even when the sun goes down there is no relief, for the heat rises from the ground as from a frying pan, and the punkah has to be used all night. Sometimes the punkahwallah falls asleep and I wake soaked in perspiration and unable to breathe.

You cannot imagine the length of these nights as I toss and turn. There is a bird here called a kokil – a kind of cuckoo – that shrieks all night on a rising pitch until one longs to shriek oneself! The countryside is parched, the grass brown, and the trees are covered in a thick layer of dust. Everyone here is praying for the rains.

Give my best love to Mama and Papa. Arthur sends his best regards.

Cecily

4th June 1856

Dear Mina,

Please do not mention this to Mama and Papa, but I understand now why Arthur has been spending so much time at the Lines. He explained to me yesterday that, since the annexation of Oudh (from where many of the troops originate) in January, there have been constant rumours that we are trying to destroy their caste and convert them to Christianity. There has been trouble in several regiments, though none in Arthur's. He says we are in no danger as his men are very loyal and he has complete trust in them. He told me that Ram Buksh saved his life during the last war against the Sikhs by standing over him with his sword when he was wounded and holding off the enemy till help arrived.

I will write again as soon as there is news.

Cecily

25th June 1856

Dear Mina,

This morning I decided to take my sketchpad and watercolours with me when I went for my ride, thinking I would paint the view for you. Yet, when I sat down and looked over the lush green landscape (for the rains have started and the parched dusty plains and hills have turned to jungle almost overnight), what came to my mind's eye was the countryside at Home as it would be now, on one of those soft June mornings when everything seems to waver on the edge of solidity. The sky is a clear pale blue, the clouds small and soft, the flocks of starlings glow silver as they turn into the low sun, the trees and bushes quiver with every passing breeze, and the whole scene is constantly transformed by the passing shadows of the clouds. I could not, of course, achieve it, for what characterises it is *movement*, yet I think I captured something of its fragility and sweetness.

As I was adding a final touch of violet to the undersides of the clouds, Ram Buksh, Arthur's jemadar, came to tell me we should return soon, as the rainclouds were gathering. (Arthur thinks it unwise for me to ride alone now and says the syce would be no use if there was trouble, so Ram Buksh, who has been exercising Arthur's Waler since he has been ill, rides with me.) He looked quite puzzled when he saw the painting and looked from it to the landscape, until I explained that I had intended to paint the scene before us but somehow ended by painting Home instead. And then I started crying like a fool, and ended up telling him about High Elms, about you and Mama and Papa and the Downs and our games, and he listened so patiently, as though he understood and sympathised with everything I said, though he could not possibly have understood even half of it, even though he speaks some English, because life is so very different here.

We think we know all about India back Home, but the reality is beyond imagining. Everything is so extreme: the heat, the sun, the wild animals and the ever-present smell of death. It is all around us, and it is not uncommon to see the carcasses of cattle and even people lying by the roadside. Arthur says when the Agra famine occurred the streets and fields were full of bodies as people were dying too fast to be burnt, and many sold their children to the Missions for a rupee each, or gave them away to anyone who could feed them, to save them from starving. I have heard some of the ladies say that it is not so bad for natives when their children die, or they have to give them up to the Missions, for they do not care for them the way we do for ours, but I cannot see why this should be true. There is a village here that I sometimes ride to and it seems to me the children's mothers care for them as much as English mothers do – perhaps more, as they do not have servants to look after their children as we do but have to do it themselves.

I cannot tell you how comforting it was to be able to talk to someone about Home. Arthur is always busy and last week we quarrelled and since then I have hardly seen him because he does not come home to sleep. I think he must be sleeping in the Lines with his men. I know you will disapprove of my mentioning our troubles, but I have no one else to talk to. Everyone here is so proper and constantly standing on their manners. Emily Tremayne seems nice, but her little girl Mabel is very sickly so she is always preoccupied, and in any case I could not talk to her about private matters.

Be kind to me, Mina, for I so look forward to letters from Home that I cannot bear it if you are cross with me.

Your loving Cecily

5th September 1856

Dearest Mina,

I am glad to hear that Peter is excited about being sent to Palestine, although I know you will miss him sadly. But he always wanted to see the world and I can still picture him wriggling through the trees on his stomach, pretending to be Davy Crockett.

You will be glad to know Arthur and I made up our quarrel, and I am slowly coming to learn something of his past. His parents died when he was very young and he and James were brought up by an uncle, who was not really interested in them, so they spent most of their holidays at school and have never really known family life. I felt so sorry for him when I heard that. I told him about our family and how much I missed you all, and how little I had understood of what married life involved. We even laughed about it. I told him that I wished to be a good wife to him and that I would try, and he was so gentle and kind with me that I think that Mama and Mrs. Welling must be right, and that perhaps in time I shall even come to enjoy it.

And there is more good news! We have just learnt that Arthur's regiment is being sent to Cawnpore, where James and Louisa are now, and that we will be leaving in November, when it is cooler, and travelling nine hundred miles overland. I am so excited at the thought of seeing them again and Arthur is happy that he and James will be together. Cawnpore is the biggest military station in India and many regiments are being transferred there because of the rumours that trouble is brewing in Oudh, but Arthur says there is no cause for worry as Cawnpore is under the command of General Wheeler, who is the finest soldier he could hope to serve under. The journey will take about three months so we shall not be in Cawnpore till early in February.

Your excited Cecily

22nd October 1856

My dearest Mina,

I know you will despair of me, especially after my last letter, but I discovered something on Saturday that was a terrible shock, for I had really thought that Arthur and I were becoming closer. But I have found out that he has been keeping a bibi, a native mistress, for years.

I did not tell you that the reason for the quarrel I mentioned back in June was that Arthur asked if I thought I should ever feel towards him as he does towards me, and I said I did not know. (This was before we had that talk and made up the quarrel.) He knew that I did not enjoy married life as he did, and I know it hurt him. I tried to tell him that perhaps if he spent more time with me and we grew to know each other better my feelings might change. But I could tell that he was not really listening and as soon as I had finished speaking he shouted for his batman to saddle Warrior and rode off into the rain. He did not come back until the next morning, soaked to the skin and shivering, and I was afraid he would be ill again but he refused to rest, changed his clothes and went straight out to the Lines. After that, until we made up, he spent several nights each week and most Sundays away from here and I had no idea where he went. I assumed he was sleeping in the Lines but now I know he was seeing his mistress all the time, and everyone knew about it except me!

I found out about it entirely by chance, for we were attending a farewell dinner before our departure for Cawnpore, and, after the ladies had withdrawn, I went to the powder room. As I entered it I heard two ladies talking – one of them Captain Melbourne's wife Lucy, who gives herself airs because her husband is the stepson of a baronet. I overheard her say, 'Poor little thing, I feel so sorry for her. He is so much older than she is and it's evident to everyone that he hasn't the slightest interest in her. Graham says he spends all his time at the Lines with his men and completely neglects her, and he's always croaking about upsetting the natives and what they might do.'

They did not see me come in and I did not want to interrupt their conversation so I remained by the door.

'Well, of course he has different tastes after twenty-five years in India,' Lucy Melbourne went on. 'It's a surprise he married at all. Everyone knows he has had the same bibi for over twenty years and Graham says he still sees her. He saw him one morning last month coming out of her house. Such a plain creature, too, and quite old, and his wife is such a pretty little thing, but then of course these native women have all sorts of tricks – ' And then she saw me in the glass and stopped talking. Both of them looked so embarrassed and left the powder room so hastily that I knew at once that they had been talking of Arthur and me.

You cannot imagine how humiliated I feel, Mina, knowing everyone has been gossiping and laughing about us. I could not face seeing them, so I sent a bearer to fetch the dogcart and to tell Arthur that I was not well and was returning home. He came out to meet me at once and insisted on accompanying me. On the way I could not hold back the tears. He asked me why I was crying, and when I would not answer he told the syce to drive out to a tank in the countryside. We walked up and sat and looked out over the water and he said, 'Would you like to tell me what has made you unhappy?'

I did not reply and he said he knew it was hard for me to be away from my home and family but that he thought we had been getting along better recently. When he said that, I felt such indignation that I burst out and asked why he had asked me to marry him when he already had a native mistress. He said that he was sorry he had not told me about her, but that when we married he had put her behind him and thought it best not to mention it because it would upset me needlessly. He had truly not intended to see her any more. It was only when he thought that I did not care for him, and never would, that he had gone back to her, but as soon as we made it up he told her that he would not visit her again.

I asked how long he has known her and he said he met her soon after he came out here – nearly twenty-five years, Mina! – and that she taught him almost everything he knows about India. I asked if they have children and he said no, and that if they had he would have married her for the children's sake. And he sends her money every month because she has given him the best years of her life.

I could tell by the way he talked about her that he still cares for her and feels guilty for abandoning her, and I cannot stop thinking about it. They have lived together since before I was born, Mina, and she must know him better than I shall ever do! When I think of the things I have allowed him to do recently, and imagine him doing the same things with her, I feel I shall die of shame.

I was mortified and angry, and told him that he had had no right to propose to me, and that he had become engaged to me under false pretences. I could tell he was upset, but he said that if I was really unhappy and wanted to go Home he would not prevent me, although it is too late to change our arrangements now. When we reach Cawnpore he will arrange my passage to England if I still wish to go.

Since then he has slept in his dressing room, and I lie awake all night unable to stop thinking about it. The worst thing is that over the past few weeks I have truly grown to love and trust him. I know you will say that it is my duty to forgive him, but I cannot stop imagining them together and I know that every time he touches me now I shall think of him touching her that way, and I cannot bear it. I have not yet decided what to do, but I do not think I can continue living with him.

Try not to think too harshly of me, Mina. I know in my place you would have acted differently, but I have never been as strong or good as you are.

Your Cecily

Lila

At fifteen, although I was not beautiful, as she was, I was starting to see something of Mother in the bones of my face, the set of my mouth. I began to dream of her, too. In the dreams I was back on the ship, leaning over the rail and watching the phosphorescence, when she swam up from the depths, one half of her face silvered by moonlight, the other in darkness. I recoiled and saw her do the same. Only when I woke did I realise that her movements had mirrored mine in every detail. I was her, and she was me.

I would wake gasping for breath and lie there in the moonlight, remembering how, when I was small, she was the princess in the fairytales Father read me: pale, beautiful and distant. I used to stand in the doorway to her room as she sat at the dressing table, at first hiding behind the doorframe; but then the fascination would draw me out to watch as the two women talked, the one facing the mirror pleading and sad, the one in the mirror harsh and cruel, spitting out her words. It was always the mirror face who saw me: her mouth twisted, her eyes darkened, one more than the other, as she spat out '*Jao*! Go!' the way she did to the servants, even to Ayah, who was closest to her.

I could still make out the faint scar on my forehead just below the hairline, a reminder of the day I had followed her rustling silk skirts from room to room, trying to catch her, thinking we were playing a game. I must have been three or four. I could hear her whimpering behind her bedroom door and when I pushed it open her voice rose to a scream: '*Please God, don't let her come in! Please God, keep her away from me!*' The room was dark – her curtains were always drawn – but sunlight was streaming through a narrow gap and refracting through something in her raised hand. Dazzled, I blinked and did not see her throw it, only felt the blow and then the warm wet on my face and saw the red spattering on to the white Kashmiri rug, and the chunks of cut glass that lay scattered round my feet. Afterwards Ayah told me it had been an accident and that I shouldn't tell Father or he would be angry with her.

I did not want to think about Mother, but it was becoming harder not to as my body began to change, outwardly and inwardly. Hair began to grow in places that had been smooth; my chest developed painful knobs of hardness, yet felt tender. I ached to be touched, and behind it all was a longing for something I could not name. It was no longer homesickness for my old life, for, although I still thought of Father, my memories of him had become fixed: pictures in an old album that had replaced the living images. The pain was no longer raw but distant, nostalgic. I missed it; in a strange way it had been comforting, keeping me connected to Father, and reminding me of who I was and where I had come from.

When I stood at my window now I still heard that rhythmic vibration – the soundless voice that seemed to be telling me something I had always known – but it was fainter now and I feared to lose it. At night I tossed and turned, unable to get comfortable, and in the day my mood swung between elation and tears. Aunt Mina noticed the changes too, which made it worse. She began to concern herself with my hair and clothes, asking Mrs. Beauchamp for advice about the new fashions.

I tried on my new outfits in front of the mirror – flounced muslin dresses in *eau-de-nil*, *café-au-lait* and dusky pink, chosen to complement my complexion and lip colour – putting my hair up this way and that, while talking to myself in my practice grown-up voice. Then I would resume my pinafore dress and my silence and go downstairs, wearing the sulky expression I knew would provoke Aunt Mina. At breakfast I pretended not to hear when she said, 'Good morning,' and slumped in my chair. One morning she gave me a lecture about being 'sulky, superior and uppish', and back in my room I whispered all the bad words I could remember in both English and Hindustani. I promised myself that as soon as I was old enough to earn a living I would leave Aunt Mina's house and never see her again.

I started spending more time with Mrs. Beauchamp, who was encouraging me to think about a career; it was important for a woman to be independent, she said, to have her own work, rather than being a parasite. She would have liked to take me with her to suffragette meetings but she knew Aunt Mina wouldn't like it. Instead she lent me books to read, books like *The Story of an African Farm* and *The Yellow Wallpaper*, both of which disturbed me, although I don't think I understood either of them then.

The boys came back at the beginning of July and Mrs. Beauchamp sent the dogcart to collect me after lunch, as she always did when they were home. Aunt Mina stopped me as I ran down the stairs. I waited impatiently as she fussed. 'Don't forget your hat, Lilian. You really must start thinking about your complexion.' I thought of Mother again: the only interest she had ever shown in me was to insist that I wear a hat when I was outside. She never went into the sun herself.

'And you're a bit old to be playing with those boys,' Aunt Mina went on. 'It was all right when you were younger but you're not children any more. It's time you made friends with some girls your own age. There's no one suitable in the village, and I've been thinking it's time you went away to school. It might rub off some of those corners. But you'd better go now, as Mrs. Beauchamp has so kindly sent the dogcart.'

I was still having lessons in the mornings and doing my prep in the evenings but it was the holidays now. In previous years when the boys were home we had spent all day together, playing Seven Tiles on the Downs, crossing back and forth across the Dyke in the cable car, or taking the train into Brighton and spending long days at the beach, where we swam or walked along the promenade to Hove or Rottingdean. Sometimes we went out with a local fisherman to fish for mackerel, or picnicked in the gardens of the Royal Pavilion, which was closed up and no longer used; people said the Queen disliked it because of its association with the disgraceful behaviour of the Prince Regent.

But Aunt Mina was right: it was different that summer. The boys were taller and the light had gone out of their faces, replaced by a brooding heaviness. At seventeen, Jagjit was well over six feet tall and he towered over Simon. His chest had broadened and the down on his face had grown into a patchy moustache and beard. His voice had deepened too, while Simon's was finally beginning to break, which I could tell embarrassed him. I was shy and self-conscious around them and began to feel in the way, fearing that they had outgrown wanting to play with the silly dumb girl but were too polite to say so. Simon was impatient and snappy, while Jagjit put himself out to be nice. It wasn't so bad when we were outside with something to occupy us, but on rainy afternoons we were trapped together in Simon's old playroom, where we passed the time playing Parcheesi and backgammon.

I began to dread these rainy days. All our old ease was gone and I found myself uncomfortably aware of Jagjit's proximity. If our hands touched by mistake I snatched mine away and then blushed. I knew I seemed unfriendly, but I could not help myself, and knowing that Simon resented my being there made me even more self-conscious. It was excruciating, but I didn't know how to extricate myself, so I started to take a book with me and spend much of my time on the window-seat, reading. Each time I told myself I wouldn't go again, but when it came to it I found myself getting into the dogcart, hoping that this time it would be different, that we would fall back into our old ease with each other.

One hot Saturday in early August, we decided to go to Brighton beach with a picnic. Being in the open, among the crowds and the activity, helped to distract us. It was almost like old times. We swam, and then the boys went off to skim stones while I lay back and closed my eyes and listened to the sea. I have always loved the sound of the sea, ever since I stood at the bow of that ship letting the wake wash the inside of my head clean.

The waves were gentler, less continuous, on this fine, almost windless day, and I had to really focus to hear them behind the chatter of day-trippers, children's voices and the cries of the gulls. The light breeze was delicious on my hot skin as I waited for a break in the pattern of sound and then began to concentrate. It started with a small rush from my right along the shingle, then a longer one from my left, then from the right again a surge, that built steadily to a rattling roar and then diminished, ebbing away along the beach. For a moment or two there was silence; then it began again. It was like an orchestra with different instruments coming in, the sound building and dying away.

There was a crunching of pebbles and I opened my eyes to find Jagjit lowering himself beside me.

'You look happy, Lila. What were you thinking about?'

I was surprised, not having known, until he named it, that happiness was what I was feeling. Without thinking, I parted my lips to answer, and saw his look of surprise and expectation. For a moment we held each other's eyes, then thought came surging back, bringing consequences with it, and I closed my mouth. I saw the disappointment in his face, quickly masked.

I touched my ear and gestured at the sea, miming waves with my hand.

He smiled his lopsided smile, holding my eyes so long that I blushed. 'Listening to the waves? Shall I join you?'

He stretched out beside me and closed his eyes. I closed mine too and tried to concentrate again, but all I could think of was his body beside mine in his navy and brown striped costume, his long brown limbs stretched out along the pebbles. Our hands were almost touching.

Silence. Then the small rush to my right. I imagined him hearing it too: the same flow and ebb through both of us. His little finger touched mine. The pressure seeming to deepen as the longer rush came from the left, a warm surge through my body, building to a crescendo as it rose into my throat and then ebbed away. The sun warmed me; the breeze stroked my skin, raising the hairs on my arms and legs. With each new sound a rush of warmth rose through my body, and I knew he was feeling it too. He turned his head and his eyes met mine, unsmiling. We looked and kept looking, beyond politeness, beyond embarrassment. Then Simon's shrill voice, calling his name, cut through the sound of the waves, the squawking seagulls and the chatter.

In the train on the way home we sat in the window-seats opposite each other. Jagjit's arm rested along the windowsill between us as he gazed out at the Downs rushing past. His long brown fingers glowed like beaten copper in the light of the setting sun, and as I looked at them I remembered his finger touching mine and the tide washed through me again, carrying a surge of warmth into my face.

'Golly, you've caught the sun, Lila,' Simon said. I realised he'd been watching me watching Jagjit. 'Your face is bright red. Your aunt is going to be hopping mad!'

Henry

6th July 1869

Since the rains started I have not been able to sit outside. The bibi never enters the house in the daytime and she never invites me into her room. When I asked her why, she said Father would not like it. So now, when my lessons are over, I read in my room or visit the Lines, and Ali, Mohan and I go fishing.

2nd August 1869

I have been ill. Kishan Lal says I nearly died. The fever came on one evening after I had been down at the river all day with Ali and Mohan. We built a dam but the river washed it away so we had to do it all over again. When I got home Kishan Lal scolded me for not wearing a hat and for spending all my time with those good-for-nothing boys.

By dusk I was shivering so hard my teeth rattled. Father was out and Kishan Lal sent the chowkidar to fetch the doctor. I don't remember much after that except the shivering and the pain in my legs. When I woke up it was dark. There was a candle on the bedside table and someone was sponging my forehead with a cool cloth. It was the bibi. She told me the doctor had been and left some medicine, and that I was to stay in bed. She gave me the medicine and asked if I'd like her to read to me. I had started to drift off, when she stopped in the middle of a sentence. I opened my eyes and saw Father standing in the doorway, looking shocked. The bibi went out and then Kishan Lal came and said that he told her that sahib would be angry if she came in the house but she would not listen. Father said it was all right and sent him away and then asked me how I was feeling and what the doctor had said. He said if I wasn't better by morning he would ask the doctor to send a nurse to look after me.

My temperature had gone down but it came back in the night and I was hot and then shivering, and I dreamt I was in a bazaar searching for my mother and I kept pulling women's face veils off and finding they had no faces, just more veils underneath, and I wanted it to stop but it just went on and on for hours and hours and hours. When I woke in the morning, the bibi was sponging me with cold water and Father was sitting on the other side of my bed holding my hand. He didn't go to the Lines that day or the next, and he didn't say anything more about a nurse.

I was ill for nearly three weeks, but I'm better now. On my birthday Father did not stay in his room but sat with me and the bibi taught us a game with dice. It was the best birthday I've ever had, even though I was ill. And after the fever had gone and Father went back to the Lines, the bibi still sat with me and we played card games. I asked her how she knew so many games and she said that women in purdah have to pass the time somehow when they can't go out. I think it must be horrible for her, living in that small room and never going anywhere, so I asked Father why she can't live in the house with us. He said it is because she isn't part of the family. I asked if she is a servant, then, but he said she isn't that either. He told me that she used to be a famous singer but she can't sing any more. I asked why she doesn't live with her own family, and he said that they are all dead.

5th August 1869

Today Father told Kishan Lal to move the bibi's things from her hut to the room Aunt Mina had. I could see he didn't like it and later I heard him say to Allahyar that it isn't right to have *her* in the house with me. But I don't mind because now I can see her every day, and sometimes we sit on the back verandah and I read to her while she sews. Father spends less time at the Lines and more at home too. We are almost like a family. I like her much better than Aunt Mina.

17th August 1869

The bibi is sick. She always looks tired but now she holds her side as if it is hurting. The doctor has been to see her and today the chaplain came to see Father again and this time I didn't need to eavesdrop because they were shouting so loudly that we could hear them in the dining room where I was having my lessons. Mr. Mukherjee tried to read more loudly but I could still hear. The chaplain was talking about the bibi and the bad example Father is setting by living openly in sin with a native. Father told him to mind his own business.

24th September 1869

I hate Father! After all he has said about not believing in sending children away, he is sending me to England to school.

Even worse, I am to spend my holidays with Aunt Mina! He won't tell me why. He just says he thinks it is time for me to get a proper education. I am going in four weeks' time, with the wife of Captain Percival, who is going home to visit her sick mother.

When he told me I ran to the bibi and begged her to tell him to let me stay, but she said he is right and that I should be with my own people. I said Father and she and Kishan Lal and Allahyar are my people. She said it is for my own good and that Father loves me very much, that he isn't a man who speaks flowery words, but he feels things deeply, and one day I will understand how hard his life has been. I told her I don't care how hard his life has been, or hers either. I said they were mean to send me away and that I hated them both. She tried to stroke my hair but I pushed her off. I do hate them both and I know I shall hate England too.

Cecily

1st January 1857

Dear Mina,

Happy New Year, though I do not know when you will receive this letter, for I am writing to you from somewhere in the jungles of northern India.

Although I was dreading the thought of this march, I find myself enjoying it. We are travelling cross-country, so the officers, and we ladies who wish to, ride, while the rest are carried in palanquins. We rise at two each morning and cover fifteen miles before stopping to make camp for the day. Fortunately it is the coolest time of year, and often quite cold when we rise.

The system of marches is splendidly organised. We have every comfort, for all our furniture (including our bathtub!) is carried on the heads of coolies. There are two of everything, including the tents, so one set can go ahead of us and when we arrive our new home is waiting, complete with steaming tub, and we are able to dismount and bathe before lunch. It is all remarkably civilised, rather as I imagine the Romans travelled. In the afternoons we rest or walk in the countryside. I take my sketchbook and try to capture the picturesque ruined temples and tombs that one finds in the most remote places, sometimes half-buried in jungle, but they never look as charming in my pictures as they do in reality. I am enclosing a few, but you will have to imagine the screeching of the crickets and rustling grass as serpents slither away!

I was dreading sharing a tent with Arthur, but I scarcely see him, he is so busy with his men. He rides alongside them when they are marching, which the other officers leave to their N.C.O.s, and goes hunting with them in the afternoons. In the evenings they have a wrestling match or a nautch. I never realised how many camp followers a regiment had until we crossed the first river and a raft full of native ladies was washed downstream and stranded on the opposite bank. A company of sepoys had to be sent to rescue them. Lt. Tremayne's wife, Emily, tells me they are fallen women who are kept for the sepoys' pleasure and then she gave me a sly look, which made me wonder if Arthur's bibi is among them, for I do not think he would leave her behind. It is horrid to think everyone is talking behind our backs.

Fortunately, perhaps because of rising so early and taking so much fresh air and exercise, I sleep very soundly, despite sometimes being woken by the howls of jackals or the weird cackling laugh of the hyaenas.

One of the other lieutenants, Lt. Thomson, and his friends go pig-sticking whenever possible, so we often eat wild boar, and sometimes venison, for dinner. Several times Arthur has been tiger-shooting with his men, for the villagers seize the opportunity of Englishmen passing through to settle their quarrels with any man-eating or cattle-killing tigers in the area. I went out with them once, and kept watch in the machan, but I was relieved when nothing came, for I cannot help feeling it is we, and not the tigers, who are out of place in the jungle.

Arthur's jemadar, Ram Buksh, has had a nasty accident. They were tracking a wounded tiger when it charged him and he ran – you will hardly credit this but Arthur assures me it is true – straight into the arms of a bear! Arthur says he does not know who was more surprised, but they grappled with each other and went rolling down a slope. Fortunately the fall must have stunned the bear, and Ram Buksh managed to get away from it before it recovered. Arthur followed them and fired at it, but it ran off into the jungle. When they brought Ram Buksh into our tent, I thought at first he was dead. He had fainted and was covered in blood where the bear's claws had raked him behind the shoulder.

Arthur sent one of the sepoys to fetch Dr. Sheldon, and he himself cut off Ram Buksh's shirt and cleaned up the wound so he could see how bad it was, while I tore up some towels to staunch the bleeding.

You would have been proud of me, Mina – I did not faint or behave missishly. Fortunately when Dr. Sheldon arrived he said it was not serious. He disinfected and dressed the wound and advised that Ram Buksh not be moved until the bleeding had stopped, so Arthur cancelled the next day's march. The servants erected another tent for us nearby and Dr. Sheldon said he would send one of those women to care for him but Arthur said he and I would do it with the help of his batman, as Ram Buksh and Durga Prasad had helped us so much when he was ill. I could see Dr. Sheldon was surprised. He looked at me as if expecting me to refuse, but it was the least I could do, Mina, after all the help they have given me. And truthfully I did not have much to do except to place wet cloths on his forehead when his temperature rose and give him his medicine, for Arthur's batman took care of everything else.

When Ram Buksh recovered consciousness he seemed so embarrassed at finding me sitting by his bed that I too felt quite shy, but by the next day we were all laughing together. I understand now why Arthur spends so much time with his men, for they are so much less stuffy than his fellow officers and their wives, who are always standing on their dignity.

This journey has been so delightful that I shall be quite sad to leave India. I shall write from Cawnpore with details of my passage.

Your loving Cecily

Cawnpore, 4th February 1857

My darling Mina,

I received your presents and letters forwarded from Cuttack when we arrived but have been unable to write for weeping. I cannot believe that Mama has been dead since November and I did not know! It is too cruel to be so far away at such a time. How is poor Papa? I wish I had been there to say goodbye to Mama and to comfort him. Oh, Mina, how shall we manage without her? I never realised how much I depended on her gentle strength. I cannot imagine her gone, or how the house will be without her.

Please give Papa my dearest love, and tell him I will be with you very soon.

My dearest love to you both,

Cecily

Cawnpore, 11th February 1857

Oh, Mina, you will hardly believe my news. I am expecting a child! I am amazed that I am able to write the words so calmly. I could scarcely believe it when Dr. Sheldon told me and I burst out crying. He laughed; he thought me so foolish not to have known it myself. 'Do your mothers teach you nothing?' he asked. He said he had suspected it for some time, when he noticed how much I was sleeping on the march, but felt it better to say nothing until we reached Cawnpore and were settled.

I do not know what to do.

Your bewildered Cecily

Lila

A fortnight before the boys returned to school, I went over to the Beauchamps' after lunch as usual. It was raining so I took a book – a novel by Maud Diver – that Aunt Mina had given me for my birthday. I hadn't looked at it before because she usually gave me books by Mrs. Molesworth or Charlotte M. Yonge, featuring pious, dutiful heroines whom I could not see myself in, but, glancing into it while hunting through the bookshelf for something I hadn't read, I found that it was set in India. I assumed she must have bought it in ignorance, since she always avoided any mention of India in my presence.

That afternoon I sat in the window-seat reading, while Jagjit and Simon played Ludo nearby in the light from the window. I had read a few pages and then put the book down and was gazing out of the window at the garden. One of the things I like about England is how different things look from day to day: some days the air is so clear and dry that one can see for miles and every detail stands out sharply, while on others the landscape seems to shimmer in opalescent colours through shifting layers of gauzy mist. But that day, through the rain-spotted window, the garden looked like an Impressionist painting, the bushes and trees blending into a palette of smudgy green and brown brushstrokes.

Behind me Simon said, 'I say, Jagjit, listen to this!' He began to read, in a put-on prissy voice, *'It was after some talk of the natives themselves, and the girl's confession that she had not yet conquered an instinctive distaste and dread with which they had inspired her from the first...'* I turned and made a grab for the book but he held it out of my reach, his pale grey eyes glittering up at me. 'No, wait, it gets better: *...that she broke a rather protracted silence with an abrupt request.'* He paused and assumed a simpering voice. ' *"Of course, I'm abysmally ignorant – you've discovered that already! But I want to know exactly what people mean by a half-caste; and why the word so often goes with a tone of contempt." Laurence shrugged his shoulders...'* Simon threw his chest out and assumed a deep manly voice. ' *"Well – I suppose one has no business to be contemptuous," he said. "But the half-caste out here falls between two stools, that's the truth. He has the misfortune to be neither white nor brown; and he is generally perverse enough to pick the worst qualities of the two races, and mix them into a product peculiarly distasteful to both. The Anglo-Indian's contempt of him is a mild affair compared to the scorn of the high-caste native, who regards him simply as a low-born, a creature without either the birthright of caste, or the prestige of Sahib-dom. Seems hard luck on the poor devils; but they really are a most unsatisfactory crew on the whole. Clever enough, some of 'em: but there's a want of grit in their constitutions, physical and moral. It's a bad business all round, the mixing of brown and white races in marriage."'*

He lowered the book and grinned at us. 'You two had better not get married, then.'

'Don't be an ass, Simon,' Jagjit said. 'I've never heard such drivel.'

'Well, it's Lila's book. What do you think, Lila?'

'Ignore him, Lila. He's being childish,' Jagjit said. There was an edge to his voice I had never heard before.

Simon flushed and his voice went up, as it always did when he was angry. 'Oh, buck up, Jug Ears! You're saying that a "high-caste native" like you wouldn't mind marrying a half-caste?'

Jagjit looked at him in silence. Then he said calmly, 'I'm a Sikh, not a Hindu. We don't observe caste; and if I found the right girl I hope I would judge her for herself and not for her parentage.'

'Just as well, since there's such a mystery about Lila's past.'

Jagjit's face changed but before he could say anything Simon stood up, dropped the book on to my lap and left the room. Jagjit turned to me.

'I'm sorry. He can be very spiteful when he's jealous.'

But why should Simon be jealous of me, I wanted to ask, when he has everything – a family, a home of his own, friends…?

'Lila – ' He knelt up and put his hand on my shoulder, but sat back down as there was a knock at the door. The Beauchamps' maid put her head round it.

'Tea is served in the drawing room, Master Simon…' Her voice trailed off as she realised he wasn't in the room. She looked at us curiously.

'We're just coming, Enid,' Jagjit said. 'I'll tell Simon.'

She smiled at him and withdrew.

I stood up and Jagjit followed me to the door. 'You *are* staying for tea?'

I shook my head and started down the stairs.

He touched my shoulder. 'Lila, don't go…' But I did not want him to see me crying, and I did not turn round.

That night, as I was reading in my room after supper, there was a loud banging at the front door. I looked at the clock on my mantelpiece. It was nine o'clock and getting dark, late for a caller. A few minutes after that there was a knock at my bedroom door and Ellen put her head round it. 'It's Master Jagjit… for you, miss.'

Alarmed, I went down. Aunt Mina was waiting at the foot of the stairs. 'That Indian boy wants to speak to you. I told him you had gone to bed but he insisted. I find his behaviour quite extraordinary.'

I waited, making my face blank.

She hesitated, then said reluctantly, 'I suppose you'd better find out what he wants. Don't be long. I shall wait here for you.'

Jagjit was standing just outside the front door, breathing deeply, as though he had been running. He took my hand, pulling me away from the door. 'Don't look so worried; it's nothing bad. I just wanted to talk to you.' He lowered his voice. 'Can you meet me in the old greenhouse in half an hour?'

I hesitated.

'Please, Lila. It's important.'

I waited till Aunt Mina was safely settled in the drawing room before I crept downstairs. I could hear Cook and Ellen washing the dishes and talking in the kitchen as I slipped out the side door. I made my way to the vegetable garden and the old greenhouse with its broken panes, where we had sometimes played when we were younger. A faint light glowed through the smeary, cobwebbed windows and, although it was a warm night, I found myself shivering.

Through the panes of the door I could see that Jagjit had pushed the old planting tables aside to make a space in the centre. He had fixed a lighted candle into the bottom of an upturned pot and was sitting cross-legged on the floor, staring into the flame. Through the dirty glass the light from the candle glowed gold, smudging and softening everything. Suddenly I was afraid. I took a deep breath to stop myself shaking and pushed open the door.

His face under his ochre turban turned towards me and he rose to his feet in one supple movement.

'I'm afraid it's not very cosy in here. But come and sit down.' He gestured to the floor where some gunny sacks had been pulled together to form a sort of rug. There was a strong smell of mildew. 'They're a bit damp, I'm afraid.'

We sat down opposite each other with the candle between us. The floor was gritty, and I shifted uncomfortably as I waited for him to speak. He seemed to be finding it as difficult as I was; I noticed his hands were trembling, and that made me nervous but also gave me courage.

'I'm sorry to drag you out like this, Lila, but I wanted to see you alone and it's impossible to get away from Simon.' His voice shook with irritation and I looked at him in surprise. He flushed. 'I'm sorry. I know that sounds unkind, but we've just had the most filthy row. You must think I'm rottenly ungrateful, especially as he and his family have been so good to me… but sometimes it feels as though he thinks he owns me.'

I shook my head, trying not to show the secret pleasure I felt.

There was a silence while we both stared at the candle and I began to wonder if he had anything to say to me at all. I could feel the damp rising from the sacks and shivered again.

'Here, put this on.' He took his jacket off and stood to drape it round my shoulders. It held his scent, and I remembered his body beside me on the beach, his finger touching mine, and again that surge of warmth travelled through me. I turned my face away and held myself perfectly still.

'Lila!' He knelt opposite me and leant forward. 'I just wanted to say that... that I really value your friendship. That's the reason Simon made that scene today... he can't bear it if I show a liking for anyone else and he's jealous because he knows that I like you. You don't mind my saying that, do you?'

I shook my head.

'It's just that I know how your aunt dislikes me. But, to get back to why I'm here... I wanted to apologise for the way Simon behaved today, and... Oh, hell, Lila, the truth is I just wanted to have you to myself! I'm sick of never being able to tell you how I feel. Don't look so surprised – you must know I care for you. It's obvious enough! Sometimes I'm afraid even to look at you when we're in company because I think everyone will see it...' He laughed uncomfortably. 'You look so blank! Do you have any idea at all what I'm talking about?'

I nodded, though I wasn't really sure. Could he really mean what I thought he did?

'Do you like me, Lila... even a little bit?'

I nodded again.

'Really? You're not just being polite?'

I hesitated and looked down. 'Yes.' It was a whisper, so I said it again, louder. A croak: the frog princess. I looked up. He was staring at me.

'Say it again.'

I cleared my throat and tried again. 'Yes, I do.' Too loud. I grimaced. 'Is that how you imagined it?'

'What?'

'My voice.'

'Absolutely. Like a sergeant-major!'

We laughed and then, somehow – and I am still not sure how it happened – we were talking as if it was the most natural thing in the world. And maybe it was the dark and the quiet and the soft circle created by the flickering candle, or maybe the forgotten warmth of being held in someone's loving gaze, but after the initial groping and fumbling for words, and stumbling over my tongue, the dam burst and everything I had locked away came pouring out, and I found myself telling him everything about my life in India, and my friends, and Father's missions, and Mother's strangeness. And finally I found myself speaking about what happened that night, as though I was just talking to myself as I watched the candle flame flicker.

When I had finished, there was a long silence and I felt empty and peaceful. Then he sighed and moved the candle out from between us and pulled me towards him. I knelt up until my face was level with his and he kissed me, first on the forehead and then on the lips. It was the most gentle and innocent of kisses, almost like a blessing, but it cannot have looked like that to Aunt Mina and Mr. Beauchamp, who chose that moment to burst into the greenhouse.

Twenty minutes later I lay in bed, seething with anger and defiance at being made to feel guilty when we hadn't done anything wrong. Aunt Mina had said nothing to me except to order me to my room in a cold voice, but I could hear the three of them talking downstairs. Then Mr. Beauchamp and Jagjit left and I heard Aunt Mina go to bed. I lay awake for ages thinking of him: how it felt to be held by him and to talk about Father without being judged or pitied; to be really listened to. I knew there would be consequences but I didn't care. There was nothing they could do to us.

I was woken the next morning by stones clicking against my window. For the first time that I could remember since Father's death I did not think of him first, but of the night before. I smiled and stretched and got out of bed, smoothing my hair back before lifting the sash. But it wasn't Jagjit. It was Simon.

'Come down!'

I dressed quickly, wondering where Jagjit was.

As soon as I emerged from the front door Simon rushed up to me, almost spitting with rage. His face was white. 'What did you do? You selfish rotter! You've ruined everything – everything!'

I stared.

'Father's sent him away! I listened at the study door when they came back – there was the most frightful row. Father said that no gentleman would have behaved the way he did with a girl as young as you are. Jagjit said nothing had happened, that you were just talking, but Father said your aunt was upset and Jagjit had to go back to school. He made him promise not to write to you and he put him on the early train, and he says he can never come in the holidays again because your aunt won't permit it! And it's all your fault – your stupid fault!'

'No, it isn't. I bet you told your father because you were jealous, you telltale sneak!'

His jaw dropped. 'You're talking!'

'Yes, but you needn't worry, because I'll never speak to you again!'

I turned and went into the dining room where Aunt Mina was having breakfast and screamed at her that I hated her and would never ever forgive her. They were the first words I ever said to her.

A fortnight later I was sent away to school.

PART TWO

Henry

Karachi, 16th August 1880

I could smell it even before we saw land. That instantly recognisable, complex scent of India – a mingling of woodsmoke, perfume, dung and baking biscuits – came out to greet us as we approached Karachi, carrying the memories that I had locked away inside me, and suddenly I felt myself again. In England I had been someone else, a pallid imitation of a person.

At school we had been discouraged from talking about India. The other boys sneeringly referred to us as 'koi hais', and using Hindustani words to each other was regarded as showing off. Standing out in any way was frowned upon, but I am more like Father than I knew, and I had no desire to fit in. I hated the regimentation, the bullying, the fagging, the enforced team sports, the tasteless food and always being cold. My childhood dream of being confined in a suffocating dark place recurred frequently, and waking the whole dormitory with my screams did nothing for my reputation.

The holidays at Aunt Mina's were a relief from school. She and I had almost nothing to say to one another, but I got on better with the boys from the village than I did with boys at school, and enjoyed playing cricket on the village green and helping with getting in the hay. They accepted me as belonging to the village, but my hopes of learning anything about my mother were disappointed.

After school I had dreamed of going to Sandhurst or Addiscombe and following Father into the Indian Army, but I discovered that he had arranged for me to go to Haileybury to train for the Indian Civil Service. I was deeply disappointed. At school, almost the only activity I enjoyed was being a cadet, enacting battles from the Zulu wars and learning to form square. My pleading letters produced a brief response – our future in India was uncertain and Father felt that if I wished to make a career in India I would have a better future in the I.C.S.

At Haileybury my fluency in Hindustani gave me a head start, but that, together with my familiarity with native customs, raised the inevitable suspicion that there was 'a touch of the tar brush' about me. I do not say I was ostracised, but I am too proud to accept being tolerated, and the only real friend I made there was Gavin McLean, whose father was Scottish and mother Chinese. He is one of the cleverest people I have ever met, and is planning a career in the Indian Political Service. We have promised to keep in touch.

Apart from school essays and letters to Father, I have done little writing since I left India. I did not keep up my journal because there was nothing I wished to remember of my time in England. It was like being suspended in a limbo that I had to endure until real life started again. While I was there, I understood Father's depressions for the first time; I felt as though I had lost everything that gave my life meaning. If I ever have children, I shall never send them away.

Rawalpindi, Northwest Frontier, 19th August 1880

When I arrived yesterday, Kishan Lal came out to greet me. His hair is whiter and his stoop more pronounced, but his smile is as big as ever. He came forward and bent to touch my feet but I caught him by the shoulders. He straightened up and we looked at each other. His eyes were full of tears.

'Sahib has become a man.'

My own eyes felt damp. 'How is my father, Kishan Lal?'

'The same as ever, God be thanked.'

The house, though different from the one I left, is a standard Army bungalow with its high ceilings and large central room divided into drawing and dining room. The furniture is unchanged and Father's steamer chair is on the verandah in the same position it has always sat. For a moment I felt as though I had stepped back eleven years.

'Where is he?'

'We were not expecting you so early. Sahib has gone to the Lines. He said to send to him when you arrived. He wanted to come to Karachi to meet you but he said you told him no.'

'I didn't want him tiring himself unnecessarily. He must be, what... seventy now?'

Kishan Lal waggled his head. 'Must be.'

I wondered how old he himself was but knew it was pointless to ask; he wouldn't know. 'He'll be retiring soon.' I tried to imagine it and failed. What would he do with himself? 'And you, Kishan Lal? What will you do?'

Kishan Lal grinned. 'Sahib will never retire. He is a lion among men. He can still wrestle with young men and win. And what would I do? No, I shall stay with Langdon-sahib till the end.'

'He's lucky to have you, Kishan Lal.' I looked around me. 'Where is Bibi? I brought her a present.'

Kishan Lal's face fell. 'Did Sahib not write it in a letter? Bibi died – must be nine, ten years ago now. The year after you went to England. You truly did not know?'

'No. He never mentioned it.'

He put a hand on my arm. 'Don't be angry with him, sahib. He must have wished not to trouble you. He knew you were not happy there.'

I bit back the obvious reply while I thought of all the inquiries I had made after her health, the good wishes I had asked him to pass on. He had never replied to any of them.

'How did she die?'

'She had something – a growth – here.' He touched his side. 'The doctor said it could not be taken away.'

I thought back to the months before I left – the doctor's visits, the way she used to catch her breath, the hand pressed to her side. 'I remember. She must have been in pain. So they knew before I went. Did it take long?'

'One year, maybe one and a half. The pain was very bad. The doctor gave her medicine but it wasn't enough. She suffered greatly at the end. Your father sat with her all day, all night, sometimes reading to her, sometimes wiping her face. He even bathed her himself because he said the bai the doctor sent was not gentle enough.'

'He must have been very lonely after she died.'

'Yes, but he has his work with the regiment. It is good to have work.'

'I suppose so. Look, don't bother to send for him, Kishan Lal. I'll walk over there. I could use the exercise after all those weeks on the ship. Have my bags put in my room, would you?'

'Of course, sahib. And sahib…'

'Yes?'

'It's good to have you back. It will make him young again. It will make us all young again.'

Father was standing on the parade ground talking to a group of native officers and sepoys as I approached. As soon as he saw me he came forward to embrace me, then gripped my shoulders and looked into my face. His white hair is as thick and his eyes as blue as ever and apart from a slight shake in his hands and a new wildness to his eyebrows he looks just the same.

'You've grown up, Henry, and become very like your mother.' He wrung my hand and stepped back. 'Here are some old friends, come to greet you. They've been eagerly awaiting your arrival.'

Two sepoys in regimental uniform came forward and saluted me, then bent to touch my feet. I stepped back.

'Sepoy Bedi and Sepoy Khan. Do you recognise them?'

'Of course I do. Mohan. Ali.'

Then all the other sepoys, ones I remembered and ones I didn't, were crowding round to greet me and welcome me home. But it is different from how it used to be. I am no longer a child they can tease. I am now a sahib and none of them, not even Ali and Mohan, would dare to pull my leg, or play a joke on me, or take me down a peg when I get too big for my boots.

As we walked back to the bungalow for lunch I understood for the first time how lonely Father's life has been. He has always been a figure apart: respected and perhaps even loved by his men, but never able to confide, share his troubles or take off his officer's mask. I wonder why he has never made friends with other British officers and whether that was always so, or whether his separateness started after Mother died. I wonder if it will be the same for me.

20th August 1880

Last night Father and I sat on the verandah and talked. Again I noticed how his hand shook as he raised his whisky to his lips. For the first time it struck me that he will die one day. The thought shocked me and made me realise how alone I shall be when he has gone.

We talked about ordinary things: he gave me the latest news of General Roberts' march on Kandahar, which he feels is doomed to failure. 'No one has ever been able to hold Afghanistan for long, and no one ever will.' I gave him news of Aunt Mina and a brief resumé of my time in England and then we seemed to run out of subjects to talk about. I watched him swirl his whisky in his glass; it's an old habit, one he uses when he has nothing to say. I have seen him do it a hundred times at the Club. I had a sudden urge to puncture his defensive shield.

'Kishan Lal tells me the bibi died.'

He looked up. 'Oh, yes. Do you remember her?'

'Of course I remember her! She nursed me that time I had typhoid fever.'

'So she did. Fancy you remembering that!'

'Why didn't you tell me she had died? I asked after her in every letter. I even enclosed some poems for her.'

'Did you? I'm sorry, it must have slipped my mind.' He rubbed a hand across his eyes.

Rage twisted through me. I remembered him telling me as a child that I surely must have known my mother's name. Perhaps that too had 'slipped his mind'.

'Was she your bibi before you married my h.
asked deliberately.

He drained his glass, picked up the small brass bell on th.
table beside him and rang for Kishan Lal.

'What I mean is, did my mother know about her?'

He laughed harshly. 'I didn't keep them both at the same
time, if that's what you mean. But yes, I knew Sabira – that was
her name, by the way – before I met your mother. I was twenty
when I came out to India. There were no Englishwomen here
then; it wasn't considered safe. In those days there was none of
this fuss about going native; we were encouraged to blend into
Indian society, to eat the food and appreciate the music and
culture. The Company was here for business, not to build an
empire, and we were healthy young men with normal appetites.
It was a less prurient time; having a bibi was encouraged. They
educated us in the ways of the country and the customs of
the people we had to do business with, or the men we would
command. Sabira was an intelligent and cultured girl, trained
in singing and poetry and dance. I was lucky to have her. I
never understood why she chose me – a green young subaltern
– when she could have been the mistress of a nawab. She
taught me to speak the court Urdu and almost everything I
know about Indian history and culture. It was after '57 when
the Crown took over that everything changed. Englishwomen
began to come out here with their husbands, and they wanted
to turn India into suburban England. They and the missionaries
and the religious zealots in the Army decided it was our God-
given mission to "civilise" the natives by pushing our customs
– and of course our religion – down their throats.' The stream
of words paused as he rang the bell again.

I was already regretting starting this conversation. As
usual he had taken something personal and turned it into a

lecture. I steered it back to where I wanted to go. 'Talking of memsahibs, how did my mother take the news of the bibi's existence? Or did she not know?'

His scar tightened, and I watched the red thread pulling the corners of his eye and mouth together. 'Naturally I gave Sabira up when I married your mother. She was a talented singer and in much demand among the aristocracy in Lucknow. After I married, she could have chosen another patron, but she chose not to.'

'She loved you.'

'Yes. God knows why.'

'So how did she end up with you after all that time?'

'I had kept in touch with her; I couldn't just abandon her after so many years. My marriage to your mother wasn't easy, but she wasn't to blame. I was too old and ignorant about delicately brought-up girls to understand her needs. And then – long after she died, when you were about ten or eleven – Sabira became ill. She had no one to care for her; she'd given up everything for me. I had an obligation to her.'

'So she was already ill when she came to live here?'

'Yes. There was no cure. It was a tubercular tumour in her side. We tried everything – she had numerous operations. They kept draining the wound but it was horribly painful and it always came back.'

'I'm sorry. I wish I had known. I was angry with her – with you both – when I left.'

He looked down into his empty glass. 'It was the reason we sent you away. She didn't want you to have to watch her die. And afterwards… it seemed better to let you complete your education.'

Kishan Lal arrived with another bottle and some fresh ice. He looked at Father's expression and shook his head at me.

'I'm sorry, Father. I shouldn't have raised the subject, especially on my first day back. But the bibi – Sabira – was very kind to me. I wish you had told me.'

He looked at me for the first time, with those painfully blue eyes. 'I'm sorry too, Henry. I haven't been a very good father to you. When your mother died everyone told me I should send you to England, to your aunt, but I couldn't bear to part with you. You were all I had.' He cleared his throat. 'It was selfish of me. You would have had a normal life there, instead of a lonely childhood here.'

'I was happy here, Father. I've always considered India my home and always shall.'

He looked thoughtful. 'We may not always be here, you know, Henry. Things are changing. Being here is no longer about ruling by force but about building a system of government that we can hand over. That's the way I see it, anyway, although not everyone agrees. That's why I wanted you to go to Haileybury. My brother James was there, you know.'

'Yes, I do know. I read his name in the Roll of Honour.'

Our eyes met. He must have known he could not keep it from me forever. I still had questions, but we had talked enough about sad things for our first night together. I decided to make peace.

'The truth is, Father, I wanted to go into the Army because I've always wanted to be just like you.'

He looked astonished. 'God forbid, Henry. I wouldn't wish my life – or character – on anyone. But I'm very glad that you're home at last. I've missed you.'

It was some time before I could speak. 'It's good to be home, Father.'

30th August 1880

I am aboard a train on my way to take up my first I.C.S. posting as an acting district magistrate. I was originally scheduled to take up a position as deputy magistrate in the United Provinces at the end of October, but the health of the incumbent magistrate at Bhagalpur has necessitated his immediate retirement, so they need an acting magistrate until a replacement can be found for him. I am to commence immediately.

It is an alarming prospect to step straight into the shoes of a full district magistrate although, fortunately, as someone invested with second-class magisterial powers, I am only allowed to impose fines or sentences of up to six months' rigorous imprisonment. Until Thornton's replacement arrives, more serious cases will have to be transferred to Patna. I am also assured that his deputy magistrate, an Indian, will give me every assistance, although I should have thought he might resent the fact that a mere griffin has been promoted above him.

I don't know whether Father was disappointed or relieved by my sudden departure. Since the night of my arrival, when we spoke so openly, he had retired into himself again. We sat together on the verandah every evening after that, and talked with apparent ease, but there was an invisible wall around him that warned me off certain subjects, just as there used to be when I was a child. And I found myself once more too timid to bring up the subject of my mother's fate. There seemed no hurry when I thought I had two months of evenings to break him down. I remember him once saying to me, 'Softly, softly, catchee monkey, Henry,' but it seems that, once again, *I* am the monkey.

Cecily

Cawnpore, 18th February 1857

Dear Mina,

I have been in two minds about what to do. Part of me longs to be Home with you and Papa, especially now that Mama is gone, but last week I dreamt of her and as I woke I heard her voice, as clearly as if she was in the room, saying those words she used to say when we had done something wrong and were afraid to confess it: 'When trouble comes, stand and face it. The further you run, the bigger it gets.' And I know she would want me to stay and do my duty, especially as Arthur has been so patient and kind to me since he heard my news. I know that he will be a good father, for he takes so much trouble with James's children, playing at soldiers with Freddie and allowing Sophie to ride on his back, and I know it would be wicked to deprive him of his child.

I expected him to be happy with my decision, but when I told him that I have decided to stay he said that now there is a baby to consider it is more important than ever that I should be safe and happy. I knew before we arrived in Cawnpore that he was concerned about the unrest we have been hearing about and was surprised to find everything so quiet, but James says it is precisely that that makes him uneasy. He says the courts have practically no work because there is no crime. When I said surely that was a good thing, he said he fears it is a sign that the natives are waiting for something to happen. There have been rumours of odd things, like chuppaties being circulated as some sort of message, but no one seems to know what it means. Louisa says she notices a different atmosphere in the bazaar too – the natives exchange glances and smiles when dealing with Europeans as though they know something that we do not. But no one wants to talk about it, and anyone who raises the subject is labelled a 'croaker'.

Some families are being sent away, but Louisa says that showing fear will only encourage the natives and she would not dream of leaving James alone. She knows India much better than I, and if she believes it safe for her children it would surely be cowardly of me to go. I cannot tell you how reassuring it is to be with her again.

The children have grown so much! Freddie, who is six now, is very like his father but is determined to be a soldier, and spends all his time playing at loading and firing 'eighteen-pounders'. Sophie is as devoted to me as ever, and the baby is the sweetest-tempered little creature. They are such a happy family and I cannot help feeling ashamed of myself when I am with Louisa, for she is always so calm and sensible. I know that if she were in my place she would have forgiven Arthur straight away.

Please do not mention anything about the situation here to Papa as I do not wish him to worry unnecessarily. Arthur has the greatest confidence in General Wheeler's abilities and says that, although he is only five feet tall, he has such resolution and authority that one glance from him can make the bravest man quail. James says if it were not for his unfortunate marriage he would have attained a much greater position, but

Lady Wheeler is a Eurasian and as dark-complexio..
native. There is some scandal about her past, but they s..
a devoted couple and two of their sons are officers in the 1st
Native Infantry, which must only be possible because of the
esteem in which their father is held.

I shall write again soon. Please give my best love to Papa.
Your loving sister, Cecily

25th February 1857

Dear Mina,

Now that we are settled I have time to tell you about
Cawnpore. It is a much larger town than Cuttack and the
cantonment stretches for quite seven miles along the river,
which is very wide. Now that I am no longer allowed to
ride, I like to walk there in the early mornings when it is
cool and peaceful. As the weather gets hotter and the water
level falls, islands are becoming visible in mid-stream; they
are full of monkeys and nesting birds and it is so pretty at
first light, when the sky is turning pink, to watch the egrets
and herons fishing in the shallows. Further along, the river
is lined with temples and cremation ghats, with steps leading
down from them to the river. Below, Brahmins can be seen
purifying themselves by ritual immersion in the filthy water,
while dhobies and women in colourful sarees do their laundry
nearby. I am enclosing a watercolour I made of the scene, but
you will have to imagine the sound of the temple bells and the
rhythmic pounding as our clothes are hammered against the
rocks. No wonder there is so much mending to do!

The town lies in the middle of a vast plain and I am
told it is quite unbearable in the hot season, when the dust

is whipped up into small whirlwinds. The soldiers call them 'Cawnpore devils' and the natives believe them to be the ghosts of unquiet spirits. Louisa and the children go up to Simla for the hot months and Arthur insists that I am to go with them. But now is the season in Cawnpore, and people travel here from all over the north and there are so many balls, picnics and entertainments that we could be out every night if we chose. Arthur usually dislikes such things but he has been so good and accompanied us to everything and made an effort to be sociable. A lady who knew him in one of his previous postings congratulated me on the change in him.

Please give my dearest love to Papa.

Your loving Cecily

4th March 1857

Dear Mina,

You will not believe who (or is it whom?) I met the other day. No less a personage than Mr. Azimullah Khan, whom you met at that ball three years ago in Brighton that time I had the mumps! I could not believe it could be the same man, but he confirmed he had visited Brighton and stayed at the hotel at Devil's Dyke. Is it not an extraordinary coincidence? He is not a prince at all, as he pretended, but adviser to one, and comes from a very humble background. It is said that during the famine of '37 he and his mother were found starving by a missionary, who took them in and gave them a home. He attended the mission school, and is so clever that he can speak not only perfect English but French and German too.

I can see how he was mistaken for a prince, for he is quite the dandy! The fact that he was a link to Home would have inclined me to like him except for his boastful manner. He bragged of the welcome he was given by the Queen's cousin, Lady Duff-Gordon, who introduced him to some famous writers, including Mr. Dickens and Mr. Thackeray, and said that he still corresponds with 'several young ladies' whom he met at Brighton. I have a feeling that despite his apparent friendliness he does not like us very much.

James says he is bitter because his mission to England failed. The prince for whom he works, one Nana Saheb Dundu Pant, who has a palace nearby at Bithoor, had sent him to appeal to the Queen because Lord Dalhousie refused to continue the pension that his father received on the grounds that Nana Saheb is an adopted, not a natural, son. Arthur says that according to Indian custom adopted sons have the same rights as natural ones, and both he and James feel that he has been treated unfairly, and that it is to his credit that he remains so friendly with us. Despite his petition having been rejected, Nana Saheb himself does not seem bitter at all. He is uncommonly hospitable to the Europeans at Cawnpore, and often gives balls and picnics for us. He has even lent Louisa a Broadwood piano, as her own was damaged while being transported to Cawnpore. James and she have become quite friendly with him and often visit him at Bithoor.

Arthur and I went with them last week (which was when I met Mr. Khan) and Nana Saheb was *most* gracious, although if I am truthful he cuts an absurd figure. He is rather plump with a round face, and wears very tight clothes made of bright shiny materials, and so many jewels that he resembles nothing so much as a gigantic Christmas tree ornament. His manners are equally elaborate, for he told Arthur that the world was ringing with his fame, that tales of his feats of courage had travelled before him and that he was honoured to meet such a legendary figure. Arthur looked astonished, but bowed politely. When it was my turn, he told me that it was beyond the bounds of belief that there could be two such paragons of beauty as Louisa and I in the same family, that our radiance put the moon to shame and that a mere glimpse of us would be worth a million pounds to most mortals!

I had to press my handkerchief against my mouth to keep from laughing, but Louisa just bowed and smiled. She tells me that such compliments are mere common courtesy among native princes and that her father often had to translate such remarks for visiting officials as: 'His Majesty says, my lord, that you are his father and mother, that the sun rises and sets by your goodwill, that you are day and night to him, and he prays that roses shall bloom in the garden of your friendship, and nightingales sing in the bowers of your affection!'

We walked through the palace gardens together and Nana Saheb reassured us that we need have no fears of a mutiny. He does not believe it likely that the troops would betray their colours but has assured us of his support. James has arranged for Louisa and the children to be taken under his protection in case of an uprising, and he very kindly invited me to join them. So you see, you and Papa need not worry!

We are invited to a ball at Bithoor on Saturday, so I shall be able to describe the inside of the palace to you. The outside is certainly not as ornamental as our own palace at Brighton, but it is a good deal larger and the gardens are very fine.

10th March

I am writing my second instalment, as promised, to tell you all about Nana Saheb's ball at Bithoor. When we arrived, the gardens were strung with coloured lanterns so it appeared as a kind of fairyland. Inside the great hall (of which every inch, including the walls and ceiling, is covered with small mirrors) dozens of candles had been lit. It was like being inside a huge glittering diamond, and the colour of our dresses reflected in the mirrors and danced with every movement. The banquet was magnificent, only the dinner service is made up of the oddest mixture of plates, ranging from the finest Sèvres porcelain to the cheapest earthenware, and one of the soup tureens was an unmentionable! Not surprisingly, the soup was politely declined by all the guests. Nana Saheb did not eat with us, for his caste does not allow it, but appeared afterwards to converse and watch the dancing.

Mr. Azimullah Khan was there, too, looking very handsome. He has beautiful manners, and moved amongst us all the time, checking that we were comfortable and had everything we wished. I made the mistake of mentioning to my table companions that my sister had seen him when he was visiting England and taken him for a prince, and a Mr. Lang – a lawyer whom Nana Saheb has been consulting about his appeal – overheard me and told us that while he was in London he too had received an invitation from Lady Duff-Gordon to meet 'Prince Azimullah Khan' who was staying with her. He laughed loudly and added, 'I refused the invitation, saying that I knew him well already for I had had my plate changed by him in Cawnpore quite a hundred times!'

He did not know that Mr. Khan was standing behind him and hearing every word. James whispered to Mr. Lang to be careful, but he laughed and said even more loudly that he was not afraid of the opinion of a charity schoolboy. I could tell James was angry but he changed the subject. He said

.vards that, if he were Mr. Lang, he would be very careful what he ate or drank from now on.

The tables were cleared and at midnight we saw a firework display, and then danced until the small hours. There were refreshments in a pavilion in the garden and we walked amongst the lanterns and under the stars until it was nearly dawn.

Your loving Cecily

P.S. Mina dearest, I am adding this quickly before the mail goes. Ram Buksh came over in the early hours to tell Arthur that he has discovered that some of the sepoys and sowars are secretly meeting at the home of a risaldar of the 2nd Cavalry. He believes Azimullah Khan is behind it. James says he has never trusted Mr. Khan and believes he is trying to turn Nana Saheb against us and that it is all the more important that we try to maintain his friendship. Louisa and I are leaving for the hills with the children in a few weeks but I cannot help worrying about Arthur and James, although Arthur assures me that there is nothing to fear.

As if things were not bad enough already, it appears that, through some oversight, the new Enfield rifles with which the sepoys have been issued utilise cartridges that are greased with tallow made from beef and pork fat. As the paper cover has to be torn with the teeth, this has upset both Hindoos and Mohammedans. When one of the sepoys at Barrackpore refused to use them last month and fired at an officer, the whole regiment was accused of mutiny and disbanded, which Arthur said was a grave injustice, and foolhardy, given the resentment already caused by the annexation of Oudh.

15th April 1857

Dear Mina,

We shall not be going to the hills after all, as the situation here is worsening daily and Arthur says is too unsafe for us to travel. He says that Ram Buksh told him that there is much talk amongst the men about a prophecy, made at the time of Clive's great victory at Plassey, that the Company would last only one hundred years, and the centenary falls this year.

Mr. Azimullah Khan is apparently telling the sepoys and sowars that England is not the large and powerful country that we pretend but a small and gloomy land where the sun hardly lifts its head above the horizon, that our Great Queen is a short fat woman under the thumb of her husband, and that he has seen white men labouring and living in filth and poverty such as no Indian would tolerate. Apparently he visited the Crimea on his way back to India and witnessed the sorry condition of our troops and the terrible losses they were sustaining. He is telling everyone of the stupidity and incompetence of our officers. Arthur says the worst of it is that it is true, and that we shall never live down the shame of our Crimea campaign. Everyone is trying to put a brave face on it but I can tell they are worried.

In case of an uprising here, General Wheeler has taken the precaution of constructing an entrenchment that can be defended until reinforcements arrive. Arthur has doubts about this plan – he says an entrenchment surrounded by buildings will be too exposed. He feels that we should use the Magazine, both to stop it falling into the hands of the mutineers and because it is easier to defend – but his respect for General Wheeler prevents him from expressing his doubts, especially as there is a group of people – boxwallahs mainly – who pooh-pooh fears of an uprising and accuse those concerned, including General Wheeler, of being croakers.

I must admit to feeling really frightened now, but Louisa insists that we must not give in to fear and reminds me that Nana Saheb has promised to protect us should anything occur.

My dearest love to you and Papa.

Your ever-loving Cecily

14th May 1857

My dearest Mina,

I am sorry not to have written for the past month, but we have been too busy. I am writing this quickly to tell you that we received news today that the troops at Meerut mutinied on Sunday. They went on to Delhi where they encouraged the troops there to join them. The whole of Cawnpore is in an uproar and all the shops are closed. Arthur has sent Ram Buksh with a note to tell me that things are calm at the Lines but he intends to sleep the night there to ensure that no one tries to stir the troops up. Ram Buksh has assured me that our sepoys are loyal. He has promised to guard Arthur with his own life and has confidence that every other sepoy will do the same. I know what trust Arthur has in his men and cannot believe they would harm him, but I am sick with fear, though I try not to show it.

I will write again by the next post.

Your loving Cecily

20th May 1857

Darling Mina,

So much has happened that there is no time to tell it all, but James and Louisa and the children have moved in with us, as it is safer in the cantonment than the Civil Lines and Arthur does not wish me to be alone at night when he is at the Lines.

I am sorry to tell you that the situation is becoming very grave. Today Arthur and James went to the Magazine with Capt. Matlock and Lt. Thomson to mine it, so we could blow it up in case it should fall into enemy hands, but they were unable to do it because the sepoys guarding it were suspicious and followed them everywhere. Nor would they allow James to remove the gold stored in the Treasury. Arthur says they assured him they were true to their salt and wondered what had come over the sahibs that they should be in such fear, but James believes it is a sign of treachery.

However, there is some good news – Nana Saheb drove over from Bithoor as soon as he heard about the Meerut uprising to assure James and Louisa of his support. He expressed his shame at the disloyalty of his countrymen and has offered to shelter Louisa and me and the children at Bithoor in case it becomes necessary. He has also promised to place his men as a double-guard on the Treasury and Magazine to stop them falling into the hands of the mutineers. On this understanding, James and the senior officers have agreed to support General Wheeler's plan of moving into the entrenchment.

I am trying to stay calm for the sake of the baby, for Dr. Sheldon says shocks and agitation are bad for both of us, but it is hard with so much uncertainty. If it were not for Louisa, I think I should have allowed Arthur to persuade me to leave, but she is adamant that showing weakness will give heart to our enemies and make things more dangerous for those who have to remain behind. In any case, Arthur says it is now too late and that we are safer here, where we are protected, than travelling in a small group where we may be ambushed. I am confident that Durga Prasad and Ram Buksh will not allow any harm to come to him or us. Let us pray that all will be well.

Cecily

27th May 1857

Dear Mina,

I am writing this from the entrenchment where we have taken shelter. I hope you get this letter, for this past week has been full of alarums and anxiety and the post has been disrupted.

Last week, during a fearful storm, an orderly came riding up shouting that all women and children were to proceed to the entrenchment. You cannot imagine the confusion, Mina, for no one knew the cause, nor whether the order was true or false, but James insisted we obey and said he would stay behind and wait for Arthur. So Louisa and I threw some things into the carriage and we took the children and their ayah and drove there as fast as we could. There was chaos when we arrived, with everyone crowding together into the small barracks, but Louisa took command and claimed one of the inner rooms, where we slept on the floor, as we had no furniture. I felt sorry for the poor Eurasian family she turned out, who had to camp on a verandah. I should not have had the heart or the courage to do it myself.

The poor gunners stood all night in the pouring rain and then it turned out to be a false alarm so we all returned home. Apparently the panic was caused by the sight of Nana Saheb's soldiers coming to take up their posts at the Magazine and Treasury. When Arthur returned from the Lines he said it was a great pity we had been seen to react with such panic, as we have lost considerable face with the troops, who are astonished at our behaviour. Captain Hayes, who came with the reinforcements from Lucknow, told Arthur that if an insurrection does take place we shall have no one to blame but ourselves for showing the natives how easily we can be frightened and, when frightened, utterly helpless.

For the past two days we have been sleeping in the entrenchment at night and returning home during the day, as washing and cooking facilities are extremely limited, but today General Wheeler instructed that we are to remain in the entrenchment. There are only two barracks – one is occupied by sick soldiers and the families of soldiers stationed at Lucknow, and everyone else has to fit into the other. Families are forced to share rooms, so all seven of us – James and Louisa and the children, their ayah Luxmibai, and I – are crowded into one small room, which is airless, and as hot as an oven in this suffocating heat. But we are fortunate compared to many.

Arthur is still sleeping in the Lines with his men; Colonel Ewart of the 1st has also been doing this, and it has proved so effective that General Wheeler has ordered that all officers must do the same.

Pray that all will be well and kiss Papa for me.

Cecily

3rd June 1857

My darling Mina,

This is probably the last letter you will receive from me until the trouble is over, for the rebels are intercepting the mails and the telegraphs. There seems little doubt now that the troops will revolt. Four days ago, General Wheeler moved his family into the entrenchment. Until then they had remained in their house with all the windows open and he was riding about the Lines jollying up the men who could not sleep because of the heat. He has been fearless, and Captain Hayes says it is only his demeanour that has kept the barrel from exploding.

Last week Mr. Azimullah Khan rode over to look at the entrenchment. James says Lt. Daniell asked him what he would call it and he smirked and suggested 'The Fort of Despair', but Daniell retorted that we shall call it 'The Fort of Victory'. Emily's husband told her that he thinks we cannot hold out for more than two days if attacked as we are so exposed. The walls are so low a cow could jump over them and when the rains come they will simply wash away. My only comfort is that I know that wherever Mama is she will be watching over us.

My hand is shaking so much that I can scarcely hold the pen. My darling Mina, if we do not meet again in this world I know we shall in the next, for we are part of each other and can never be separated. I am enclosing a letter for Papa, but *do not give it to him unless you hear all is over*. Please forgive me for anything I have ever done to hurt you and remember that I shall be, for all eternity,

Your loving sister, Cecily

Lila

In the spring of 1914 I was nineteen. Although I had been living at High Elms since leaving school, I spent most of my time with Mrs. Beauchamp, for I had still not forgiven Aunt Mina for Jagjit's banishment.

It was four years since I had last seen him but after his departure I had continued to write to him every week in defiance of Aunt Mina's wishes, and of the school rule that forbade writing to members of the opposite sex unless they were relatives. Although our correspondence was vetted, on Sundays we walked from school to church in a crocodile along Hove seafront and I took the opportunity to slip my letters into a post box. I did not expect a reply. I knew Jagjit well enough to know that he would keep his word to Mr. Beauchamp not to communicate with me in any way, but I had made no such promise.

I did not see much of Simon either, except at Christmas. Over the last few years, in the parliamentary recesses, Mr. Beauchamp had taken both the boys travelling. They had visited all the great cities of Europe, gone walking in Bavaria and the Pyrenees and skiing in the Alps. With the trouble in Servia continuing, and the possibility of a European war looming, Mr. Beauchamp wanted to show them Europe while it was still possible. I suspected it was also his way of enabling Simon's friendship with Jagjit to continue, since Jagjit could no longer visit their home.

Each summer I received a postcard from Simon. The year before the picture had been of an alpine meadow full of wild flowers, with a small stone church surrounded by fruit trees and, hanging above them, the snow-capped peaks of the Dolomites. On the other side it said:

Dear Lila,

We walked over these mountains from Austria. Austria was ripping and we went swimming in the lakes. We are going to Florence next and then to Venice.

Father says to give his regards to your aunt.
Simon

I read the postcards with envy, both for his opportunity to travel and see the world, and because he was with Jagjit.

At school I had made no effort to form friendships – what was the point, when everyone I cared about was always taken from me? Aunt Mina had told me that she hoped school would make me less sulky and superior, but I knew the other girls thought me stand-offish. I did work at my studies, though, partly to keep myself busy, and partly because I was determined to leave High Elms able to earn my own living, and the only way to achieve that longed-for independence was to be well educated.

Mrs. Beauchamp was too busy with her suffragette work to accompany her husband and Simon on their trips to Europe. After the great demonstration in June 1908, when hundreds of thousands of people had converged on Hyde Park dressed in the W.S.P.U. colours of purple, white and green, the Liberal

Party had pledged to support votes for women. Two years later they reneged on that promise, and the suffragettes had become increasingly militant, demonstrating outside Parliament, courting arrest and going on hunger strike, throwing stones and setting fire to post boxes. Mrs. Beauchamp's friend Mrs. Clarke had been active, despite her frail health, in organising a campaign of window-breaking in Brighton, bravely facing down the rowdies who frequently attacked suffragettes in the street, but in November that year she was arrested at a protest march in Brighton. Mrs. Beauchamp was arrested alongside her but the police released her, despite her protests, when they realised she was the wife of a local M.P.; Mrs. Clarke was taken to Holloway, where she went on hunger strike and was force-fed. She was released a few days before Christmas.

That first Boxing Day after Jagjit's banishment, I had gone over to the Beauchamps' to thank them for our presents. Enid had answered the door and gasped, 'Thank goodness you've come, miss.' She showed me into the drawing room, where I found Mrs. Beauchamp sunk into an armchair, with a white face and shaking hands. Her beautiful narrow skirt, patterned in shades of green, was stained red, and at first I thought it was blood, until I saw the empty wine glass on the floor.

'What is it?' I asked, sinking down and taking her hands to hold them still. She could not speak, so I unfolded her fists to rub them warm, and found a crumpled telegram in one. It was from Mrs. Pankhurst, saying her sister, Mrs. Clarke, had died the previous day. The autopsy later showed that she had died from a burst blood vessel in the brain, probably caused by the stress of force-feeding.

Afterwards, Mrs. Beauchamp threw herself even more passionately into the campaign, organising local groups and writing to the papers. I knew she missed Mrs. Clarke, and

145

when I was home in the holidays I always offered to help, although I knew Aunt Mina disapproved.

As the end of school approached, Mrs. Beauchamp suggested that I study for university entrance exams and then apply for a one-year pre-medical course at London University to see if I might be interested in being a doctor. Aunt Mina would of course have to pay, but she was thinking along different lines, because soon after I left school she invited Mrs. Beauchamp over to ask her if she would be willing to present me at Court for my coming out.

'A *débutante*?' Mrs. Beauchamp said. 'Do you think that's the right thing for Lila? A lot of girls don't bother these days. It was important when a girl's only prospect was marriage, but these days women have more choices. Lila's an intelligent girl; her school results show that. She could be anything she wants – many of the professions are opening to women these days.' She hurried on before Aunt Mina could say anything. 'There's a very good pre-clinical course at London University. It would be a way for Lila to find out if the medical profession would suit her. And, if she wanted to return to India, women doctors are badly needed there.'

She could have said nothing better designed to turn Aunt Mina against the idea. India had always been a taboo subject between us and I knew it would remind her of Jagjit. Realising her mistake, Mrs. Beauchamp added quickly, 'As you know, our dear late Queen was very keen to encourage women to train as doctors.'

'Amelia, we are old friends,' Aunt Mina said, 'but you have your opinions and I have mine. When Lilian's f... when I agreed to take Lilian in, I gave my word that she...' she paused and then turned to me '...that you would always have a home with me.'

146

The awkwardness I felt as I met her eyes made me realise how seldom we addressed one another directly. We were strangers living in the same house, skirting round each other, understanding nothing of what the other was thinking or feeling.

As though reading my mind, she went on, 'I know we have not always seen eye to eye, Lilian, but I hope there will never be any question of your having to support yourself. My home will always be yours, and I hope you will continue to live here after I have gone – unless, of course, you marry.'

This was the first I'd heard of the house becoming mine, but the picture of myself trapped in Aunt Mina's suffocating life made me want to run screaming out of it. I hoped it did not show in my face. I could think of nothing to say except, 'Thank you, Aunt Mina.'

'Lila, you know Jagjit Singh, who used to spend holidays with us…?' Mrs. Beauchamp said casually one morning as I sat at the dining room table copying out, in a fair hand, letters she'd drafted to the newspapers. She was careful not to look at me and I was grateful.

'Yes, of course,' I said, keeping my face lowered to the letter I was working on.

'Well, he'll be visiting us at the beginning of August and, as you were childhood friends, I thought you might like to meet him again.'

My first reaction was elation. I had kept track of Jagjit's progress from the Beauchamps and had continued to write to him even after he left school and went up to Cambridge to read law. I remembered that his father had intended him to go on to study for the I.C.S., which meant he would be in England for another three years. I thought of him all the time, and often fantasised about meeting him accidentally. It had been one of the attractions of going to university in London that we might be free to meet in London or Cambridge. I even conducted conversations with him in my mind: he was the one person I felt I could say anything to and expect to understand. My letters had become a sort of diary – a record of my thoughts and feelings – with no expectation of a response. Writing to him was like talking to another part of myself. However, now that the prospect of meeting him was in front of me, I was terrified. I even found myself hoping that Aunt Mina would object, but after four years she must have thought the danger was past.

The one consolation was that Simon would be home too. He was at Cambridge as well, reading history, having gained admission after Mr. Beauchamp had 'had a word with his old tutor'. Like Jagjit, he had joined the Officers' Training Corps and usually he would have been home already, but that year they had stayed up for extra training for the war that everyone feared was approaching.

A few days before their arrival, war was finally declared. It is strange, looking back, to realise that I barely gave it a thought. Our life was so quiet that the events of the wider world seemed hardly to concern us. And I was preoccupied with thoughts of meeting Jagjit again.

As the day of his arrival grew closer, I became more and more apprehensive. I cringed as I reviewed my outpourings, artlessly confided with no thought for how they might be received. What must he have thought of me, continuing to write to him for all those years with no encouragement? What could my letters possibly have meant to him? Had he even bothered to read them, or had he left them unopened, as I had Aunt Mina's letters to me at school? As the day grew closer I found myself wishing for something to happen – anything to prevent us coming face to face.

The day of their arrival was unusually hot, even for August. After lunch I went up to my room and tried on costume after costume until my bed was covered with rejected garments. Finally I chose a simple cream muslin dress with a square neck edged with *café-au-lait* lace. I looked at myself in the mirror. I knew I was no beauty, but perhaps I was pretty. My oval face and regular features were unobjectionable but my dark eyes and straight dark eyebrows gave me an intense look. At school I had often been reprimanded for scowling and urged to assume a 'more pleasant expression'. My skin was clear but had a definite olive tinge, not helped by my refusal to wear a hat. Not for the first time, I wished that I had inherited Mother's pale skin and delicately arched eyebrows.

The path along the foot of the Downs was powder-dry, and by the time I reached the Beauchamps' house I was perspiring and the hem of my dress was brown with dust. I wiped my face and hands with my handkerchief before entering through the french windows into the sitting room.

As my eyes adjusted to the change of light, a genie materialised in front of me. He was wearing a dark blue suit and a pale pink turban, and if I had met him in the street I should not have known him. He was taller than ever, but with a new breadth of shoulder. His moustache and beard were neatly shaped and his deep-lidded eyes and high-bridged nose no longer seemed too big for his face. But it was his expression – grave, thoughtful, dignified – that made me realise how much he had changed from the awkward, lanky boy I had pictured as I was writing my letters.

The hand he held out to me was large and warm and swallowed mine completely. 'Lila,' he said, smiling. He reached for my other hand and stood back to look at me. 'You've grown up, but I would have known you anywhere.'

I glanced towards the tea table, where Simon was standing to greet me. Mrs. Beauchamp smiled at me. 'Come and have some tea, Lila.'

Jagjit pulled out a chair for me and I greeted Simon and sat down.

Mrs. Beauchamp explained that Mr. Beauchamp was in London, caught up in war planning, but would be back for the weekend.

Jagjit sat down opposite me. I found myself unable to raise my eyes to him and fixed them on the cakes and sandwiches on the table. I felt paralysed with shyness and could think of nothing to say.

Mrs. Beauchamp explained that the suffragists had decided to put aside their campaign for the duration. 'Of course we must support our men, who are fighting to defend us.' She looked at me. 'Simon has joined up,' she said flatly.

These were the first words that penetrated my paralysis. I looked at Simon in astonishment. He smiled awkwardly. 'I don't know why everyone is so surprised. I thought you'd be pleased.'

Mrs. Beauchamp unfolded a napkin and spread it over her lap. She said levelly, 'Well, I thought it might have been wiser to complete your degree first. You're young and there's plenty of time. And you've never been strong.'

'So you've always said. Anyway, they say it won't last long and we didn't want to miss it.' He glanced at Jagjit, who looked away, towards the french windows. 'We decided to join up together yesterday, before we left Cambridge.'

Startled, I looked at Jagjit, but his face was as stony as Aunt Mina at her best.

Simon said hesitantly, 'We... we'd hoped they'd put us in the same regiment, but – '

' – they wouldn't take me,' Jagjit cut in. He sounded bitter. 'The officer who was interviewing us told me Indians weren't eligible to be officers. He said I would be of more help if I went home and took up a temporary place in the I.C.S., thereby freeing an Englishman to fight for his country.'

'I'm sure your mother and father would be grateful,' Mrs. Beauchamp said. 'They must be eager to see you after so many years.'

'But it isn't fair,' Simon said. 'Jagjit was the senior boy in the O.T.C. at school. He won all the shooting medals.'

'Anyway, they can't keep me out,' Jagjit cut in. 'Indians may not be eligible to be officers, but I shall join up anyway as soon as I get back to India. I've booked a passage from Southampton on Tuesday. I just hope I can get back here before it's all over.'

It was as though he was talking about being left out of the cricket team – as if all that mattered was his stupid desire to be part of this game called war. He did not even glance at me.

A painful lump formed in my throat, bringing tears to my eyes. I thought of Father saying goodbye to me before one of his missions with Uncle Gavin: his airy manner, dismissive of the idea that something might happen to him, his refusal to see how terrified I was at the thought that I might be left alone with Mother forever. I pressed my lips together to stop them quivering and stood up, rocking my chair backwards.

'Lila, my dear, what is it?' Mrs. Beauchamp said, as I stumbled towards the french windows.

Familiar thoughts drilled through my head: *You can't trust anyone. They always leave. In the end you're alone. Stupid, stupid! How could you have forgotten that you don't matter... that there's always something more important? Surely Father should have taught you that lesson?*

As I crossed the garden, tears streamed down my face. I dashed them away furiously. *You fool, you fool, what are you crying for? What did you expect? That he would sacrifice a chance to be a hero for you? Idiot! But I don't care. I don't need anyone. He can go to hell!*

I was ripping at my skirts, which had caught in the brambles by the fence, when his deep voice said, 'Stand still.' His long fingers reached around me and freed the cloth from the thorns. 'I'm afraid you've torn it.'

I waved my hand without turning.

He took my arm and pulled me round. 'Lila, what is it?'

I stared at his suit lapels. Close to, the navy blue fabric was patterned with fine pink stripes made up of thin dashes of red and white.

He bent to look in my face. 'What is it? Why are you so upset? Is it something I've done?'

I looked away.

'Won't you even speak to me? Why did you run off like that? You don't know how much I've looked forward to seeing you.'

He reached for my hand but I jerked it away. I wanted to shout at him but the jagged lump in my throat choked me. I swallowed hard and managed to jerk out in a shaking voice, 'Stupid... So s-stupid...'

'Who's stupid? Do you mean me?'

I looked up at his bewildered face. 'Yes, you... *stupid!*' I said, and reached up and slapped him.

He stepped back, and I turned and ran all the way back to High Elms.

Aunt Mina was out in the garden with her cream parasol, dead-heading the roses in her white gardening gloves. She turned in astonishment as I rushed past her. I went up the stairs at a run, sobbing loudly, and slammed the door of my room behind me. I threw myself on to the bed. My whole body felt light, as though I might float away. There was a painful pressure in my chest, a buzzing in my head, and the sour-tasting lump in my throat was strangling me. I was sick with rage, with the desire to break something, to tear this room, this house, the whole world apart. I felt like that six-armed black statue of Kali I once visited with Father, the floor around her awash with the blood of sacrificed goats, whose heads lay piled at her feet. I understood her dance of destruction; I too wanted to trample and slay and burn, to rend limb from limb, to leave nothing standing.

I curled up on the bed and wrapped my arms around my knees, trying to hold my anger in, contain it where it could hurt no one but me. My heart felt like a stone in my chest. *'I don't care, I don't care, I don't care,'* I chanted, but the words turned to sobs and then I lost all sense of where I was. Far away I could hear someone wailing and screaming, 'Fa-a-ther… Fa-a-ther…' in an absurd histrionic way.

When I came round, Jagjit was sitting on the bed beside me, stroking my hair and talking to me softly. I sat up and looked around me. We were alone.

He smiled at my surprised face.

'Your aunt sent me up. No, she hasn't had a change of heart; she's outside. You frightened her. You frightened me too.'

I put my hand to my head. My hair had come loose on one side and was hanging in tangles. My eyes and throat felt swollen and my head ached.

'Am I ill?'

'Upset, I think.'

I looked at him blankly.

'Don't you remember? I think it might be because I told you I was going to join up.'

I turned my back on him and stared at the wallpaper, a pattern of oranges made of dots, with interwoven branches and green pointed leaves. The lump started to form in my throat again but this time the tears flowed freely. He put his hand on my shoulder and turned me to face him but I pulled away and lay down, hiding my face in my arm.

I felt his weight shift on the bed and then he lay down behind me and his arms went around me, gathering me into his chest. One hand smoothed the hair away from my ear. He whispered into it, 'Lila, don't be angry with me. I've missed you. I loved reading your letters, every one of them. I wanted to write back but I'd given my word. All I could think of was when I could see you again.'

'And you thought the best way was to get yourself killed!'

'Come on, Lila. It won't be forever. They say the war won't last long.'

His tone was indulgent, as though I was making a fuss over nothing. It was the first time I'd ever heard him do it – assume that false bravado that boys use to cover up their gentleness, vulnerability and fear. His truthfulness was what had always set him apart from Simon and other boys.

'It really doesn't change anything,' he added. 'And afterwards I can come back and finish my I.C.S. training. Will you wait for me, Lila?'

'No, because you'll be dead!' I did not add, *and I'll be alone again.*

'Sshshshsh.' He laughed softly and began to rock me. His body was strong and warm around me. I wanted to hate him but I can't remember, even now, a time when I felt safer or more loved. 'I'll come back. I promise. *Will* you wait?'

There was a knock at the door.

'*Go away!*' I shrieked.

He said admiringly, 'I never knew you were such a virago!'

'You don't know anything about me.'

'Not as much as I'd like to, but then I want to spend the rest of my life getting to know you.'

'Not long, then.'

He sat up and pulled me round to face him. 'I have no intention of dying, Lila. Now, I think we should let your aunt in, before she gets really worried. But you haven't answered my ques– '

I put my hand over his mouth and called, 'Come in!' Then I knelt up and kissed him hard. We were still kissing when Aunt Mina opened the door.

A few days later I accompanied the Beauchamps to Southampton to see him off. Aunt Mina made no attempt to stop me; she was still shocked by my outburst and must have comforted herself with the reflection that Jagjit would soon be nearly five thousand miles away.

In the carriage I sat between Mr. and Mrs. Beauchamp, with Jagjit and Simon on the seat opposite.

'I'm going to miss it all,' Jagjit said, gazing out of the window. 'All the different seasons – the first snowdrops, followed by the apple and cherry blossom, and the bluebells in May, and then poppies, and bringing the hay in, and the falling leaves, and the snow. We don't have all this variety where I live.'

'What is it like there?' Mrs. Beauchamp asked.

He smiled. 'Very different. We have just three seasons in northern India. The hot season, which lasts for months, where everything is baking hot and dusty, until we long for the rains. Then the monsoon, which is always welcome – it was my brother Baljit's and my favourite season. Everything is washed clean after all those months of dust, and the fields all fill up with water and reflect the sky. And then there's the cold season, which is nothing like as cold as here, but the evenings are beautiful.'

He paused and I remembered that first time when he had come over to High Elms alone to see me and talked of those winter sunsets when the ground mist rose as the villagers were making their way home from the fields. We shared something that no one else could understand.

My eyes filled with tears. I wanted to beg him to take me with him.

Once aboard the ship we admired the saloons and state rooms, then stood around awkwardly, waiting for the warning bells. Jagjit stood head and shoulders above everyone else and I noticed people surreptitiously glance at him and then at us, wondering what we were to each other. As always, he seemed indifferent to the curiosity he aroused.

Simon offered to help him carry his cases down to his cabin, which he was sharing with another Indian. They seemed to be gone for an age, and when they came back Simon looked pale and upset. I tried to catch Jagjit's eye but I could tell he was preoccupied, his mind travelling ahead of him. Mrs. Beauchamp tried to make conversation but eventually gave up. The minutes stretched out as we waited for the warning whistle and I wished I hadn't come, that I had said goodbye at the Beauchamps' instead of here, with all these people watching and him already gone from me.

Then the first whistle blew and people around us began to take leave of each other. Jagjit shook hands with the Beauchamps and thanked them for all their kindness. He turned to Simon and hesitated, then moved to embrace him, but Simon stepped back. He put his hand out, avoiding Jagjit's eyes. Jagjit took it and said, 'You will write from wherever you're posted? I'd like to know how you're getting on.'

'Of course.' He turned to his parents. 'Shall we wait on deck?'

Mr. Beauchamp looked puzzled. Mrs. Beauchamp grasped his arm and steered him away, with Simon following.

Jagjit turned to me and took my hands in his, ignoring the stares. He said softly, 'I'll come back for you when it's all over. And if I'm sent to Europe – as I hope I shall be – I'll use my leaves to visit.'

'I still don't see why you have to join up… It's nothing to do with you. Please…'

'Don't, Lila. I don't have time to explain; it's just something I have to do.' He lifted my hand to his lips. 'Goodbye, my darling.'

'Wait.' I unbuttoned the high neck of my blouse and pulled out my lucky Sussex stone. 'I want you to have this. To bring you back safely. It was Father's.'

'Lila, I couldn't possibly…'

'He would want you to have it. Bend down.'

He bent and I placed it round his neck, just as I used to do with Father. He tucked it inside his collar and smiled at me. 'I promise I'll keep it safe till I can return it to you myself.'

I stood on tiptoe and raised my face to his. He hesitated, then bent his head and kissed me. The conversation around us died for a moment and in the silence the second whistle went and it was time to go.

That night I dreamt Father was alive again. I was back in the bungalow in Peshawar, with the white muslin curtains lifting in the breeze, but this time there was a figure half-concealed behind them, silhouetted by the moonlight. A thrill of fear went through me but I found myself compelled to move closer. Then, as the curtains lifted again, I recognised her. Mother, in a white dress, smiling, but her eyes were as clear and empty of life as chips of green sea-glass. I turned and ran and found myself standing outside Father's study door, which was outlined in a glaring white light. With a feeling of dread I put my hand on the smooth brass doorknob and turned it. The door opened and there was Father, sitting behind his desk, with the statue of the dancing Shiva on the shelf behind him.

'Hello, Lila,' he said, as though nothing had happened.

I said, 'But it can't be you.'

He looked amused. 'Why can't it be me?'

'Because you're dead,' I blurted, and then realised that he didn't know.

He laughed. 'You can see I'm not!'

'But I was here. I saw it...' I looked up the wall behind him but it was clear of stains. Had I dreamt it? 'Then where have you been? Why did you go away?'

He looked surprised.

'I was with Gavin... on one of our missions. You know I would never leave you. Why didn't you wait? You must have known I would come back.'

I shook my head. 'I thought... But you were... I saw...' I swallowed hard, tears coming to my eyes, thinking of all those years wasted.

He smiled indulgently. 'O ye of little faith! You still don't believe me, do you?' He pushed his sleeve up and held his arm out across the desk. 'Here, touch me. I'm real. You know you can't feel things in dreams.'

I reached out and took his arm between my hands, feeling its weight and warmth, smelling the sun-warmed skin, seeing the skin wrinkle under the pressure of my fingers. It was real. Tears welled up in my eyes. He was alive! Joy flooded through me.

Then I woke up.

Henry

Taking over as acting magistrate from Thornton has proven
to be more challenging than I expected. On my arrival here
I went to introduce myself to him at his house, since he was
unwell. Even as I greeted him, it was apparent what the
cause of his 'illness' is, for over the course of the evening
he consumed almost a whole bottle of whisky. His briefing
consisted of a rambling complaint that India was a 'hellhole',
the job 'thankless and deadly boring' and that he would be
glad to quit it. His exact words were, 'You don't want to
believe a word those native sewers tell you. Pigs and liars, the
lot of them. Doesn't really make any difference whose favour
you find in. Hindu, Mussulman, Christian – they're all as bad
as each other.'

I met his deputy magistrate, a Bengali Muslim called
Hussain, the next day. Indian DMs are very rare so I knew
he must be a man of considerable ability. He showed me a
huge backlog of cases awaiting trial or sentencing. He did not
need to tell me that Thornton has not shown much interest
in his job: he had invited me to watch a session of the court
that morning and I have never seen a man look more bored; it

was worse than watching Father when he was forced to attend a social event. He yawned loudly, whacked about himself with his fly swat and even sang to himself once or twice, while the lawyers were speaking. After lunch he fell asleep, but the lawyers carried on unperturbed, as though used to it. I wondered how Thornton would cope when it came to the summing up and verdict, but when both parties had finished presenting their cases Hussain woke him and there was a brief adjournment while they went into another room. When they returned, Thornton gave his verdict, which seemed a sensible one.

It is apparent to me that Hussain is the magistrate in all but name and would make a useful ally. He seems – on first inspection anyway – to be an honest man and reminds me of Mr. Mukherjee. Since it is clear that he has extensive experience and has actually been running the show, I wonder if he resents my being promoted over him. I hope not, as I shall be quite reliant on him until I develop an ear for the local dialect. It looks as though the work is going to be rather more challenging than I had expected. I am expected to tour the area for at least ten days a month, but this territory is so large that Hussain says some of the remoter areas have never been visited by Thornton, and justice is administered by the police without trial, often by a beating. This is something I am determined to remedy.

30th November 1880

With the help of Hussain, I have worked my way though most of the backlog of files. I have found his knowledge of local conditions invaluable: he knows the history of many of the disputes, and my fears that he might be biased in favour of one or other party have proved to be unfounded. It is undoubtedly due to his competence and integrity that Thornton has been able to continue in his role for so long. I feared Hussain might see me as a usurper and resent the demands I am making on his time, for we work late into the night and I have extended the court hours so that we can begin to clear the backlog of cases, some of which have been waiting for years to be heard. But he seems pleased that I am taking an interest and that I value his opinion.

One embarrassing episode occurred on my first day in court. I had already noticed that Hussain always refused my invitation to sit down when we were working together, saying he preferred to stand, but now I understand why. One of the local landowners came to my office to see me during the lunch break to introduce himself and I offered him a chair. He stood hesitating, and to my astonishment the chaprassi pulled away the chair facing my desk and fetched another from against the wall – an ancient broken-down wreck of a thing. When the landowner had left I asked the chaprassi what he thought he was doing. He didn't understand at first but then explained, as though puzzled that I was unfamiliar with the concept, that it was the 'babu' chair. I looked at Hussain, not quite believing my ears. He said, 'Mr. Thornton kept a special chair for Indian visitors.'

I could not think of anything to say, except to order the chaprassi to get rid of it. 'Sit down, Hussain,' I said, indicating the remaining chair.

He demurred.

'For God's sake sit down, man!'

He sat.

I thought afterwards that perhaps I should not have been so sharp, but the next morning he asked if I would care to take lunch with him and his wife, and seemed delighted when I accepted. I was surprised that his wife sat with us, which is unusual for a Muslim woman. She is an educated woman from Bengal and, like her husband, speaks Hindustani, Bengali and English. She is also an avid reader, so we conversed a little about literature. Her ambition is to open a girls' school in Calcutta one day.

Over lunch I asked Hussain why he chose to join the civil service, and he told me that he had been inspired by a story he read in a book when he was at college, about the magistrate at Delhi, a man called Metcalfe. The story goes that during the Mutiny he was escaping along a road on foot, pursued by mutineers, when he stumbled upon a holy man sitting by the roadside. The sadhu, sizing up his situation, indicated a cave in the hillside and advised Metcalfe to hide in it. Having little choice, he entered it with misgiving, knowing he would be trapped if the sadhu betrayed him. When the mutineers arrived, they demanded of the sadhu whether he had seen anyone. The sadhu said he had not, but the mutineers, seeing the cave, proposed searching it. The sadhu told them in a loud voice, designed to reach Metcalfe's ears, that there was a red demon that lived in the cave, which liked to decapitate men before eating them. Upon hearing this, Metcalfe took up a position, sword in hand, just inside the entrance to the cave and, as the first man stooped to enter, he decapitated him with one blow of his sword. The head rolled down the hill and the mutineers fled in terror. Later, Metcalfe thanked the sadhu and asked why he had saved his life. The sadhu replied, 'I was up in front of you once and I know you are an honest man.' 'I must have found in your favour, then,' Metcalfe replied. 'No,' the sadhu said. 'You found against me. But you were right.'

Hussain smiled at me.

'For some reason that story inspired me.'

I laughed. 'Do you think it true?'

He chuckled. 'Unfortunately not. I did some research into Sir Theophilus Metcalfe later. He was magistrate at Delhi during the rebellion and his life was apparently saved by a nawab of his acquaintance, who sheltered him and whom he subsequently rewarded. But after the recapture of Delhi he was so maddened by revenge and so bloodthirsty in his reprisals that the Commissioner removed him from the city, saying that the sooner the power of granting life or death was removed from him, the better.'

Something came to my mind:

> 'My friendless heart's a city reduced to ruin,
> The great world has shrunk to a patch of rubble.
> In this place, where love was martyred,
> What now survives but memories and regret?'

'Mir,' he said. 'How do you come to know that?'

'I had a Bengali tutor when I was a child.' I'm not sure why I didn't mention the bibi; perhaps I was afraid that he would think less of Father.

Hussain told me that when he joined the I.C.S. he was warned by one of his tutors that he would never reach the highest echelons of the service because there would always be junior Europeans promoted above him. 'I have a verse for you too,' he said.

> 'High on the mountain
> the fruit is seized by the croaking crow
> while the lion who bullies bull elephants
> growls hungrily below.'

He smiled. 'But please do not imagine, Mr. Langdon, that I am comparing myself to a lion, or you to a crow.'

It is certainly true that as deputy magistrate, if he had been a white man, he would have been promoted to the job that I have now; but we both know that no European would submit to being judged by a native. It is also clear to me that Hussain is not in awe of Englishmen and that I shall have to win his respect.

In the meantime I have had practical matters to deal with, like finding somewhere to live. I cannot afford, on an assistant magistrate's salary, to continue living at the Club, nor to take over Thornton's bungalow. Fortunately, I have made the acquaintance of a 'Yellow Boy', a newly arrived member of the 1st Bengal Cavalry – otherwise known as 'Skinner's Horse' – who has suggested I share quarters with him and a fellow officer, as they have a spare room. Roland Sutcliffe is everything I am not – tall, blond, handsome, and a favourite with the ladies – and he appears to great advantage in his regimental uniform with its long yellow tunic and blue and gold striped puggree.

He has undertaken to educate me and advises me that flirting with unmarried European girls is unacceptable because it raises their hopes, but that married women are fair game as long as one is discreet. Eurasians are the best bet of all, he tells me: because a man knows they are using all their wiles to trap him into marriage, he need feel no guilt about seeing how far he can get without committing himself. Roland is already carrying on a flirtation with the wife of an officer who is out of station, and the cynical part of me cannot help wondering whether he has befriended me because I offer no competition in the looks department.

From what I can see, there is not much to do in Bhagalpur except attend the various dances and balls, and I have been warned that it is a full-time occupation to avoid being trapped into matrimony with the hundreds of young girls who flock out every year, and are known as the Fishing Fleet. Civil servants are not bound by the same restrictions as Army officers, who are discouraged from marrying young, so despite my lack of charm I am actually more eligible than Roland, even though, having no private means, I could not support a wife on my pay.

1st June 1881

I have been here almost nine months now and I feel at last that I am making progress. Hussain and I work well together and I am beginning to acquire a sounder grasp of the local conditions and to understand the dialect. I enjoy the tours especially – they remind me of the manoeuvres on which I used to accompany Father as a child. In some places we stay in dak bungalows, in others we camp in airy and comfortable 'Swiss cottage' tents, and during the day we hear cases. Where there is no building available, we hold court in the open air, sitting under the trees. Since there are no roads, reaching the further places on horseback can take several days, so I am often away for two or three weeks.

Before I left on my last trip, Roland told me he had met a girl at a dance. Her name is Rebecca Ramsay and she is the daughter of a 'boxwallah', as he insists on calling people in trade. He says she is the most exquisite creature he has ever set eyes on and promises that when I meet her I shall fall head over heels in love with her. I told him that in that case it might be better not to meet her, since he is so obviously in love with her himself. In the event, she went off to the hills with her ayah for the hot season before I had a chance to make her acquaintance. She must be special, since he still speaks of her almost three months later, and looks forward to her return when the rains start. However, I notice it has not stopped him from flirting with the Eurasian girls who attend the hot season balls, now that all the Englishwomen are in the hills.

30th June 1881

I have met Miss Ramsay at last and she lives up to Roland's description. I have never seen anyone as exquisite as she. She is very slender and has a cloud of curly dark hair and pale skin. The most fascinating thing about her is her eyes. They are slightly different shades of blue-green, and the greener one has a splash of brown on one edge of the iris, an imperfection that, strangely, adds to her beauty. I felt when I met her as though I was meeting a creature from another world – a sprite, or water nymph. There is something fragile and vulnerable about her that makes one long to protect her.

Roland introduced us and almost immediately left us alone together while he went to fetch her some fruit punch. At times like that I envy him his ease with ladies. I stood there tongue-tied until she smiled and suggested we take some air. I followed her out on to the verandah, feeling awkward and foolish. Standing there in the moonlight, with the smell of night jasmine wafting in from the garden and her pale face glimmering in the moonlight, I felt for a moment as though I was in a tale from the *Arabian Nights*.

'Roland tells me you're an assistant magistrate,' she said.

'Yes.' Then I launched into an account of some of the mishaps I had encountered in my open-air trials. I had just made her laugh by telling her about the time when a cow lifted a file of papers from a table placed under a tree and wandered off with it, and the poor court clerk had to run after her to retrieve it, when Roland came back with the drinks. Although she tries not to show it, I can tell from the way she looks at him that she is in love with him.

Back at the bungalow, I reminded Roland about what he had said about not flirting with unmarried girls but he just grinned at me. 'There's always an exception to every rule. Don't you think she's the most delectable creature you've ever set eyes on? She's almost worth losing one's commission for.'

'Do you mean you'd consider marrying her?'

He laughed. 'If I were to consider marrying anyone it would be her, but the C.O. would never give his permission, and I'm not cut out for any other work. I'm not clever like you, Henry, and I have only a small private income. No, I was always destined to be cannon-fodder. I know I shouldn't raise her hopes, but you must admit she's enchanting. If only that ayah of hers would leave us alone sometimes, I could at least snatch a kiss.'

I laughed. 'She obviously doesn't trust you. And if Miss Ramsay has no mother to watch out for her…'

'Yes, but the woman's insufferable. If we're on the verandah, she hovers nearby in the garden shrouded in her veil, like some sort of ghoul or banshee.'

'I didn't notice her. What about Miss Ramsay's father?'

'I've hardly seen him. As soon as they arrive he's off to the card room. Doesn't come out till it's time to go, and then he can hardly stand.'

Something else she and I have in common, then. But it must be harder for a girl to grow up with no mother; nor does she seem to have any female friends. I suspect the fact that she is country-born and -bred, like me, doesn't help, and her beauty and the fact that she is inundated with requests for every dance must provoke envy among other girls.

24th July 1881

I have found out a bit more about Miss Ramsay. She grew up in Assam on a tea plantation; her father was a planter but is now a steamboat agent. I met him briefly at the Club one evening and would never have guessed who he was if I had not been introduced to him by name. He is short, stout and ruddy-faced, and what little remains of his hair is a faded red. She must get her beauty from her mother. Miss Ramsay was two when she died and does not remember her; she was raised by her ayah, who is devoted to her and never leaves her side – for which I must admit I am grateful, because I fear Roland is completely smitten and too used to having his own way to resist the temptation to take advantage of her innocence.

20th September 1881

Roland has been away with his regiment for almost a month now, and I must confess, with some shame, to having taken advantage of his absence to get to know Miss Ramsay better. Despite not being one for balls and parties, I have continued to attend them in Roland's absence in the hope of seeing her. When she failed to appear I even plucked up the courage to call on her and ask if she would like to go for a drive. I could tell she only agreed because she was bored, and all she did on the drive was talk about him. Her ayah sat up front with the syce, with her headscarf pulled tightly around her face, but I was aware of her watching and listening to every word we said, though I don't know how much she understands.

Generally speaking, servants understand a lot more than we think.

Miss Ramsay brought her embroidery with her and kept her head bent over it and would hardly meet my eyes, though she seemed pleased when I admired it, and indeed I have never seen such fine embroidery or such strange designs or combinations of colours: trees, birds and flowers of a shape and form I have never seen before. She says they are all her own design and come from her imagination. 'You must have a very vivid imagination,' I said, and she said that her father told her that her mother, who was Irish, used to read her stories when she was very young. She does not remember her mother, but thinks some of the pictures from the stories must have stayed with her. And then she lifted her beautiful mismatched eyes to mine and I saw that they were full of tears, and I ached to hold her in my arms and kiss them away. I have never felt so tender towards anyone.

I know that I am poaching on Roland's territory, but I also know his intentions are not honourable, and with his penchant for clichés he would be the first to say that all's fair in love and war.

29th October 1881

I must take care, as my feelings for Miss Ramsay are getting out of hand. Yesterday I found myself thinking about her in the middle of a case and Hussain had to draw my attention to the fact that the plaintiff's lawyer had finished speaking. I had to call for a brief adjournment so he could brief me on what I had missed. He made no comment but I wondered if he was thinking of Thornton, who presumably had started off at least trying to be competent. I apologised for my inattention, which astonished him. I know it is not sahib-like behaviour, but one thing Father taught me was always to apologise when I am wrong.

10th November 1881

Roland is back. Tonight we met Miss Ramsay at the Club and the moment she saw him her face lit up. It was obvious they wanted to be alone so I left early. I have been trying to work, but while I look through the case of Gobind Chunder, who is trying to register a claim on land that his Muslim neighbours say belongs to them, all I can see is Rebecca Ramsay in Roland's arms, and hear that maddening dance music over and over in my brain, compounding my misery. I have put aside the work, but even three whiskies have not helped to deaden the pain and jealousy.

I suppose this must be what they call being in love, because when I am with her it feels as though the whole world is illuminated and every moment is precious and I would not exchange it for anything, and when I am away from her everything seems empty and meaningless. I wonder if this is how Father felt about my mother. For the first time I have some inkling of what her loss might have meant to him.

Bhagalpur, 2nd April 1882

The hot season is with us again. We have gone through the upheaval of the yearly exodus of women and children to the hills and it seems very quiet. Miss Ramsay did not go with them. She says that her father is unwell and cannot be left, but I suspect that none of the mems has offered to take her under her wing. I do not know whether through Roland or some other agency, but it seems word has gone round about Mr. Ramsay's past – it appears that he may have lost his job as a tea-planter because he could not keep his hands off the tribal women – and, as a result, Miss Ramsay has become increasingly isolated. I believe jealousy to be the true reason, however, for it has been apparent from the first that the mems have never warmed to her because she makes their daughters look plain. I have heard spiteful comments being made in voices loud enough for her to overhear, and the other girls no longer speak to her. She pretends not to notice, but she looks paler and more fragile every time I see her and my heart aches for her. I know from school what it is to be isolated and friendless, and once again I am regarded with suspicion because of my friendship with Hussain.

Roland is as obsessed with her as ever, and I have become useful again as a chaperone now that the winter season of balls is over and there are not so many opportunities for them to meet. So we all three, accompanied of course by her ayah, drive out to the tanks and sit by the water, or ride in the early morning before Roland goes to the Lines. I know I am being made use of but I find it hard to turn down the chance of spending time with her.

20th May 1882

Last night a party of us – some of Roland's fellow officers, some Eurasian girls chaperoned by their mothers, and Roland, Miss Ramsay and I, closely shadowed by her ayah – drove out to one of the tanks that provide the town's water. Miss Ramsay was wearing a spotted white dress made of yards and yards of some diaphanous material that made her seem more ethereal than ever. The party began to walk around the lake, the young ladies trailed at a discreet distance by their chaperones, but when Miss Ramsay's ayah tried to follow us Miss Ramsay turned on her and hissed something so ferocious that she dropped back. After that I began to feel uncomfortably *de trop* so I decided to take a walk up a nearby hill to a small temple on top that promised a good view of the tank. It was a bright moonlit night and from the top of the hill it was easy to follow the progress of the party as they walked. As I approached the temple I thought I saw a movement inside.

'Who is it? Show yourself!' I called in Hindustani.

A dark shape moved forward but remained in the shadows, the brilliance of the moon illuminating only the base of a fluted pillar and a pair of sandalled feet, which, marbled by the intense light, looked like those of a Greek statue with their high arches and long, elegant toes.

'Come into the light.'

The figure came forward hesitantly and I recognised Miss Ramsay's ayah. She salaamed, her hand pulling her veil closely around her face as she turned to leave.

I said quickly, 'Wait. Don't go. You were here first.'

She turned back and said in a panicky voice, 'I must go. Missie Baba may need me,' but I knew her real fear was of leaving Miss Ramsay alone with Roland.

I said reassuringly, 'They're not alone. Come and look. You can see them quite clearly from here.'

She stepped towards the edge of the platform and I pointed to Miss Ramsay, whose white dress made her easy to pick out from the other girls. She stopped near one of the pillars, looking down, her face turned away from me.

In an attempt to make conversation, I asked her how long she had been caring for Miss Ramsay.

'Since she was born, sahib.'

I noticed that her voice was low and her speech refined. Her accent reminded me of the bibi's. 'You're from Lucknow?'

She glanced round, surprised, then lowered her face again. 'Yes.'

'And you knew Miss Ramsay's mother?'

She nodded.

'What was she like?'

She hesitated. 'She was a good woman.'

'Is Miss Ramsay like her?'

'How?'

'Was she very beautiful?'

She shrugged. 'Some say so.'

I sensed her reluctance to answer and wondered why, but before I could press her further she said abruptly, 'What kind of man is Sutcliffe-sahib?'

'What do you mean?' I asked, taken aback by her presumption.

'Is he a good man? A man of honour?'

I said pompously, 'I hardly think it's your place to ask such a question.'

She said quietly, 'I mean no offence, sahib. I want only what is good for her. She has no one else to care for her.'

'Surely she has her father?'

She made a sound of contempt that surprised me, considering she was speaking of one Englishman to another, and I was about to say something sharp when she gave a gasp of alarm and I followed her eyes. Below, most of the walkers had returned and were sitting in small groups by the side of the tank. There was no sign of Miss Ramsay's white dress. Before I could react the woman had taken off down the hill, so fast that I was afraid she'd fall.

I caught up to her and said, 'You look on this side of the lake. I'll take the other.'

I knew Roland wouldn't thank me for disturbing his *tête-à-tête*, so it was a relief, when I finally found him, to learn that Miss Ramsay's ayah had discovered them first and insisted on taking her home. Roland was seething. 'I'd only had a few minutes alone with her before that virago found us. Oh, Henry, she's the most mesmerising creature. Sometimes she's all ice and at others she's all fire.'

'Roland, you didn't…'

He snorted. 'Chance would be a fine thing! We were getting on splendidly and then… then that harridan burst in on us. I'd made a bit of a mess of Rebecca's dress and if looks could kill I'd be dead now. She told me she'd tell Rebecca's father… if he complains I'll be up before the C.O., but it would be worth it. I just wish I'd had a little longer alone with her.'

I wanted to hit him, and yet I am no better than he, because lying in bed last night I found myself fantasising about what it would be like to be with her and I knew that Roland was right: she would be wild, passionate. I have never envied anyone the way I envy him. I would give anything for her to care for me, but she has eyes only for him. I cannot bear to watch them any more so I have decided to take some of the leave I have due to visit Father. Perhaps this time I can find out a little more about my own past.

Cecily

Dearest Mina,

You will probably never receive this letter as the mail has ceased, but writing to you comforts me. It is the worst thing, waiting for something to happen. Everything is quiet, yet we can feel the tension in the air: a storm waiting to break. It is horrible being cramped up here in the dark in this little room, and I am so filled with fear, but of course we cannot show it for the sake of the children, who are as happy and excited as if we were on a picnic. To them it is all a game. I heard Freddie say to Sophie this morning, 'You fire shells and I'll return shot from my battery,' and despite our fears Louisa and I exchanged a sick smile. She is, as always, brave and resolute. How I wish I were like her, but I am not. All I can think of is the terrible things they say were done at Delhi to pregnant women and innocent children. Louisa says I must not think of them, but I cannot get the pictures out of my mind. How could human beings be so cruel, and why do they hate us so much?

The heat and dust are stifling. Yesterday the lid of my writing bureau, my wedding gift from Mama, split in two.

Later

We have just heard the news that Capt. Hayes and Lt. Barbour are dead – cut down by their own sowars. General Wheeler had sent them out a few days ago to rescue any civilians who might have survived. Today he recalled two patrols of Arthur's troops, who are trustworthy, and instead sent out some troops from the 56th, who have been showing signs of disaffection. Everyone knows his purpose is to get rid of them. Their poor officers went bravely, not showing that they knew their fate. One of them is Lt. Tremayne, Emily's husband. I do not know how she will manage without him.

All the officers have now been ordered to sleep in the entrenchment. Arthur alone is permitted to sleep in the Lines because his troops are the only ones who have shown no sign of disaffection. I truly do not believe that Ram Buksh and Durga Prasad would allow their men to hurt us, but I cannot help remembering that many of the worst atrocities in Delhi were done to helpless women and children by their own servants. When Ram Buksh came back with Arthur I felt so guilty for doubting him that I could not meet his eyes.

5th June 1857

Our case now seems hopeless. This morning we were woken by shots and went out to discover that the 2nd Native Cavalry had rebelled and shot their risaldar-major who tried to stop them. I was frightened for Arthur, but he and his men turned out on to the parade ground, together with the remainder of the 56th under the command of their native officers, where they remained standing to attention and ignoring the pleas of the rebels to join them. Soon after, the 56th too rebelled, firing at Col. Williams who rode out to intercede with them.

To my relief, General Wheeler summoned Arthur to the entrenchment along with his native officers, but then, for some reason that no one can understand, Gen. Wheeler ordered our native gunners to fire upon Arthur's men, even though they were standing quietly in their ranks and showing no signs of rebelling. Arthur tried to stop them but Gen. Wheeler overruled him. When the first shot landed near them they looked startled but seemed to think it was a mistake and remained at attention, but when two more landed among them they broke ranks and ran for their Lines.

No one knows why Gen. Wheeler should have ordered such a thing, but James thinks it may have been to test the loyalty of the native gunners, who have been behaving sullenly. If so it was a mistake, for they became so uncooperative afterwards that Gen. Wheeler offered them an opportunity to leave the entrenchment and they all took it.

I have never seen Arthur so upset. He begged for permission to go to his men but Gen. Wheeler forbade him to leave the entrenchment. Arthur went white and for a moment I truly thought he would attack the general but at that moment Ram Buksh leapt on to Arthur's horse, which he had been holding, and rode away. Our sentries fired after him but fortunately missed. He told us when he got back this evening that he had remembered that our guards were on the Treasury and Magazine and, fearing that when they learnt that their fellows had been fired upon for no reason they would hand the buildings over to the mutineers, he had ridden off to stop them. But it was too late, for when he got there he found that both were already in the hands of the rebels and that *Nana Saheb has assumed command over them*! It is strange how calmly we took the news, almost as though we expected it, although poor James feels terrible about having trusted him.

General Wheeler has recalled all the officers and assigned them a position along the walls. As Arthur no longer has any men to command, he has volunteered to serve under Captain Moore. It must be humiliating for him to take orders from a junior officer, but he says this is no time for pride and every man is needed now. Ram Buksh has been allowed to remain, along with a few other loyal native officers. Durga Prasad wanted to join them but Arthur asked him to go out and round up their men. He returned with them a few hours ago but when he asked them to collect their rifles they refused to pick them up for fear we should fire upon them again. Gen. Wheeler will not to let them enter the entrenchment, so they are in a barracks outside, where Arthur says they are exposed to fire from every side. Durga Prasad is to command them. Arthur and James have given him all the money they have for food and provisions, as it is of no use to us now.

When Arthur came back from parting with Durga Prasad and his men, he broke down and wept. In the last few days I have seen his strength, courage and kindness, his unfailing generosity and patience, and the comfort and reassurance he dispenses to everyone around him. I truly have grown up, Mina, and if – through God's mercy – we survive this, I shall never doubt him again.

My darlings, if I do not see you again in this world, I know I shall see you in the next.

Your ever-loving Cecily

6th June 1857

James has just told us that General Wheeler has received a strangely courteous note from Nana Saheb stating his intention of attacking us at ten o'clock. It is now ten minutes to ten. May God have mercy on us.

Lila

After Jagjit left for India, I went into a kind of hibernation. That summer was the hottest and driest I can remember in England. Day after day the sun shone, and seemed to mock my misery. There was a weight in my chest formed of grief and dread that threatened to rise into my throat and choke me. I woke with it in the morning and went to bed with it at night.

Each day I took a book from my great-grandfather's library and went up on the hill behind the house to my old hideout. Books had been my comfort throughout childhood when Father was away; imaginary worlds filled the emptiness of knowing that no one cared for me most, not even Ayah, because Mother's needs always came first. I had lost myself in stories then, but they could not console me now; I could no longer forget who I was and become poor orphaned Pip or Jane Eyre, alone and friendless, taking comfort in my shared unhappiness. But the story I went back to repeatedly was 'The House of Eld', puzzling over the meaning of Jack's tragic story.

About a fortnight after Jagjit's departure, Aunt Mina called me into the morning room. She was reading through some papers, and looked up at me.

'Sit down please, Lilian.'

I pulled up a chair to the desk and sat opposite her, wondering what she wanted. Again there was that feeling of awkwardness between us. I had lived with her for seven years and still we did not know what to say to each other.

She put down the paper she was holding and looked at me. 'Do you still wish to go to university in London?'

I did not know what to answer. The application date had passed and I had given up the idea. Nothing had seemed to matter very much except the fact that Jagjit might be killed. Although I tried not to believe it, I could not help feeling that everyone I loved was destined to be taken from me.

'I don't know, but it's too late now, isn't it?'

'I spoke to Mr. Beauchamp a few weeks ago and he agreed to speak to the Provost for me. Because so many students have joined up they have unfilled places, and if you are still interested you could go up for an interview next week.' She handed me the letter.

'But I thought you didn't want me to go.'

'It may seem to you, Lilian, as though I make a point of always standing in your way, but I know what it is to live in uncertainty. I have always found it better to keep oneself occupied and not have too much time to think. Studying may be the answer for you.'

So she had noticed my unhappiness. Once again I was lost for words. 'Thank you, Aunt Mina.'

In the event I never did get to university, because in the next few weeks it became apparent to the authorities that this was a war different from any they had ever known. As the scale of the slaughter became apparent, and the casualty lists grew longer, the recruitment drive intensified. Mr. Kipling was touring the country, making inspiring speeches with his

new anthem, 'Jerusalem', set to music by Mr. E.
Pankhurst suspended the Votes for Women movement th.
war was over and transferred her energies into recruiting men
to go and fight, handing out white feathers to those who were
laggardly, while Mr. Keir Hardie, who was an ardent pacifist,
was trying to organise a general strike to protest against the
war. Mr. Beauchamp told us he had been jeered in the House
of Commons for addressing anti-war demonstrations and
defending conscientious objectors. He was no longer invited
to the house.

Meanwhile, Mrs. Beauchamp, like the mothers of many
young men who joined up, had thrown herself into war
work and arranged for me to join the Women's Voluntary
Aid Detachment in Brighton. So, less than two months after
Jagjit's departure, I was working at the new military hospital
on Dyke Road.

Being a V.A.D. opened my eyes to many of the things
Mrs. Beauchamp and her suffragette friends had talked about.
For years I had heard them discuss the lot of working class
women, but now I experienced for myself what it was like to
do hard physical work all day. Unqualified to nurse, V.A.D.s
did all the menial jobs: washing unending piles of greasy
dishes, emptying bedpans, serving meals. My hands were raw
from eczema and being scrubbed with carbolic; my muscles
ached. At night I was so tired that I fell asleep on the tram
back to the nurse's hostel, and barely had the energy to make
myself a cup of cocoa before collapsing into bed. For the first
time I thought about the life of our maids, who rose at five
every morning to scrub the grates and make up the fires and
went to bed after we did.

I think the tiredness took some of the edge off the shock
of the other sights we saw. For the first few months I worked

mechanically, scrubbing and cleaning, fetching and carrying, following orders. We were treated with impatience by Matron and with contempt by the professional nurses, who regarded us 'lady nurses' as spoilt and useless. But to complain was unthinkable. When one saw the state of the young men, little more than boys, who were being brought in, it was impossible to feel sorry for ourselves. We were called upon to help hold limbs steady while they were bandaged, to carry amputated limbs to the sluice room, to help bathe men who were the same age as ourselves, to sit with dying men and to comfort shocked and grieving relatives. Overnight, girls who had led sheltered lives were exposed to a level of suffering that was unimaginable to them. In some ways I adapted better than some of the others because I could understand at least something of what these young men had been through. I knew what it was to see violent death; I knew what the inside of a man's head looked like. I knew what it was to have one's world come to an end.

Simon came home from France on short leave that November. I was shocked when I saw him. His face was grey, his hands shook and his occasional stammer had worsened. At lunch he seemed abstracted, hardly speaking and ignoring all Mrs. Beauchamp's attempts to draw him into the conversation. All through the meal he rested one elbow on the table – something we had never been allowed to do – and crumbled pieces of his bread roll between his fingers, letting the crumbs drop on to the floor. I could see it was irritating Mrs. Beauchamp, who eventually said in a chivvying voice, 'Lila has come to see you, Simon. You could try to be a little less gloomy.' He shot her a look of such hatred that I was astonished.

After lunch we walked in silence up to the top of the Dyke. I could feel the tension in his body as he stood beside me looking north over the Weald. It was a still grey day, and a hush hung over the countryside. It had been a wet, cold autumn following the glorious summer, and I wondered what it was like out in the trenches.

He gave a deep sigh. 'It's so peaceful. You'd never think that just across the Channel such carnage was going on.'

'It's very bad out there, isn't it?'

He glanced at me. 'I wouldn't know where to begin, Lila. It's worse than anyone can imagine, but you must know that, working where you do.'

I thought of the neurasthenic patients, shaking and stammering, gripped by amnesia or headaches, or dumb from shock. 'One sees the state they're in, of course, but for the most part they put a brave face on things.'

'Or perhaps they've just grasped the truth, which is that no one really wants to know about how beastly it is. Everyone is constantly trying to cheer one up as if one's the doomsayer at a picnic, or dishing out advice when they don't know the first thing about it. But I should be used to it by now... Mother never really cared about me... she always wanted a girl: someone she could involve in her bloody Women's Movement.'

'I'm sure she does care, Simon. It's just hard to imagine what it's like out there, even for me. One doesn't like to ask. Perhaps if you told them about it you'd find they would understand.'

He snorted. 'Strange advice from you, Lila. It's not as if you were a great talker yourself. You've never said what happened out in India before you came here.'

I was silent.

He smiled. 'So you see, we're not so different. Some things are just too hard to talk about.' He pushed his pale hair back from his brow. 'Do you hear from Jagjit?'

Jagjit had written several times. He told me that his brother, Baljit, had signed up too. They were in the same regiment. In his last letter he had said that they would be leaving India at the end of the month.

'He does write. He doesn't seem terribly happy now he's in. He says he realises that it makes the officers uncomfortable when they find out that he was a public schoolboy, because they don't know how to treat him. It's easier if he pretends not to speak English too fluently, and he thinks they would disapprove of a sepoy being friendly with an Englishwoman, so he won't be able to write freely once they're in the field. Apparently their officers read all their letters.'

'Yes, we do that to make sure the men don't give anything away. And of course to ensure they don't say anything about what it's really like out there. Have to keep up the morale of folk at home, don't you know? But I can imagine he might find it difficult. Do you know, Father told me some MPs protested when the use of Indian troops was first proposed? They felt it was all right to use Indians to fight other Indians in their own part of the world, but unacceptable to employ them against our fellow Europeans. I can imagine that Army life is not what he envisaged – in the O.T.C. we were all treated the same. Do you know where they're sending him?'

'No. He hopes Europe, so he can visit. But surely he writes to you?'

'No.'

'But you were such good friends.'

His mouth twisted.

'I thought so; obviously he didn't. When we parted he said he'd write – they were his last words – but he hasn't. Not once.'

I remembered that atmosphere of awkwardness between them on the boat as they said goodbye. 'Have you written to him?'

'The ball was in his court.' He looked at me suddenly and grimaced. 'I'm sorry to be such bad company, Lila. It was good of you to come.'

'It's all right, Simon. I do understand.'

He looked at me properly for the first time. 'Do you, Lila? Yes, I think perhaps you do. You know, your quietness used to annoy me when we were younger, but I like it now. It's restful being with you. I find it hard to talk to most girls… I never know what to say to them. One can't stop thinking about it, you know, even when one's away from it. At least I know you understand. You've always been different.'

After Simon had gone, I thought about what he'd said about my being different. It was true that even as a child I'd always felt separate, apart; I had thought it was to do with being an only child, but now I wondered if it was more than that. The servants had always teased me about my solemnity, and I knew other V.A.D.s at the nurses' hostel thought me odd and stand-offish.

I had made only one friend at the hospital, a sister called Barbara Melton, who took a shine to me for some reason I was unable to fathom, because we could not have been more different. In her starched uniform and cap she was all professionalism, and the other V.A.D.s were afraid of her, but out of uniform she was the most unconventional person I'd ever met, with her cropped dark hair, red lipstick and short skirts. She said she liked me because I wasn't silly or squeamish, and just got on with the job. All of us were naïve and none of us was used to performing menial tasks, but some of the girls were so incapable that they were more of a hindrance than a help, and others became coy and giggly when having to deal with tasks like administering bedpans or helping with bed baths. Barbara had no patience with them; she herself was an Honourable, the daughter of a baronet, and had become a nurse before the war, despite the opposition of her family, who did not consider it a profession for ladies. Her fiancé, Ronald, was at the front.

Less than a fortnight after Simon's departure, plans were announced to transform the disused Royal Pavilion in Brighton into a hospital for Indian soldiers. Barbara was one of the sisters picked to work there, and she decided to take me with her. V.A.D.s were not wanted at the Indian hospital because all the manual work was done by Indian orderlies – the nurses were forbidden to touch the men – but Barbara thought my knowledge of Hindustani would come in useful.

The preparations were extraordinary. Every effort was made to respect the different religious observances: there were separate water taps, separate cooking facilities, even separate operating theatres and orderlies for Hindus and Muslims. Hindu and Sikh temples were set up in tents in the grounds and arrangements were made for Muslims to be taken to worship at the mosque in Woking. The floors were covered in linoleum and rows of white-sheeted beds and screens created a hospital environment at ground level, while, above, the painted domes, palm tree pillars and magnificent chandeliers that gave the former royal palace its oriental feel remained. For men recovering consciousness, it was disorientating to find themselves in what seemed like an Eastern paradise, and they sometimes had to be reassured that they were not dead or hallucinating. But, for me, it was like coming home. Listening to the buzz of Hindustani took me back to my childhood, playing in the compound and listening to the servants gossiping as they worked. And hearing the Sikhs speaking Punjabi reminded me that it was the language Jagjit would speak at home, and made me eager to learn it.

I enjoyed being with the men, helping them with the reading and writing of letters; I was grateful to Father who had taught me to read and write Hindustani. Gurmukhi – the Punjabi script – was beyond me, but I found Punjabi itself quite easy to pick up because of its similarity to Hindustani.

The work I liked best was sitting with the dying. I have never seen a baby born but Barbara tells me that witnessing the presence of a being where no being existed before is nothing less than a miracle. For me the moment of death was no less profound. Father used to tell me the story of how Savitri outwitted Yama, the Lord of Death, to save her young husband, who was fated to die. Savitri, the faithful wife, was the heroine of the story but I liked Lord Yama best, because he was compassionate enough to allow himself to be outwitted, knowing they would both come to him in the end.

Having witnessed many deaths in the last years, it seems to me that it is not death itself that is terrible but the process of dying, and that is what haunts me about Father: that he died without comfort, with the sense that there was nothing left to live for. I cannot help feeling that I failed him by not providing him with a reason to live.

Often as I sat with patients, talking, they would ask me about the war. They were puzzled. A young Jat soldier asked me once if it was true that the Kaiser, the King and the Tsar were related and, if so, why they were fighting. 'It's just like the *Mahabharat*,' an older sepoy told him. 'Cousins fighting each other.'

Some were so awed by the magnitude of the destruction, the shells that obliterated whole villages and destroyed fertile fields, that they thought it must be the final battle of the last age, the Kali Yuga, when Shiva opens his third eye and the world is destroyed before being reborn. Used to fighting face to face, and giving respect to the enemy, they could not comprehend the honour in a war where men fired shells at men they had never seen, and in turn cowered in ditches while bombs rained down on them. But all remembered the enthusiasm with which they had been greeted by the French when they'd arrived in Marseilles. Women had come out to greet them with flowers. Some had even embraced and kissed them. And on the hospital train they had been nursed by Englishwomen who had changed dressings and administered bedpans. 'They were not like memsahibs but angels,' an old N.C.O. told me.

And since they had arrived in England there had been more angels. As soon as the hospital opened, the ladies of the town descended bearing flowers, fruit and other gifts. The soldiers were invited home for tea, or taken for rides along the seafront. For most of them hospital was not a depressing place. They had spent the autumn and the first part of winter digging trenches in the pouring rain, while standing knee-deep in water; many had lost toes to frostbite and, to make matters worse, their winter uniforms had never arrived so they were still in their tropical uniforms, and would continue to be until the following spring. Remembering how cold I had been that first summer in England, even indoors, I could not imagine what the trenches in winter must be like for them. So to be in a warm, comfortable environment, with all their

190

needs supplied, playing cards and dice, or standing on the balconies waving at people passing on the trams, who waved back, was an enjoyable experience.

During that winter the Indians were involved in some of the heaviest fighting on the Western Front. As I later discovered, Jagjit and his brother were at Ypres, where almost half their regiment would be killed or wounded, but I learnt nothing of this from his letters, in which he addressed me with stilted formality, knowing his words would be read by his company commander.

As the months passed I found myself increasingly reluctant to expose my own feelings and our letters became more and more like those of casual acquaintances.

In March 1915, the Indians were involved in a huge battle at Neuve Chapelle and there were so many casualties that we ran out of beds; men were lying on stretchers on the floor. Unlike previous patients, who had been cleaned up and bandaged at casualty clearing stations or field hospitals, these soldiers had been put on the train straight from the battlefield, in muddy pus-soaked field dressings and stinking lice-ridden uniforms. The smell of gangrene hung in the air and the incinerators were struggling to keep up.

The wounded had started coming in the night before and, no matter how fast we shifted them, more kept coming. Most of us were well into a double shift, and it looked as though we would be there all night again, taking short breaks when we could no longer go on.

Having no set role, that day I was working as a general dogsbody, carrying cups of tea to the exhausted surgeons who gulped them down between operations, ferrying instruments from the operating theatres to be sterilised, carrying buckets of discarded body parts to the sluice room, and doing anything that no one else was available for. Towards the end of the second day, when things began to settle a little, I was helping the orderlies to sort through piles of uniforms to decide which were worth repairing and which were fit only for the incinerator, when I picked up a uniform jacket which was so soaked in blood that whoever was wearing it must almost certainly have died of blood loss. It seemed astonishing that he'd survived long enough to be put on the train for England, and I was laying it on the pile for incineration when something fell on to the floor with a clink. I looked down and my stomach lurched as I saw a knobbly pendant on a cord, covered with dried blood. I picked it up and my fingers recognised the shape before my eyes did. It was Father's lucky Sussex stone.

Henry

29th June 1882

I have been at Father's for almost ten days now. The rains started two days after I arrived here and it has been raining ever since. The noise on the corrugated roof is deafening but I find it strangely soothing – it is one of the sounds of my childhood. The scent of the night-flowering raat-ki-rani drifts into my room and last night I woke and thought myself back in my childhood bed and remembered the bibi's cool hands on my fevered forehead.

Yesterday I screwed up my courage and raised the subject of my mother again.

Father sighed. 'You must know what happened, Henry. Everyone knows what happened at Cawnpore in '57. You must have learnt about it at Haileybury, surely?'

'So you're saying that my mother died at Cawnpore? That it wasn't my fault?'

He looked astonished. 'Your fault? How could it be? Did you really think that?'

I shrugged.

He stared at me for a moment then looked away, out into the darkness and the rain, and I thought he was going to

193

retreat into himself and shut me out, as he has done so many times before, but instead he said, 'I suppose you have a right to know, and you are old enough now to understand. But it's a long story.'

'I have plenty of time, Father.'

He sighed. 'The truth is, your mother shouldn't have been here at all. She was supposed to return to England when we discovered she was pregnant, but things escalated before I had time to take her to Calcutta. When it was clear there was going to be trouble, I arranged for her to travel with my brother's family but then Louisa – my brother James' wife – refused to go, and Cecily decided it was her duty to stay. She got it into her head that her mother, who had died recently, would have wanted her to. Our marriage had not been easy and she was trying to be fair, to do what was right for me, but sometimes our best intentions lead to the worst consequences. I should never have allowed it, of course, but I was afraid if she returned to England I would lose her, and you. It was selfish of me, but I don't think any of us expected the barrel to explode the way it did. And then it was too late: we were trapped. It was my fault, my selfishness. I should never have let her stay... let any of them stay.'

'So what exactly happened?'

He took a deep breath. 'Wheeler had built an entrenchment in Cawnpore. You must have learnt something about this at Haileybury...'

And of course he is right. I have known what happened at Cawnpore for years. It was hardly possible to avoid learning of it in England, for everyone who has relatives in India lives in fear of a recurrence. I have read Mowbray Thomson's and Fitchett's accounts, both of which came out while I was at school, but I did not know that my mother or I were part of that story. 'Yes, of course,' I said. 'The James Langdon in the Roll of Honour. He was your brother.'

He nodded. 'We were all there together – your mother, pregnant with you, and James and his wife Louisa and their three children…' His voice thickened and he cleared his throat. 'Suffice to say it was unimaginably terrible, and through it all your mother was remarkably brave. She was very afraid, as anyone would be, especially in her condition, but she behaved with great courage, helping Louisa with the children and even volunteering to work in the makeshift hospital until it burnt down. It was very distressing – there were hideous injuries from the round shot and wounds got infected and we had very few medical facilities even before fire destroyed the hospital. The screams of the sick and wounded were dreadful to hear… I was concerned that in her condition she would find it too upsetting, but she coped admirably. In the end it was Louisa who fell apart… after James and…' He paused and covered his eyes with his hand. 'I'm sorry, Henry. Even after all this time I can't talk about it.'

'What were you doing during all this?' I was trying to distract him but it sounded almost accusing. 'Sorry, I didn't mean…'

He gulped his whisky. 'I was serving under the commanding officer of a British regiment, a Captain Moore. He was junior to me but I had no men of my own to command – Wheeler had thrown all the native troops, except a few trusted officers, out of the entrenchment. My men were completely loyal, as would be proved later, but by then Wheeler didn't trust any of them. It was a mistake that sealed our fate, because it turned even those who were loyal against us and allowed the Magazine and Treasury to fall into Nana Saheb's hands.'

He took a breath.

'It's hard to describe… unimaginably hellish. It's astonishing that we held out as long as we did. Any competent army could have taken us in a day, but of course they had no leadership… The entrenchment walls were so low that they provided no cover at all. We were effectively out in the open, in the blazing sun at the hottest time of year, and under constant fire, day and night. We didn't even have access to water: the well was targeted by snipers even in the dark; they could hear the splash of the bucket and the creak of the rope. Those who volunteered to get water did so at the risk of their lives. We got used to drinking water with blood in it, and by the end all there was to eat was handfuls of gram flour mixed into a paste with a little water. When the hospital barracks caught fire, there was no time to evacuate the wounded and all our medical supplies were destroyed. It meant bullets could no longer be extracted and even the slightest wound was a sentence of death.

'At first we were sheltering in the barracks, but we had to abandon them because the walls had great holes in them and they were in danger of collapse. After that we camped in the shallow trench under the walls – it had been dug so we could walk about without being picked off by snipers. Our clothes were just rags. We had given up our shirts for bandages, and the women had given their petticoats and were walking about half-naked… but we were past caring about things like that. You cannot begin to imagine, Henry, how degraded suffering can make people. We were filthier than the filthiest beggar.

'Your mother was heavily pregnant by then and finding it hard to move around. I gave her what help I could, but during the day I was busy with the defence… We were under constant attack.' He gave a staccato laugh. 'I remember your mother telling me that Colonel Ewart fumed at the incompetence of his sepoys after one of their attacks had failed: "Have they learnt nothing from me at all?" he said. He was in hospital then, having been wounded in the arm. But to answer your question – as I said, I volunteered to defend the walls under the command of Captain Moore. He was a good man, young but very competent. Later he sent me out to lead sorties against the enemy, which is how I survived. I wish to God now I had stayed behind. It's foolish to imagine I could have saved her... but at least I would have shared her fate.'

I watched him struggle to hold back his tears. 'It's all right, Father. You don't have to talk about it.'

He held his hand up. 'No, I may as well finish. On that particular day I'd gone out with a party, including one of my native officers – a jemadar called Ram Buksh – to clear some mutineers away from a disued barracks. They'd been using it as a base from which to attack us. We had just managed to chase them out when we were charged by a group of sowars. One of them rode straight at me. I was on foot – we'd eaten all the horses by then. I shouted to Ram to get the others under cover and tried to dodge under the horse's belly but the sowar brought his sword down... It gave me this – ' he touched his scar ' – and sliced into my shoulder, breaking my collarbone. The next thing I knew, I was lying on a bed of grass in a hut. Some of my sepoys, who had been sheltering in a nearby ravine, had found me and carried me to a village where the villagers looked after me. The headman knew me because your mother and I sometimes rode out that way and she was popular with the children.'

Tears came to his eyes. 'I wish you'd known her, Henry. She was so... so full of life. Rooms lit up when she walked into them. I used to watch her with the village children. They loved her too. When I met her the world became a brighter place… and when she died…'

I looked away as he struggled to control his face. He took a swig of whisky to steady himself and went on grimly, 'They packed my wounds with some native recipe and bandaged them up tight but the shoulder got infected and I was delirious for some days. When the fever finally passed I was too weak to move. But my sepoys kept visiting me and bringing me news. They told me that the relief column, which had left Calcutta at the end of May, was stuck at Allahabad, having halted all along the route to burn villages and erect gallows. They had created such terror that word of their approach emptied villages before them, so they could find no food or supplies, and no coolies to carry them. It was this time of year, and the rains had started. Hard conditions for a marching army.'

He paused and stared out at the sheeting rain, but I knew what he was seeing was then, not now. 'I knew Wheeler could not hold out much longer because the walls would simply wash away. And sure enough I heard a few days later that he had surrendered to Nana Saheb and that the survivors of the entrenchment had been promised safe passage by boat to Allahabad.'

He was silent for a long time then, and I did not urge him to go on, for every English man and woman knows the meaning of the phrase *Remember Cawnpore!*

Cecily

I do not know what day it is. We have been here two or three days, prisoners of Nana Saheb. I do not know how to write the terrible news. Freddie, James, Louisa, Sophie and the baby are all dead. Arthur is missing after going out on a raid outside the entrenchment. Ram Buksh saw him cut down and went back to recover his body but it was not there.

The sights I have seen are imprinted on my mind and I cannot get them out. I see them when I close my eyes and when I sleep I dream them. At night I am woken by my own or other women's or children's screams. Scenes from the entrenchment roll over and over in my mind – little Mabel Tremayne dying of shock when the first bombardment started; Freddie shot through the head by a sniper's bullet, dying in his father's arms; James with his insides spilling out and Louisa trying to push them back in; the screams of the wounded when the hospital burned down; Luxmibai with both her legs blown off while trying to fetch water for the children; Louisa, crazed with grief, dying of fever and the baby fading like a flower in a few hours. Towards the end we no longer cared whether we lived or died; children ran out among the bullets and no one tried to stop them. Poor Arthur saw his whole family killed, except Sophie and me.

After he was gone Ram Buksh did everything for me – he cared for poor Sophie, who was dumb from shock and would not eat. Even after he was wounded, he brought us food and water from the well at the risk of his life.

General Wheeler surrendered on the 25th, and we left the entrenchment on the 27th, after a delay because there were not enough palanquins for the sick and wounded. But as soon as we were outside they dragged the servants away and our luggage was all left behind. We knew then we were betrayed, but it was too late. We were filthy and dressed in rags and the natives jeered and taunted us as we made our way to the river. I saw Colonel Ewart's own sowars drag him from his palanquin by his wounded arm while he screamed in pain. They mocked him and demanded to know why his shoes were not polished, then they cut him to pieces in front of his wife. They told her she could go but when she turned they cut her down too. Ram Buksh tried to shield me from the sight, but when we got near the river they dragged him away, shouting that he was a traitor, and put him in irons. He fought them to stay with me but they beat him with their rifle butts until I screamed at him to go with them. I am so ashamed now that when we agreed to surrender no one thought to ask if safe passage applied to the native officers who had risked their lives for us.

They were waiting for us at the river, lining the ghats, their rifles loaded and ready. We managed to scramble aboard the boats but the water was low and they stuck fast in the mud. Capt. Moore was shot through the heart and Gen. Wheeler cut down in the water by a sowar on horseback. I pushed Sophie down on to the floor but before I could get down beside her a sepoy grabbed me and pulled me from the boat. It was one of Arthur's men and he was shouting something to me about Arthur, but I did not listen, for I was fighting to get back to Sophie. At last he let me go, but when I reached the river again I could not find the boat. They were all on fire – everyone in them burnt alive. Women and children jumping into the water were speared like fish. I cannot write any more.

Next day

We are being held captive in a building in the garden of a larger house. After the river we were taken to another place by Nana Saheb's soldiers, who taunted us and threw grain on the floor for the children to scrabble for, and called us vermin. Yesterday we were brought here, where we are guarded by mutineer sepoys. It is dark and hot and there are so many of us that we cannot lie down together but have to take turns. But our guards are not unkind; they allow us to draw water from the well and wash our clothes and some of the women have cut off all their hair to be rid of the lice. The natives climb on to the walls to watch us and mock at us but we are beyond caring. The things I have seen go round and round in my head.

Some of the ladies pray to keep themselves calm, or read aloud from the Bible, but I cannot. I do not understand how God could allow such terrible things.

Two days later

Today General Wheeler's servant brought my bag, which he had been carrying for me, and handed it back through the window. He asked after the family and wept to learn that they are dead, unless any escaped in the boat that got away. Other servants came to the barred windows to ask after their masters and to bring us food or possessions they have salvaged. Mrs. Anderson gave them some notes to carry to the rescue force, which they say has reached Allahabad, asking them to make haste.

They told us that the native officers are still alive but Nana Saheb intends to try them for treason and make an example of them by cutting off their hands. I cannot bear to think of it. I realise that I no longer think of Ram Buksh as different from us. He is closer to me than anyone else on earth, closer than Arthur, or Mama or Papa, or even Mina, for he and I have shared something that no one else could ever understand.

July ?

Nana Saheb has sent us meat, beer and wine and a native doctor to care for the sick. The sepoys say that when he saw the conditions in which we are held he was shocked. I no longer know what to think. Perhaps what was done at the river was not by his orders and he does not intend to kill us after all? The doctor is a Bengalee and seems a kind man. He said my baby will come soon and that all will be well.

July ?

Two of the servants carrying notes to Allahabad have been caught, and to punish us Nana Saheb has sent us a woman to be our jailer. We are to call her the Begum. We hoped a woman would be kinder but she is not and even the sepoys dislike her. To humiliate us, she has ordered that our food is to be served by the men whose job it is to clean away the night soil. She makes us grind our own corn too, but we do not mind, for any activity is a relief.

Fourteen died of cholera today and were dragged out to be thrown in the river.

July ?

Today we heard the guns. They are here at last! We all cheered but the Begum told us not to be too happy, for Nana Saheb's army has gone out to meet them and will wipe them off the face of the earth.

14th July

My baby is born. A boy. He was delivered at dawn by Mrs. Moore with the help of the native doctor. I asked him what date it was so I would know my son's birthday. He lies beside me now, sleeping so trustingly that I know I would do anything to save him – that if we all perish, he must live. It is the last thing I can do for Arthur, to leave a son who will carry on his name now that he and James are dead.

15th July

We were woken by the guns this morning. After breakfast Nana Saheb's soldiers came and took out the men and boys from the Futtehgurh party, who were kept in a different room, and shot them. They took the doctor away too, though he pleaded to stay, saying he was needed. This afternoon they shot him too, along with the servants who were caught carrying messages.

The Begum told Mrs. Anderson that Nana Saheb has ordered our execution. When Mrs. Anderson begged for the children's lives she said that when one cleans out a serpent's nest one does not leave the eggs. I do not understand why she hates us so much. She said every sepoy would give his life willingly to rid their country of every white-faced serpent, but this afternoon she ordered the guards to shoot us and they refused. They say they will kill any number of men but not a single woman or child. Then she called for Nana Saheb's general, who ordered them to shoot us through the windows, but they fired into the ceiling and the plaster fell down on us. The Begum screamed at them that they were cowards and she would find some real men who are not afraid to do a man's work. She has been gone for an hour now. Mrs. Anderson and Mrs. Moore have ripped up their dresses and tied the door handles together.

I have placed the baby in my bag with my lucky Sussex stone around his neck in the hope that it will preserve him. The others are all praying. I tried to pray with them but I could not, for I find that I no longer believe in God. Strangely, I am no longer afraid.

Lila

'You really are a dark horse,' Barbara said when the rush was over and everything had calmed down. 'A Sikh boyfriend and you never mentioned it.'

I was sitting by Jagjit's bed, waiting for him to come round, and still recovering from the shock of finding the pebble. Barbara had said that an orderly had come running to tell her I had fainted. She had revived me with smelling salts and made me sit with my head between my knees. 'You were white as a sheet. I thought you'd just overdone it until you started crying and calling his name. Of course we didn't know who he was then.'

I had no recollection of any of that, nor of what I did while I waited for her to bring me news of him. I could not believe he was alive, even after she told me that the blood on the front of the jacket was not his. I realised then that I had never expected him to come back.

The surgeon had removed pieces of shrapnel from his shoulder and back.

'He's a lucky chap,' he told me, when Barbara took me to ask what he'd found. 'This –' he held up a jagged piece of shrapnel ' – was stopped by his scapular, but he still has some fragments in his skull. I can't operate without shaving some of his hair and we need his permission to do that; we don't want another mutiny on our hands.'

This was the policy with Sikhs, whose religion forbids the cutting of hair. There was an elderly Sikh jemadar on the ward with a fractured skull who, for this reason, was refusing an operation that might have relieved his paralysis. And despite my pleas that I knew Jagjit, and was willing to take responsibility, the surgeon would not budge.

'He really is a dish,' Barbara said admiringly. 'He looks completely at home here…' She gestured up at the great painted dome. 'With any luck he'll come round soon. Shall I pull the screens round and leave you two lovebirds alone? I'll keep an eye out for Matron.'

'He's just a friend. I've known him since I was thirteen.'

'I believe you; thousands wouldn't. Don't worry, your secret is safe with me.' She winked at me, pulled the screens round us and went away.

Jagjit was lying still, his head bandaged and his skin yellow-grey against the white pillows. I stared at him, feeling a mixture of relief and anger. Why had he not listened to me? Why had he insisted on signing up for a war that had nothing to do with him? Why did men have to play at heroics without thinking of the consequences, not just for themselves but those they left behind?

A wave of exhaustion overcame me. I leant back and closed my eyes, and when I opened them it took me a few moments to register that he was looking at me.

'Lila? What…?' His eyes left mine and travelled round the room, pausing on the chandeliers and palm tree pillars. 'Where the hell…?' He tried to sit up and sank back with a grimace.

'You mustn't move. You've had an operation.'

'An operation? But why? What is this place?'

'It's a hospital. In Brighton.' I steadied my voice, not to alarm him.

'Hospital? What kind of hospital? And what are those bells?'

'I can't hear any bells; you may have tinnitus. You're in the Indian Hospital in the old Pavilion... where I work. I wrote to you about it.'

He blinked and raised a hand to his bandaged head. 'What happened?'

'A shell, we think. You've lost some blood so you'll feel weak for a bit. Are you in pain?'

'Er...' He shifted a bit and winced.

'Try not to move. You don't want to start bleeding again. There are still bits of shrapnel in your head. They need your permission to shave your hair so they can operate. You will give it?'

'Of course.' He looked round again and then back at me. 'Don't look so worried.'

'I should let them know you're conscious. And Matron won't like me being alone with you with the screen closed.'

'Come here.'

He held his hand out and I took it, feeling the weight of it in mine, the warm skin under my fingers. A feeling of unreality came over me. What if he was dead and this was a dream, like the one about Father being alive again? I remembered the jacket and shivered.

'What is it?'

'Nothing. Just a goose walking over my grave.'

'You looked so cross a moment ago... Are you angry?'

'Of course not. Just tired. And worried.'

He pulled me towards him. 'Come closer.'

I leant over.

'Kiss me.'

'If Matron sees us I'll be out on my ear.'

'Damn Matron.'

I bent over him, careful not to jog his shoulder, and touched his lips with mine. A tear dripped on to his forehead and I straightened up quickly, wiping it away. 'I think you've got a temperature. How do you feel? Can you remember anything? What happened or how you got here... anything at all?'

He frowned. 'We were advancing... I think it was raining. Baljit...' his voice sharpened '... Baljit was next to me.' He began to struggle up.

I pushed him back. 'Stay still! You can't get up yet.'

'But Baljit... I've got to find him. I remember now... he was wounded... bleeding. Is he here too?'

I thought of the jacket. 'I don't know, but I'll ask.'

'There was so much of it... I couldn't stop it... It just kept coming...' His lips began to tremble.

'Just rest now. I'll try to find out.'

As I stood up, he reached out and grabbed my wrist. His grip was surprisingly strong. 'If something's happened to him, I'll never forgive myself. He signed up because of me. If he's... If...'

'Sssshh. Stop it. He might be all right. I'll go and ask now.'

He lay back and closed his eyes. Tears squeezed out between his lids.

I bent and kissed him on the forehead. 'I'll have to go. I promise I'll ask about Baljit.'

But there was no record of a Baljit Singh being admitted. 'It's possible he was taken elsewhere,' Barbara said. 'But if that was his blood on your friend's uniform, it doesn't seem likely that he survived.'

Jagjit's wounds healed well and, apart from a few scars and the tinnitus, there was no lasting damage, but I could tell he was suffering. A few days later he received official notification of his brother's death together with a tobacco tin containing one of Baljit's little fingers, wrapped in a cloth. He told me that when bodies could not be recovered the other sepoys took a finger so that some part of their friend could be cremated.

A few weeks later, when he was stronger, we were taken by bus to a place on the Downs, just north of Brighton, where there was a cremation site for Hindus and Sikhs who had died at the hospital. All the soldiers well enough to walk came to pay their respects, and Barbara arranged with Matron that I should accompany them. We stood on the Downs on a glorious clear morning with the shadowy blue Isle of Wight visible in the distance, and the fields yellow with buttercups, and the larks singing above us, and listened to a Brahmin read the sacred rites while the bodies were fed to the flames. Jagjit went forward and placed Baljit's finger on a pyre and stood back. Then flowers, fruit and sandalwood were thrown into the fire and, as the breeze carried the smell of burning flesh to our nostrils, I watched the ashes rise into the clear blue sky and pictured them flying upwards, to be caught by the trade winds and carried round the world until they came at last to rest in the lap of Mother Ganges.

Jagjit's body grew stronger but his depression did not lift. He dreamt of Baljit often and woke shouting or crying. The Beauchamps came to visit him, and in May, when Simon was given a fortnight's leave, they asked if Jagjit could complete his recuperation at their house. It was an unusual request but because the boys had been at school together it was permitted. Things were quieter at the hospital by then and I managed to take some leave too.

Simon looked even thinner and paler; his nerves seemed shot to pieces and his hands trembled constantly. I had told him in my last letter that Jagjit had been wounded but received no reply and I was hoping that their quarrel, whatever it was, had been forgotten. I expected that their experiences in the trenches would have brought them closer, but Simon was withdrawn and Jagjit seemed too preoccupied to notice. At mealtimes Mr. and Mrs. Beauchamp did their best to keep up the conversation but I have never been much of a conversationalist, and Simon and Jagjit barely spoke.

Mrs. Beauchamp invited Aunt Mina to lunch on the second day and to my surprise she made an effort to speak to Jagjit as well as Simon, asking after his family and expressing regrets for the death of his brother. He replied politely but the conversation soon lapsed and she left as soon as lunch was finished.

I followed her outside and apologised. 'I'm sure he didn't mean to be rude... it's just – '

'There's no need to apologise, Lila. I can see they're both exhausted. How could I feel anything but grateful when they're fighting to defend us?'

It was only after she'd gone that I realised she had called me Lila.

Time seemed to drag and yet the days flew past. The three of us rose late, dawdled over breakfast, went for long walks in the woods or on the Downs. By mutual consent we retired to the playroom in the evenings, where we sat and read or gazed into the fire. I could see this was what they both needed – quiet and time to heal – but to me it felt like time wasted, time when I could have been alone with Jagjit.

One morning, towards the end of the first week, after the Beauchamps had left the breakfast table, Simon asked Jagjit if he could speak to him in private. I watched them leave the room together and walk off down the garden. When they came back Simon's face was closed and set. The next morning he announced he was going to spend the rest of his leave at the flat his father used when he was up in London. His parents naturally wanted to go with him, but were concerned about leaving Jagjit and me alone together.

'Your aunt wouldn't like it,' Mrs. Beauchamp said, 'and I understand her concern. There would be talk. And Jagjit can't stay here alone with only the servants to care for him.'

As luck would have it, Barbara was due some leave and agreed to come and stay. As an older person – she was twenty-seven – and a qualified nurse, she could chaperone us and also be responsible for Jagjit's welfare.

As always, her presence brought things to life. She refused to humour Jagjit's moods and insisted on keeping us busy every moment of the day: we went riding, picnicked in the bluebell woods, strolled along the barbed-wire-covered promenade at Brighton and went to the Grand for tea. In the evenings she insisted we dress for dinner and kept us laughing with tales of the scrapes she had got into during her nursing training. She even managed to get Jagjit to join in the conversation, something I was unable to do. On the fourth day she was there she withdrew to her room after dinner, saying she needed to write some letters. That afternoon she'd handed me a small package, telling me to open it when I was alone. Wrapped in a paper bag inscribed with the words *'Carpe Diem!'* was a packet of French letters.

After she retired to her room that evening, Jagjit and I sat in silence at the table, at a loss what to do. It was he who eventually suggested retiring to the playroom. It was familiar, a place in which we felt safe, except that suddenly we didn't. In hospital I had been able to assume the mantle of 'nurse', but here I felt like a child in the presence of a grown and brooding man. I understood his need to grieve – who better? – but once again I experienced how painful it was to be shut out.

Jagjit sat down on one end of the sofa. I wasn't sure if he wanted me to sit beside him so I took the armchair by the window. We sat in silence, staring into the fire. Even though it was May, we had a fire every evening because he was cold; he was always cold these days, he said.

'I wish I could do something to help,' I said, hearing, even as they left my lips, the pathetic inadequacy of those words, remembering Simon's comments about inane talk from civilians who didn't know the first thing about what the war was really like.

The light began to fade outside and the fire filled the room with moving shadows. The silence lengthened until I could no longer bear it. I looked across at him. He seemed to have forgotten I was there. Tears came to my eyes and I was about to leave the room when he spoke to the fire.

'No one can help, Lila. It's indescribable out there. But for me the horror and the discomfort aren't the worst thing… because that's the same for everyone. We're all in it together. It's the little things that get to you… the inequalities and injustices that rankle… Of course, I knew racial prejudice existed, but… I'd never experienced it myself, not really.

Everyone has always behaved well to me. But on the ship to France we were sharing a hold with some Tommies... it was horribly hot and crowded so everyone was irritable, but they were so appallingly rude – both to and about us – that we had to be moved. They complained that we stank... they didn't like the fact that the men ate with their fingers instead of a knife and fork... if we met them on the gangways or in the corridors they swore at us and told us to get out of their way. I reminded one of them of his manners once and was hauled over the coals by the C.O. – told I would have to learn to behave myself once we got to Europe. They even cancelled the meetings where we could express our grievances to the C.O. They were a special concession for Indian troops, to prevent resentment building up, but they don't want to hear it now... And the men *do* feel resentful... about the fact that our victories are never reported and that they're the only troops barred from using the brothels. Even the North Africans are allowed to, but then the French don't share the British horror of miscegenation.'

He looked across at me and grimaced.

'I'm sorry, Lila. Sometimes I forget who I'm speaking to.'

Had he forgotten, I wondered, glad that the fire was camouflaging my blush, or was this part of the new hostility I sensed in him?

'The one good thing about getting in trouble... it made the men trust me. They'd been uncertain about my loyalties. They knew that I'd lived in England... thought I might be carrying tales to the officers. It was difficult for Baljit too... they weren't sure about him either. But after that they started to ask me things. Most of them had never even seen the sea... everything was new to them: how to use a European toilet, how to eat with a knife and fork. I gave the quartermasters French lessons too, so they could haggle for food and supplies.'

I noticed that his speech, like Simon's, was more hesitant than it had been before the war, and that he held his hands locked together to control the tremors.

He fell silent and I watched him staring into the fire, his face sombre, heavy, with new lines around his eyes and mouth. He yawned suddenly like a cat, his teeth white in the firelight, then looked at me as though he'd woken from a sleep. 'I'm sorry, Lila. I'm being a whining bore.'

'No, I want to hear about it.'

He smiled.

'You're just being polite. It's nice of you not to say I told you so. You were right, of course… about me being a fool to sign up, I mean. I wanted to play my part but I realised… in training… the officers feel uneasy around me. I'm not quite one of them but… all that guff they spew about izzat – honour – and all that rubbish. And the regiment being our father and mother. They even issued all the Sikhs and Hindus with a copy of the *Bhagavad Gita*… to persuade us this is a holy war.'

'You're bitter.'

'Yes, but I have no right to be, do I? I was stupid, acting out a schoolboy fantasy. And I don't mind paying the price for my own stupidity, but Baljit…' He looked down, his throat working. 'He trusted me, you see. I was his burra bhai, who knew what we were getting into… I was supposed to look after him. He'd only been married a few months. His wife is expecting a child. '

'How did it happen?'

For a moment I thought he wasn't going to answer, then he said, 'We were advancing. We'd been reminded that we

214

had to walk slowly and hold the line. Baljit and I were next to each other. He must have seen or heard something I didn't, because he shoved me... knocked me into a crater and jumped in beside me... and a second later a shell landed right where we'd been. I don't know how he knew... sometimes you just have an instinct.

'Of course at first you're disorientated by the shock and the noise. I remember the sudden silence... and then... this... this tremendous feeling of calm. Just lying there and watching all the debris – the earth and... bits of shrapnel and clothing and other bits and pieces – flying through the air above us, silhouetted against the sky. It was really quite beautiful. I didn't know till later that I'd been wounded. Baljit was lying on top of me... his face was on my chest... he was shaking. I thought he was just shocked. I pushed him off and then I saw the blood... I got out a field dressing but it wouldn't stop; it just kept coming...' He paused. 'And then the strangest thing happened. It was as if I was floating, looking down at myself trying to staunch Baljit's wound, and then I was even higher, right above the battlefield, and I could see it all... had all the time in the world to explore every detail... the scarred fields and the barbed wire and the wounded and dying men. I could even see the layout of the German trenches, so much straighter and better made than our own, and I felt nothing – no grief, or hatred or enmity – just a sense of wonder and calm, as though none of it mattered... none of it meant anything. And the next moment I was back in the mud and the filth, scrabbling to stop the blood, panicking... knowing it was hopeless and that I was losing him...'

He closed his eyes; he was trembling.

I heard a buzzing in my head and saw a red fountain spraying up the wall and the god dancing in the moving shadows. I stood up and went to him and he put his arms around me. His shoulders heaved and shook as I held him, feeling his hot tears soaking through my blouse.

The next day I suggested a visit to Shaves Wood to see the bluebells. Barbara begged off, saying she had some shopping to do in Brighton, so we went alone. I took him, I think, in a bid to reawaken his memories of the happy times we had spent there – those warm sunny days when I had gathered flowers to make crowns and bracelets for us all. But this time the day was overcast and still. It had been a wet spring, and the soldiers in the trenches were floundering deep in mud. In the wood, the mostly untrodden paths were firm underfoot, but the smell of damp humus lingered in the air. The air felt muggy and the sharp bursts of birdsong sounded faintly threatening, like warnings in the silence.

We were silent too. There was a distance, a heaviness between us, as though we both knew something needed to be said or done, but neither had the energy to initiate it. I could tell he was depressed and I myself was close to tears. Too much had happened, in us and in the world. I wondered if it would be possible for us ever to be happy again.

We walked quietly one behind the other until at last I said, 'Shall we sit?'

He shrugged and followed me into a clearing. The bluebells had withered already, as had the anemones. The undergrowth was scratchy and unfriendly and nettles bloomed everywhere, encouraged by the rain.

I found a log, which smelt of fungus, and perched on one end. He sat down, leaving a gap between us. I looked sideways at him as he squatted, hunched over, long hands hanging between his knees, staring at the ground. Anger flared in me at his depression, his withdrawal, and yet I knew he could not help it. I felt for a moment as though I were in one of those fairytales where the prince is transformed into an animal and the princess has to undertake a dangerous journey to prove her love. But it was he who would be going on the dangerous journey while I waited, helpless, at home. I berated myself for my disappointment. What mattered was not my romantic dreams but the reality of his suffering. And yet I could not help resenting it. I had hoped that I could comfort him, but once again I was not enough. He needed rest, boredom, normality; not emotion, not more intensity.

I stood up and walked away, over towards a pond I remembered, and leant against a tree looking at it. It was stagnant now, the water still and unmoving, and there was not a sound. Even the birds had stopped. I heard twigs crack as he came up behind me. He was standing so close that I could feel his breath on the top of my head. I leant back until I was resting against his body and he slid his arm around my waist and pulled me into him, burying his face in my hair.

We stood like that for a long time, and then I turned in his arms and looked up at him.

'Lila,' he said, in the way only he could say it, with that lilt in the middle. Then he bent his head and kissed me. When he started to draw back I put my hands on either side of his face and held his mouth with mine. He made a small sound and then I felt his body relax and he began to kiss me back, pulling me close into him until I could feel the whole hard, trembling length of his body against mine. One of his hands moved up to my throat, stroking the skin, and then slipped down on to my breast. I felt myself slide into that world of sensation; everything faded away except the sweetness of his mouth on mine, the warmth of his hand. I shivered and then, without warning, he pulled away so suddenly that for a moment I lost my balance and had to steady myself against him. I looked up at him, shocked by the precipitancy of his withdrawal. His face was grey.

'What is it?'

He shook his head. 'We'd better get back.' He turned and began to make his way through the wood. His strides were so long that he was out of it before I caught up with him. He had slowed and was walking with his head hanging.

I felt a flare of anger. 'What is it, Jagjit? Tell me.'

He said dully, avoiding my eyes, 'I think it's better if we call the whole thing off. You should try to forget me. Things were different then... before. I was different. I thought then we could make a life together – be happy... but now it's all...'

'All...?'

He shook his head. 'Better to forget it... just be friends. I should go back tomorrow.' He forced a smile.

'But why?' I wanted to say, should have said; I should have forced him to explain, but the old familiar misery rose up and choked me. I wasn't wanted. I couldn't give him what he needed. I wasn't enough, just as I hadn't been for Father. I would never be enough.

We walked back to the house in silence.

The next day he returned to the hospital and three weeks later he was passed fit for duty and given compassionate leave to visit his family in India before being transferred to a new area of operations.

Henry

14th July 1882

It has taken me a fortnight to be able to write down the story as Father told it to me, and as far as possible I have tried to do it in his own words. Today is my twenty-fifth birthday. It has rained all day and Father has stayed in his room. It has brought back to me the many birthdays I spent alone as a child, feeling guilty because I believed myself responsible for my mother's death, while he was drowning his depression with drink. Despite the pity I feel for him, I cannot help resenting him for never thinking to reassure me.

This evening Kishan Lal urged me to speak to him, so I went to his room. His eyes were red and I could tell he had been drinking, but to my surprise he got up, washed his face and came to the dinner table. Afterwards we sat out on the verandah listening to the rain rattling on the corrugated roof. I had given up any thought of conversation so was surprised when he picked up his narrative without prompting.

He told me how, as he lay ill, his sepoys had brought him news about the massacre at the boats where Nana Saheb, having accepted Wheeler's surrender and promised the garrison safe passage to Allahabad, had ordered his troops to open fire on them at the river. One of his sepoys later told him that he had tried to rescue my mother but she fought him off, perhaps fearing he was trying to abduct her. Later, Father learnt that some of the women and children had survived and been taken captive, but he had no way of knowing if my mother or Sophie were among them. Desperate to do something, he had pleaded with his sepoys to take him to join the rescue column, but they had heard that the men under the new command of Brigadier General Neill were hanging every native they could lay hands on, regardless of guilt or innocence, and they refused. Finally he had persuaded them to carry him in a palanquin to the road down which the column was approaching and to leave him there to be discovered.

'I have never seen an army in such a state, Henry. The rain was unrelenting – ' he glanced out at the drenched garden ' – much as it has been today – and the tents being carried on bullock carts had swelled and become so heavy that the bullocks died of exhaustion. The column was forced to abandon all its supplies, the soldiers eating only what they could carry and sleeping out in the rain. They were filthy and exhausted, but when they heard that the women were still alive every man of them expressed their willingness to fight to the death to save them.

'Nana Saheb's forces came out from Cawnpore to meet us. Both sides fought with courage and skill – loath as I am to admit it, his general, Tatya Tope, was magnificent, but our men fought like tigers. The battle lasted for three days until eventually the enemy was defeated. Then our men collapsed and slept where they fell. I was desperate to go into Cawnpore that same night but General Havelock would not allow it. He promised me that first thing in the morning he would despatch a detachment of Highlanders, led by Captain Ayrton, to the rescue and that I could accompany them. I could just about sit a horse by then, with the support of young Peter Markham, who by some strange chance was in the relief force. He had been my rival for your mother's hand, and later became engaged to your Aunt Mina – his regiment had been transferred from Palestine to help put down the Mutiny. When he heard that I was alive he came to see me and we rode in together. He died a few weeks later, of the cholera, poor boy.'

He paused for a long time then and I could tell he was gathering the strength to go on. I don't think I shall ever forget his description of what followed next.

As they rode into Cawnpore that morning, they saw a lot of subdued Indians standing with their heads bowed. Some came forward timidly to offer milk and sweetmeats, which some of the Highlanders accepted. Inside the city they were hailed by a man in shackles who turned out to be Jonah Shepherd, a Eurasian who had been in the entrenchment but had been sent out as a spy by General Wheeler. He had been captured by the mutineers and was now looking for his wife and daughters, whom he had last seen in the entrenchment. He offered to lead them to the house where he had been told the women were being kept.

'Seeing what was left of Cawnpore through the eyes of the Highlanders was a shock. All the European bungalows had been burnt down, the church burnt out and despoiled. When I saw the entrenchment from the outside it seemed inconceivable that we could have survived there for so long. It was a mere furrow in the earth, surrounding the ruins of the two barracks – just heaps of rubble. We paused to look over the wall. Every yard of it was scarred with shot and shell and covered in broken bottles, old shoes and half-buried round shot. Everywhere vultures and crows were picking at the bones that still lay about in the open. I shall never forget the smell…'

I felt suddenly hot. My breath shortened and that familiar feeling of suffocation came over me. 'Father…'

But he was beyond hearing me, caught in the grip of his inner vision. 'We passed the ravine where my sepoys had sheltered after General Wheeler threw them out of the entrenchment and I pointed out to Ayrton the barracks where I had been wounded. And then we came to the river. The smell was worse… Soon after we came to a group of men who looked at us fearfully…' He paused and took a deep breath. 'A little further on we saw another group standing by the roadside in silence, and when they saw us they looked at us with sorrowful faces and silently pointed through some compound gates. The men all fell silent; I think we all knew then that we were too late.

'As we passed through the gate the stench was heavier… the air seemed weighted with it. Part of me wanted to stop, but our horses just kept walking. It was like being in a dream. Just inside the gate was a great pile of women's clothing and possessions… When Jonah Shepherd saw this he stopped and went back to the gate to wait. I wish now that I had done the same.' He took a shuddering breath.

'It's all right, Father. I know what happened.'

He shook his head. 'I can still remember the flies – a great black cloud of them and the buzzing – and my feet sticking to the floor… And then I…' He closed his eyes and for a moment I thought he was going to faint. Then he went on, 'Peter must have helped me back to the gate. The officers came out – words were unnecessary – their ashen faces told the story. Shepherd, who was weeping, asked if they had found any bodies. They shook their heads. Then we heard a shout – some Highlanders who'd been exploring the garden. We followed them. There was a bloody trail through the bushes that led to a well…' His head dropped.

'Father!' I stood up, filled his glass and pressed it into his hand. 'Drink this.'

He raised his head and took a long swallow. I had heard enough and wanted to stop him, but now that the festering wound was open he seemed to want to purge it completely. 'I begged the Indians who were standing there to tell me if anyone had been spared. I told them my wife had been expecting a baby. Had they seen her? They were silent.

'At the enquiry, witnesses said that they saw four men with swords enter the garden. Their leader was the lover of the woman who was guarding the prisoners. They were butchers by profession…'

We sat in silence for a long time. Kishan Lal, coming through to trim the lamp wick, paused and stared, then looked at me and shook his head reproachfully. Father ignored him.

'They were never buried, you know. Never even counted or identified. Sherer, the magistrate who later conducted the inquiry, arrived soon afterwards and ordered the well filled in. Havelock gave permission, to prevent the spread of disease.'

'Then you can't be sure?'

He looked at me with those naked blue eyes. 'Don't you think I've hoped, Henry – hoped and prayed that by some miracle she might have been spared? I even consoled myself that she might have been abducted – some of the Eurasian women were, you know, General Wheeler's daughter among them – and they might have mistaken her for one… She was dark, like you. I knew it was a fantasy, because she would have done anything to get back to you, but even the most absurd fairy story was preferable to imagining and dreaming, as I did every day and every night for years – and sometimes still do – what her end must have been.' He raised his eyes to mine at last. 'So now you know.'

I had, of course, known the story already, but I had not known my mother was among the victims of the bibighar, and that made all the difference. I could understand now why he had never talked of it; how those pictures must have played through his mind over and over again as he imagined my mother's fate. How had she died, in what terror and pain? Had she been one of the women thrown into the well alive to slowly suffocate under the bodies of her companions? In his guilt and shame, he had felt responsible, and I could see that it had never occurred to him that I might feel myself to blame.

'I still don't understand how I survived.'

'I was told that when we got back from the bibighar I collapsed and raved like a madman for two days. And then Peter came to me and said that a native had come forward with a baby and they thought it might be Cecily's. I knew it was impossible, that no baby could have survived, but they brought the man to me.' He raised his eyes to mine. 'He told me he had heard that there was a sahib who was looking for a baby and that he had found you in a carpet bag he bought in the bazaar... a more likely explanation is that he had thieved it from that pile of possessions in the garden and was shocked to find a baby inside.'

'Then you don't actually know that I'm... that I'm your s...' My throat closed on the word.

'There's no doubt at all in my mind, Henry... no doubt that you are my son, and hers. Apart from the fact that you look like your mother – you have her eyes and her smile – you were found in her carpet bag with some letters to her sister that she wrote while in the entrenchment, and you were wearing her lucky Sussex stone, which she placed around your neck. Do you still have it?'

I reached into my shirt and pulled it out. My throat was tight with tears.

'Henry, the last words she ever wrote were about you. She knew those butchers were coming to kill them and she hid you in the bag in the hope that you wouldn't be found. It was lucky that you slept, but the darkness and airlessness in the bag must have helped, and even if you had woken they would never have heard your cry amidst all their screams. You were her gift to me, Henry, the most precious gift I've ever been given. When I held you in my arms I felt…'

I knew I must not look at him or we would both weep. I cleared my throat. 'Thank you for telling me, Father.'

He waited until I looked up and his eyes met mine and held them. 'I should have told you long ago. I'm sorry, Henry, but I couldn't bring myself to speak of it.'

I managed, past the lump in my throat, to stammer out, 'I un-understand, Father.'

'The truth is, I have spent years trying not to think of it, yet thinking of practically nothing else. The odd thing is, since I started telling you the story, the dreams have stopped. I've slept better in the last two nights than I have at any time since she died.'

I did not add that he and I have talked more in the last week than in the entire rest of my life.

15th July 1882

Today is the anniversary of my mother's death. Last night I had the old dream again. I woke in terror, as I often have before, to find the screams were mine. Father was shaking me by the shoulder. 'Henry, wake up. Wake up. It's all right, you're safe.'

He sat with me till the terror faded and I could go back to sleep. When I woke this morning, he had gone to the Lines.

Tonight, without prompting, he told me what happened after the massacre: how everyone had seemed to lose their reason and sense of restraint. Soldiers, beside themselves with rage and guilt at not having got there in time, vowed to avenge themselves on any native they encountered; souvenirs from the bibighar were treasured; a Highlander had shown him a bloodstained handkerchief and said that, if he was ever tempted to trust a native again, he would look at it and it would remind him of his desire for revenge.

'It was as though we were all possessed. Discipline went out of the window and Neill lost complete control of his "Lambs", so called because they were devout Christians. They spent all their time drunk, rampaging through the town, killing and burning. And Havelock's men – known as "The Saints" for their sobriety – joined in, until Havelock ordered all the liquor bought up. Indian women were ravished in the streets; children were burnt alive. Even the Sikhs joined in, shooting any Indian they saw. Poor Sherer was forced to issue notices for respectable citizens to affix to their doors, absolving them of any part in the Mutiny.

'More and more extreme punishments were devised to frighten and humiliate the mutineers and to break down their defiance: beef or pork was forced into their mouths; they were smeared with cow's blood or sewn into pigskins; Hindus were told they would be buried and Muslims burnt to ensure their eternal damnation. We even revived the old Mughal punishment of blowing men from cannons.

'It seemed to me that we had all died and gone to hell – a hell like in one of Bosch's paintings... Caught up in an ecstasy of wickedness. General Neill – a man who prided himself on his Christian faith – came up with a punishment the Inquisition would have been proud of. Every condemned mutineer was to be made to clean up a portion of the bibighar – with his tongue! We thought we were superior... that we were civilised, because we could control our impulses and they couldn't. When I think of our behaviour I shudder with shame. But who am I to judge, after what I did?'

'What do you mean?'

He paused, struggling to find the words. 'I myself betrayed someone... a man far better than I shall ever be. His name was Ram... Ram Buksh. He was a jemadar in my regiment and had shown me nothing but loyalty... he saved my life at the risk of his own during the first Sikh campaign, when he was just a boy. I took him under my wing and we became friends... In the second campaign he did so well that I promoted him. That created some resentment, because promotion in the Indian Army is, as you know, usually by seniority. But he was an exceptional soldier with a fine intellect. I have never found another companion with whom I shared so much.'

I waited for him to go on.

'I knew your mother liked him. He had taught her Hindustani and used to ride with her when I was recuperating from an attack of malaria. He was one of the few native officers whom Wheeler allowed to remain in the entrenchment. After I was wounded, he protected and cared for her. When Wheeler surrendered the entrenchment he was captured by Nana Saheb and sentenced to have his hands cut off, but the sentence was never carried out. Afterwards he was brought before a temporary magistrate – some boxwallah who had been appointed to judge the natives' guilt or innocence. To most of them – and he was no exception – the only evidence of guilt required was a brown face. Ram Buksh told him that I would vouch for his loyalty, so the magistrate reluctantly brought him to me. At that time I was still weak from my wounds and half-crazed with grief.'

I noticed his scar had tightened and his right eye was twitching. 'Henry, I can't begin to explain the frame of mind I was in. I was beside myself with grief and anger – anger with myself and with him for failing to save her. And I was jealous. We'd had our problems, and he was young and strong and handsome – in the letters she left behind she'd talked of being closer to him than anyone else on earth. It was all perfectly innocent, of course – I knew that later, when I reread her account and realised that nothing had really happened – but that was later.' He was silent, absent, his eyes haunted.

At last I said, 'Father, what is it that you blame yourself for?'

He sighed. 'When they brought him before me he wept with joy to see me alive and tried to touch my feet. And I… I pushed him away and demanded to know what he had done with her. He must have thought I meant he hadn't done enough to save her, because he wept and begged me to forgive him, and of course that confirmed my suspicions. The magistrate, an impatient man with no brief for natives, asked me whether I would vouch for him or no, and I said – ' he closed his eyes ' – I said that I could not vouch for his actions after I left the entrenchment, as I had no knowledge of them.' He paused and cleared his throat. 'When he heard me say that, his face changed. He got to his feet and did not look at me again. I told the magistrate to speak to Lt. Thomson, who

228

had been in the entrenchment for the whole time and would know more than I.'

His eyes met mine over the rim of the glass. 'Henry, I swear I thought Thomson would bear out Ram Buksh's story and that they would release him. But Thomson was supervising the building of the new fortifications outside Cawnpore and was not available. I was told later that the magistrate asked if Ram Buksh wanted an adjournment so they could call Thomson as a witness. He replied that if his senior officer, under whom he had served for eighteen years, would not vouch for his loyalty, he had no further defence to offer. I should have remembered how proud he was. The officiating officer told me he was taken to the bibighar first, to carry out Neill's penance... but when he saw the room he wept so bitterly that the officer excused him the punishment. He was hanged that same afternoon.'

He paused, as though waiting for me to say something, but I could think of nothing. The memory came back to me of that night after the chaplain's dinner – Father standing on his verandah, crucified against the moonlight, crying 'Ram! Ram!' into the darkness.

His shoulders dropped and suddenly he looked old.

'But that wasn't all. When Wheeler refused to let my sepoys enter the entrenchment I had given them each a letter vouching for their loyalty. After Ram Buksh was hanged, a group of them, including my subhedar-major, a man called Durga Prasad – the best and most loyal officer who could be imagined – were summoned before the court. They produced the letters and their cases were dismissed, but as they left the court a group of English soldiers standing at the gate bayoneted them all.'

'That, at least, wasn't your fault, Father.'

'I should have been there, Henry. They had given up everything for me and I owed it to them. If I had been there I might have stopped it. But the truth is I was too caught up in my own grief to care. I suppose if I'm honest I wanted revenge too… I'll never forget the sight of James, cradling poor dead little Freddie in his arms…'

I looked away as he struggled for composure. 'I don't understand why you stayed on. I'd have thought you'd have wanted to get away, go home.'

He laughed. 'I have no home, Henry. I've lived in India since I was twenty. My parents died when I was a child. James and his family were my last remaining relatives. I stopped believing in our mission here long ago, but the army and my sepoys are the closest thing I've had to a family. And you, of course.'

I wished that I could say something to comfort him, but there is nothing. I understand now why he never wanted to speak of the past.

16th July 1882

Today I asked Father something that has been puzzling me since he told me the story of my mother's death, namely how it is that I am not famous as the sole survivor of the bibighar.

He explained that in all the hysteria that surrounded the discovery there was a lot of confusion, and rumour was rife. 'Soldiers made up stories to feed their desire for revenge and justify our own atrocities – stories of women being paraded naked in front of Nana Saheb's troops, of rape, of babies' bodies found hanging on hooks – as if the truth wasn't bad enough! There were so many rumours that contradicted each other that no one really knew what to believe.

230

'Afterwards I avoided any mention of it and no one dared to raise the subject with me. They talked, of course – no one could stop that – but that was just speculation. No, the only time I was concerned was when I learnt that Lt. Thomson was writing a book about the events at Cawnpore. As soon as I heard of it I wrote to him and asked him not to mention you – you were still a child and I didn't want that notoriety for you. And he was kind enough to agree.'

It is humbling to realise that the mystification about my birth that I have resented all these years was devised in order to protect me.

18th July 1882

Yesterday, on an impulse, on my way back to Bhagalpur, I alighted from the train at Cawnpore and went to look at the site where the entrenchment had been. Nothing, of course, remains. The buildings have all collapsed, their materials scattered, the mud walls washed away long ago, and it has reverted to the patch of barren waste ground, populated by scavenging pariah dogs, that it must have been before it was selected for that most hopeless of defences.

In the evening I went to visit the memorial gardens that have been planted where the bibighar once stood. There is a British soldier stationed at the gate to prevent Indians from entering. An octagonal pierced marble screen conceals the well, now filled in and covered over. I stood for some time looking at the guardian of the well – a marble Angel of the Resurrection with cast-down eyes and a sombre, brooding expression. Crossed palm leaves fan out above his folded hands.

The bibighar – my birthplace – in the gardens of which the well stood, was originally built in the grounds of his house by an Englishman for his bibis. It was demolished soon after the Mutiny and the memorial was raised some years later, paid for by public subscription in England and fines levied on the citizens of Cawnpore.

The inscription reads:

Sacred to the Perpetual Memory of a great company of Christian people, chiefly Women and Children, who near this spot were cruelly murdered by the followers of the rebel Nan Dundu Pant, of Bithur, and cast, the dying with the dead, into the well below, on the XVth day of July, MDCCCLVII

The white purity of the monument conveys nothing of the terrible event it memorialises.

I waited there for some time until the tomb glowed pink in the short but spectacular sunset, hoping for some flicker of memory, some buried instinct to stir, but I felt nothing.

Lila

A few weeks after Jagjit arrived in India I had a letter from him.

My dear Lila,

Please forgive me for being such poor company when I was last with you. I was haunted with guilt about Baljit's death and it seemed wrong to pursue my own happiness when, through my fault, my parents and his wife and son – born just a month ago – have lost their child, husband and father. I cannot replace him, even in my parents' affections, for we are almost strangers to each other.

My real life is in England and I feel closer to you than to any of my blood family. If I did not make love to you it was not because I did not want to, but because I could not bear the thought of leaving you bereaved if anything were to happen to me. Please believe me when I say my heart has not changed, and that I fully intend to keep my promise if it is humanly possible, but from what I have seen of this war so far it is impossible to predict what might happen. I can no longer believe that the world will be a better place for all this slaughter.

I realise now that I allowed myself to be drawn into this war simply to prove myself, and that that motive has dictated most of my behaviour over the last ten years, ever since I came to England. I can no longer even remember who I used to be. After this war, if I survive, I will have to spend some time finding out who I really am. What I have always admired about you is that you go your own way.

With all my love,

Jagjit

Although he sounded unhappy, this was the first letter I'd had from him in which he shared his thoughts with me as openly as I had done with him. I thought about what he had said about me. Was it true that I went my own way, or was that just a reaction too? Had I not learnt that from Father, who, like Akela, always walked alone and whose only friends – with the exception of Uncle Gavin and Uncle Roland – were the Indians he worked with?

I, too, felt more comfortable with Indians, but by then I was no longer working at the Indian Hospital. Shortly after Jagjit's departure all the English nurses had been removed, all visitors banned and patients were no longer allowed to leave the premises. The fences were heightened and barbed wire put along the top. Despite protests that the patients felt imprisoned, and appeals that it was bad for their morale, the military authorities stood firm. It was felt that the Indian soldiers were becoming too friendly with the local women, and that this familiarity might negatively influence their behaviour towards Englishwomen when they were back in India. By the end of 1915 the Indian hospitals were closed down and the treatment of Indians shifted to France. Over the same period, most of the Indian troops were withdrawn from the Western Front.

According to Mr. Beauchamp, the M.P.s who had argued against the use of Indian soldiers felt vindicated by the difficulty they seemed to have had in adjusting to trench life, attributing it to a lack of moral fibre. It was decided that the troops withdrawn from the Western Front should be sent to Palestine, Egypt and Mesopotamia, where conditions were closer to those they were accustomed to, and where they would be fighting other brown-skinned races.

In the autumn of that year, Jagjit was sent to the Mesopotamian Front, or – as it would later be referred to by soldiers on the Western Front – 'the Mesopotamian Picnic'. At around the same time, Aunt Mina's house was requisitioned by the Army as a convalescent home for wounded officers and I was offered a job and a room there. Aunt Mina moved in with the Beauchamps for the duration of the war.

The last uncensored letter I received from Jagjit was written soon after his arrival in Mesopotamia.

My darling Lila,

I have been in Basra for almost a week now, waiting to join my new regiment. The other relieving troops and I are stuck here because there are not enough boats to carry us upriver. I do not want to worry you unnecessarily, but I shall not get another chance to write freely once I join my regiment. I am sending this letter in the care of a wounded officer who is waiting for a passage to England. He is a captain with a Sikh regiment and he told me that the 3rd Battalion, to which most of the Sikh regiments belong, has received more than double its original strength in replacements since April. In other words it has been wiped out twice over. This perhaps explains the letter that was waiting for me on my arrival informing me that I have been promoted directly to the rank of jemadar, I presume as a result of my time in the trenches. As promotion is strictly by seniority, I don't need to spell out the implications.

As if to underline it, the first sight that met my eyes when I got off the troopship was a pile of new pine coffins the size of the great pyramid at Giza. Ironic, as there is a shortage of almost everything else – tents, medical equipment, mosquito nets, water-sterilising equipment, and especially the shallow draft boats needed to transport equipment and men upstream and bring down the wounded.

While I kick my heels, waiting for my orders, I have been helping to unload some of the wounded from the river transports. After travelling downriver on the open decks, most of them are suffering from heatstroke and sunburn. Many are still wearing their field dressings. It is so bad that one can smell the arrival of a hospital boat long before one can see it.

On a more cheerful note, the campaign has made tremendous progress under Gen. Townshend, who they say is a great tactician. He made a reputation for himself in your father's part of the world and has earned the sobriquet 'The Hero of Chitral' for defending a siege there with a tiny garrison while besieged by Afghans. So far his forces have won every battle and it is said his objective is Baghdad. Despite the conditions, it will be good to be mobile and not stuck in a trench for months at a time. But once we are on the march I do not know how easy it will be to write. Please remember, my darling, if you do not hear from me for a while, that I love you more than these feeble words can ever express.

Jagjit

I received a few short letters from him after he joined his regiment but they were constantly on the march and had little time to write, and once again letters were being censored, this time by an official censor based in France, which meant they sometimes took months to arrive. But through the newspapers and Mr. Beauchamp's offices I received regular news of General Townshend's rapid progress towards Baghdad as he defeated the Turks in battle after battle.

News of his triumphs helped to alleviate the terrible news that continued to come in from the Western Front, until November, when his forces were defeated at Ctesiphon with enormous casualties. Weeks of uncertainty followed as families waited to learn the names of those killed or missing in action; for me it was even longer because Indian names did not appear in the casualty lists. My only hope of news was through Jagjit's family, but it was weeks before I could expect a reply to my enquiries. When it came it was to say they had heard nothing.

News came at last that Townshend had been driven back to Kut-el-Amara, a small shanty town lying in a fold of the River Tigris. Kut was completely surrounded by the Turks: no letters went in or came out, and attempts to drop supplies and mail by plane were abandoned. For five months there was no further word. Those months were the darkest of my life as I struggled to keep hope alive, knowing that everyone thought I was deluding myself. Only the fact that I had patients to care for kept me going; while I was working I had no time to think, and my own anxiety and grief opened my mind to their suffering.

Kut finally fell at the end of April 1916, and the whole garrison became prisoners of the Turks. Once again there was hope that we might find Jagjit's name in the records of those taken prisoner, but prisoners' names had been phonetically transcribed by Turkish guards in their own script, and records were chaotic.

Over the months that followed we learnt something of the conditions at Kut. Thousands had died of disease and towards the end the garrison had been starving. As news from the Red Cross became available, we learnt that prisoners had been marched many hundreds of miles into the desert and some of the prison camps were so far into the interior, where there were no roads or railways, that the Red Cross had been unable to trace them.

Finally, after nearly two years of hearing nothing, in August 1917 I received a letter from the War Office.

Madam,

I am directed to transmit to you with regret the enclosed letter/s addressed to Jemadar Jagjit Singh which has been returned from Turkey with an endorsement to the effect that Jemadar Singh is dead.

No confirmation of this information has reached this office, but it is feared that, unless you have heard from him recently, it may possibly be correct. An enquiry is, however, being sent to Turkey with a view to learning whether the report is confirmed, and, until the result of the enquiry has been ascertained, the report will not be accepted for official purposes; but I am to point out that a considerable time will probably elapse before an answer can be expected.

I am to express the sympathy of the Army Council with the relatives in their anxiety and suspense.

Your obedient servant,

F. Weatherstone

A bundle of my letters to Jagjit was enclosed. He had never received any of them.

PART THREE

Henry

19th July 1882

Everything has happened so fast that I can scarcely believe it; it has been less than a month since I went on leave and in that time everything has changed.

I arrived back last night to two pieces of news. The first is that Thornton's replacement – a Mr. Farraday – has at last been appointed and will be arriving at the beginning of August, and that I am to stay on as an additional district magistrate at least until he finds his feet. The second, and more shocking, is that Miss Ramsay's father collapsed at the Club a few days after I left and died of a heart attack. Roland tells me he left nothing but debts – he owed money everywhere and was in arrears with his rent. His employers have agreed to pay Miss Ramsay's rent for two months to give her time to make other arrangements. Roland says people were expecting her to go to relatives in England or Ireland, but she seems to have none – or none willing to take her.

'How is she?' I asked. 'She must be very distressed.' I can imagine her grief more vividly perhaps because of hearing so recently about the circumstances of my mother's death. It seems like another connection between us.

To my considerable surprise, Roland admitted that he hasn't seen her since it happened; she'd been unwell and he didn't think her ayah would welcome a visit from him. He must have seen my incredulous stare, for he added, 'The truth is, I wouldn't know what to say to her. I'm no good at this kind of thing... Damn it, Henry, it's all very well for you to look like that but it's a damned awkward situation. It's not as if I promised her anything...'

'But you implied it.'

'Well, let's just say she made certain assumptions that I failed to dispel.' He smiled that lopsided smile that women seem to find so disarming. 'And now of course she expects me to come to her rescue. But I can't do it, Henry. You know how I feel about her but, even if my C.O. gave permission and I could afford it, marrying now wouldn't do my career any good.'

'I had no idea you were so ambitious.'

'It's not ambitious not to want to ruin one's career. And it's not as if I don't care... I do feel badly about it.'

'Well, I wouldn't worry too much. Since she's disliked by the other women, no one will blame you for letting her down.'

He glared at me. 'I don't know why you're being so damned superior. Would you marry her in my place?'

'I'd feel honour-bound to if I'd encouraged her hopes as you have.'

'Well, if you're so damned honourable, why don't you ask her? You don't imagine I haven't noticed how you feel about her, do you?' He laughed. 'Only we both know that she wouldn't look at you while I was around. Well, now's your chance – she's desperate enough to snatch at any straw.'

'You arrogant bastard!'

I had forgotten that all that riding has made his stomach muscles as hard as rock. He stood watching me curse as I bent over my hand, nursing it, and then turned to go. 'Good luck,' he said from the door. 'You'll make the perfect couple. And, if you need someone to give the bride away, don't hesitate to ask.'

I would never have thought Roland clever enough to be capable of sarcasm.

20th July 1882

I don't know whether to feel hopeful or terrified. I have asked Rebecca to marry me. It happened almost without a conscious decision on my part and I can't help wondering if Roland was right about her desperation. And yet she did nothing – it was all my doing.

I went to see her today to ask about her health and, to my surprise, her ayah recognised me and invited me in. Rebecca was sitting on the back verandah in a steamer chair. She was dressed in a high-necked white cotton nightdress and her hair has been cut off to conserve her strength. Sitting there, with short dark curls framing a face almost as pale as her nightdress, she looked like a beautiful boy.

Spread across her lap was a large piece of embroidery of extraordinarily fine quality: a detailed depiction of a banyan tree with hanging roots. I looked closer, intending to say something complimentary, and saw there was a woman peering out from in between the multiple trunks, her mouth open in a scream of terror or despair. She appeared to be trapped, manacled by the hanging roots, which had coiled around her wrists and ankles. Her right breast and leg appeared to have been absorbed into the tree trunk but the left breast was bare, the nipple hidden by a spreading root that had sunk its gnarled fingers into the flesh around it as though

243

seeking out her heart. I barely had time to get an impression of the whole before her ayah snatched it up and began to fold it away.

I greeted Rebecca and sat down but I was too disturbed by her embroidery to meet her eyes, so I focused my gaze on her bare feet, which had been exposed by the removal of the fabric. They are exquisite – slender and high-arched, with four long, slim toes and one short one. With a curious feeling of *déjà vu*, I saw in my mind's eye a pillared temple illuminated by moonlight. Some picture I'd seen, perhaps? But it was gone before I could grasp it.

Rebecca appeared not to notice that her embroidery had been removed. She sat up and eagerly demanded when Roland was coming to see her. I stammered some excuse and watched her eyes brim with tears.

'I'm so sorry to hear about your father,' I said, feeling the inadequacy of the words.

She shook her head. In daylight her eyes appear darker than they are because her pupils are so large, and her irises are not one shade but made up of many different colours – pale grey, different shades of blue and green, and even some flecks of gold and russet; and then that strange brown blotch in her greener eye. In the light, the difference between them is even more striking.

'I was making him a picture,' she said, and looked around for her embroidery. 'It's nearly finished.'

For a moment I was puzzled, until I realised she meant Roland. I caught the eye of her ayah and looked away, imagining what he would make of such a gift. 'Try not to worry,' I said gently. 'You need to rest and get stronger. I shall do everything in my power to help you.'

The tears brimmed over.

'You are very kind, but what can you do? We shall have to move from this house.'

'Where will you go?'

She wiped her tears away.

'I don't know. She – ' she glanced at her ayah ' – she says we can make napkins and tablecloths and… other things… and sell them door-to-door.' Her voice faltered and she added with touch of pride, 'People have always admired my embroidery.'

I tried to picture her knocking on doors like a beggar and being turned away, or being taken advantage of by men like Roland who would see her destitution as an opportunity. I thought of my mother, dirty and half-naked, her clothes in rags, being jeered at on that long march to the river, and of Father's regret at being unable to save her. I could save Rebecca. It was in my power.

'Why don't you marry me?' The words surprised me as much as they did her. She stared. 'I mean it.'

She looked down at her twisting fingers.

'Look, I know you don't love me. I don't expect anything from you. I know your affections are engaged… elsewhere… but I don't think you can expect anything from that quarter. I would like to help you and this is the only way I can see to do it.'

She looked at me, seeming genuinely puzzled about my motives. It touched me, for in male company she has always appeared so confident of her allure.

I leant forward and took her hand. 'I won't press you now, but promise me you'll think about it?'

She nodded, and once more her eyes brimmed with tears.

As soon as I was out of sight of her I wondered what had possessed me. Do I want her answer to be yes or no?

22nd July 1882

I did not expect an answer so soon, but when I got back from the Club last night – Roland was out at a mess dinner – the chowkidar told me a woman was waiting for me on the verandah. My heart began to jump, and as I approached the bungalow I broke into a sweat. It was her ayah.

'You have a message from Miss Ramsay?' I was astonished how steady my voice was.

'She said to tell you that she agrees.'

A flood of adrenalin surged through me, whether excitement or panic I still can't say.

She stood waiting for me to speak.

I said stupidly, 'Do... do you think it's the right thing? For her, I mean?'

She lowered her eyes. 'It is not for me to say, sahib, but I know that you are a good man, a better man than Sutcliffe-sahib.'

'Do you think she could ever care for me?'

She shrugged. 'Husbands and wives learn to love each other. Or so they tell me.' Her tone was ironic. I can see why Rebecca dislikes her.

Can she ever love me? Or am I repeating Father's mistake by falling in love with someone who will never love me in return?

30th August 1882

Rebecca and I were married a fortnight ago, as soon as the banns were complete. John Moxton, who shares our quarters, stood in as my best man, but Roland did give me a good send-off. The night before the wedding, he, John and two other officers took me to the Club and got me royally drunk; then, when we were politely requested to take ourselves off, he dragged me round the opium dens in the bazaar, where we drank some vile home-made liquor and smoked a couple of hookahs. I have never smoked opium before but I think my nerves finally got the better of me. All I remember is a sudden expansion of time, as though I had lived for centuries – aeons even – watching civilisations rise and fall. Vast landscapes opened before me, populated with dizzying cliffs and vast deeps, all accompanied by a clarity of thought I have never experienced before. I sat absorbed in my imaginings, while around me people smoked and expectorated long streams of brown saliva into spittoons. Roland and the others sang along to the jangling music and the drums, while the houris danced, undulating their bare bellies in a way that made my head swim. I remember Roland egging one of them on to undo my trousers as he rode one of his fellow officers around the room, while the Pathans laughed.

In the early hours we staggered back to the cantonment, where we were challenged by a sentry. No one was able to remember the password, which, in any case, we were laughing too hard to be able to say, so eventually an officer who knew Roland was summoned to identify us and we were allowed to pass. The next thing I recall is being in bed, with Roland and his friends peering at me through the mosquito net, and throwing something at them. I discovered next morning it was a folder full of court papers that I had brought home to read.

That night I had a dream that has stayed with me vividly. I was alone in the middle of a vast desert that stretched to the horizon in every direction. Directly ahead of me stood a temple that must have been built by Titans, because its top was lost in the clouds. In the centre of the wall facing me was a great carved gate, several storeys high and built from black timber so weathered that it looked more like stone than wood. As I approached them, the great doors began to swing open and people swarmed out of nowhere to line up on either side. I joined them and waited.

From where I stood, to one side of the gate, I could hear a strange sound, like the timbers of some colossal ship creaking and groaning, and a low rumbling chant that seemed to spring from the earth itself. Then, through the open gates, a procession of men came, the tendons and muscles in their arms and chests straining as they hauled at thick ropes attached to a great wooden chariot. It was the height of a three-storey house and fantastically carved, with great iron-bound wooden wheels. Sweat ran down their backs and legs, and, when one fell, the others stepped over him and went on. At the very top of the chariot, dressed in silk finery, was an idol: a simple log of wood painted black, with round, staring white eyes and a red blob for a mouth.

As the chariot passed in front of me the crowd thinned and I saw that men were pushing forward to lie down in the path of the great wheels, which crushed them like bugs. I could hear their bones crunching, hear their screams, and see the narrow streams of blood filming over as they trickled through the dust. Then I felt myself being propelled forward and, try as I might, I could not struggle free. Eager hands pushed me down and I saw the rim of the great wheel poised above me, heard the renewed chant of the crowd. I felt its weight descend on me and my ribs begin to collapse.

I woke, or dreamt I woke, to find a naked woman sitting on my chest, like a succubus, her long black hair falling into my face. Her skin glimmered in the moonlight and as I opened my mouth to scream her head darted down and her lips fastened on mine like a snake striking. Her tongue probed mine and I felt myself rising under her. Her sinuous body writhed above mine as we wrestled and panted, and it seemed to go on for hours in an endless cycle of lust and satiety, like one of those feverish dreams one cannot shake off. At last, drained and spent, I fell back exhausted and lost consciousness.

I woke with a pounding head and dry mouth and a very queasy stomach, to find the sun streaming in the window. As I dressed in a stupor, with the help of Roland's batman, I tried to put the dream out of my mind but was filled with a sense of dreariness and foreboding. What had possessed me to offer for Rebecca, whom I hardly knew and who loved another man? The dream felt like a premonition, and as I imagined Rebecca walking towards me down the aisle I found myself picturing the serpent woman of my dream and I shuddered, even while a febrile excitement filled me.

'Cold feet?' Roland asked cheerfully as I entered the dining room. He was eating eggs and bacon, the sight of which made my stomach turn.

'Did you send a woman – one of those houris from the bazaar – to my room last night?'

He raised an eyebrow. 'You've been having opium dreams, my boy. Fun, aren't they?'

In the small church I stood under the effigy of a naked, tortured Christ nailed to a cross, understanding how men must feel who flee on the eve of battle. I felt a surge of resentment against Roland; he should have been in my place, instead of sitting in a back pew, so easy and handsome in his bright uniform, with a shaft of sunlight striking gold from his hair.

Then the organ struck up and I turned to watch my bride walk towards me on John's arm. In the shadowy light from the narrow arched windows she could have been anyone – virgin, houri, demoness – and I felt my heart sink with dread. Then she was beside me and I saw that her face was as white as mine felt, and she was trembling so hard that her bouquet of cream roses had shed a trail of petals across the grey stone floor. She looked up at me timidly and I smiled and took her hand, and, as I felt it quivering in mine, I knew that I had made the right decision and that she is the only woman I shall ever want to marry.

Lila

The morning after receiving the letter I did not get up from my bed. I lay and stared at the ceiling and had no thoughts; my mind seemed to be filled with clouds or cotton wool. People came and went around me and I barely noticed them. That interlude, which lasted for several weeks, is a blur to me now. I can remember visits from a doctor, being spoon-fed soup by Mrs. Beauchamp, Aunt Mina sitting knitting in an armchair by the window and Simon trying to talk to me, but I can remember nothing of what was said. It was a comforting time – like being wrapped in a fleecy blanket that protected me from the sharp corners of the world – but gradually the world began to creep back in, despite all my attempts to block it out.

One morning I noticed that I was hungry, and, although I tried to ignore it, my body would not be denied. A couple of days later I realised that my back was aching from spending so long in bed. I got up and walked weakly to the mirror and saw Mother, pale and weak after days spent lying in a darkened room with one of her headaches. I wondered then if she had been grieving for something – why had I never thought about that before? I suppose because children do not think about their parents' problems; they expect their parents to think about them. And Mother never had. *Why* had she never loved me? Surely it was natural for a mother to love her child? I used to tell myself that she wasn't really my mother, but, looking in the mirror then, there was no question that I was my mother's daughter.

'I hear you're feeling a bit better.'

Simon smiled at me and I smiled back weakly. He pulled a chair up to the bedside. 'It's hard coming back, I know. But I'm glad you did. It was lonely without you.'

I looked at him, surprised. It wasn't like Simon to admit to his feelings. He had been invalided out of the Army in June after being wounded in the leg at Messines, an injury that had left him with a permanent limp. Since coming home he seemed to have turned in on himself, as many men who survived the trenches did. I had been working when he came home from hospital and had only been able to visit him briefly, but I could tell he was depressed.

He reached out and took my hand. 'I'm sorry about Jagjit.' He saw me flinch and his hand tightened on mine. 'It's the worst thing, not knowing, because you can't start getting used to it, and I've learnt that you can get used to anything once you accept it. But you can't accept what you don't know.'

'You miss him too.'

'Yes.'

We sat in silence for a long time. Then he stood to go, still holding my hand in his. He smiled down at me. 'I'm glad you're back, Lila. I've missed you.' He lifted my hand and kissed it before placing it back on the cover.

Somehow, during the time that I was absent, Aunt Mina and I got used to each other. Perhaps I had just become accustomed to seeing her sitting by the window, knitting or sewing quietly. I think she might even have read to me from time to time, though I couldn't say what it was she read. At any rate, her being there seemed natural, so when I woke to find her sitting by my bedside I raised my head and said sleepily, 'Hello, Aunt Mina.'

She asked me how I felt and, when I had given the usual answers, our eyes met and I saw her colour rise.

'Lilian... Lila, I am so sorry... I know how hard it is — just to wait, not knowing, when someone you care for is in trouble.'

Her voice was shaking and I reached out and took her hand.

'Your grandmother — my sister, Cecily — and her husband were out in India during the Mutiny. We knew they were at Cawnpore, but all the news we got was months out of date and often incorrect. I can still remember that feeling of waking each morning with a sense that something dreadful was hanging over one... the taste of fear that never went away...'

I looked into her cloudy brown eyes and wondered what she saw when she looked at the ceiling; whether all these years she too had been living in a cotton-filled world, not fully experiencing anything. How else had she managed to bear such a stifling, uneventful life?

She looked away from me. 'I'm sorry. I probably shouldn't be talking about this now, when you're feeling low.'

'It's all right. I'm interested. Go on.'

'There isn't much to tell. We'd been getting her letters and then they stopped and we knew they were under siege by the rebels. We got occasional news of attacks repelled, of relief attempts — just as you have had — but no real news. What we read in the papers was weeks out of date. We knew people were dying but we had no way of knowing if Cecily and Arthur were among them.' She swallowed. 'My fiancé, Peter, was with the relief column. They got there too late. He... he'd been in love with Cecily before. I think he still was. After Cawnpore he wrote to me. I could tell he was – that he would never be able to forget what he'd seen. And then he caught the cholera. He died out there. Your grandfather wrote and told me...

'I still wake sometimes with that sick feeling, and for a moment I'm back there, wondering and waiting... before I remember it's all over.' She fixed her brown eyes on mine. 'What I am really trying to say is that I'm sorry about your friend. I know what it is to care for someone and never have the chance...' She pressed her handkerchief to her lips with a trembling hand and stood up. 'If it's any comfort, this is the worst time. It doesn't get any worse... even if one's fears are realised.'

While I was considering the implications of this, she rose and left the room. Somehow I stopped resenting her after that, and from that day there was peace between us.

'If Jagjit is still alive he must feel pretty bitter,' Simon said. He had been given a desk job with the War Department in London – something to do with military transport – and only came home at weekends.

It was a cold rainy day in January 1919, and Simon and I were spending it in the old playroom, as we had done so many times in our childhood. I always felt in this room that Jagjit was close to me, hovering somewhere just out of my line of vision. Sometimes I felt his presence so strongly I would turn my head, trying to catch him.

The war had ended the previous November and all prisoners-of-war had been officially released, but Christmas came and went and still neither his father nor I had received news of Jagjit. Some of the returning British officers, after treatment in hospital for dysentery, malaria and beri beri, were sent to High Elms to convalesce. They had few complaints about their treatment in prison. They had been held in comfortable conditions, with sufficient food and exercise, and had grown friendly with their guards, playing cards with them and even being allowed out on excursions to nearby towns. Their main complaint was of boredom.

My heart lifted when I heard that Indian N.C.O.s had been held in the same camps, and I eagerly enquired if anyone had encountered a Jemadar Jagjit Singh, until a captain who had been at Kut told me that the British and Indians did not mix. 'The Turks treated us all the same to begin with, even serving our meals at the same tables. Our C.O. had to point out that in the British Army it isn't done for British officers and Indian N.C.O.s to mess together. After that we didn't see much of them. They kept themselves to themselves.'

It was a different story for the rank and file from Kut, already weak with starvation and many suffering from wounds, cholera and other illnesses. After their gruelling march through the desert, many dying on the way, they were held in camps where they spent twelve hours a day breaking rocks and laying railway lines with no protection from the burning sun. When the war ended, these camps were often abandoned by their guards, leaving prisoners, with no food or supplies, to make their own way hundreds of miles through the desert to the coast. Most died of thirst or hunger or were killed by the Marsh Arabs. The officers who visited the few survivors who had made it back were shocked by their condition and their stories. I thanked God that Jagjit was an N.C.O.

I looked at Simon. '"If"? Have you given up hope?'

He wiped a thin hand wearily across his eyes. 'There's always hope, I suppose. They say they're still finding stragglers from some of the more remote camps, but they're all rank and file, not officers. It doesn't look good, Lila. We may never know what happened to him.'

I thought I could bear anything except that – never to know, always to be wondering, imagining.

'Father says Townshend gave his Indian troops a particularly hard time,' he went on. 'He blamed them for everything, and now it appears that when they ran short of food at Kut he made no allowance in the rations for the fact that Indians were vegetarians. Many of them starved or developed scurvy. Everyone is disgusted with him. We lost twenty-five thousand men trying to relieve him, and since the surrender he's been living in luxury as a guest of the Pasha while his men have been dying in the camps. And Father says his only concern seems to be to negotiate a good war settlement for his Turkish friends. Wouldn't you be bitter if you were Jagjit?'

'Why did you stop writing to each other?'

He sighed. 'What does it matter now?'

I wanted to say, *If I'm never to see him again, I want to know everything*, but I could see he was upset, so I said nothing.

We sat in silence, gazing into the fire like an old married couple, and I had a sudden presentiment of us sitting there years from now, our heads filled with the husks of memories sucked dry, wondering what had happened to the future we once imagined lay before us.

Henry

23rd September 1882

I have been putting off writing to Father because I could not think what to say: how to explain my sudden decision to marry, only a month after seeing him, a woman whose existence I had failed even to mention. However, I am now obliged to ask if he is able to make me a small allowance; supporting a household is proving more expensive than I had anticipated, even with the minimum staff: a bearer, cook, gardener and watchman and, of course, Rebecca's ayah.

Rebecca is still very wary of me. We sit on the verandah after dinner, she with her embroidery and I with my papers, pretending to be absorbed in our work, but her slightest movement, or even the rustle of her dress, distracts me and I lose the thread and have to start again. From what I have observed, her embroidery does not progress very fast either.

So far we have not found much to say to each other, for referring to our past acquaintance raises the spectre of Roland, who has tactfully kept away.

7th October 1882

I received Father's reply today and was surprised to find him wholly accepting of the situation. He offers his congratulations, and informs me that he forgot to tell me when I was there that I have some capital of my own: apparently the grandfather for whom I was named – Mother's father – put some money into a trust for me after her death, to come to me on my twenty-fifth birthday. That at least makes things somewhat easier.

Since he is due some leave, he has promised to visit us next month. I wonder what he will make of us.

3rd November 1882

All my fears about Father's visit have proved unfounded. From the start he seems to have sensed Rebecca's fragility and addresses her with a sensitivity and gentleness I have never seen in him. It puts me in mind me of Kishan Lal's account of him tending the bibi in her last illness.

Rebecca seems to like him too, for she behaves towards him like an affectionate daughter, pressing another serving on him at dinner and making sure his glass is full, and I can see that he likes it.

After dinner we sit on the verandah and he reminisces about his youth. Last night he talked of the death of his parents and how he and James were brought up by a bachelor uncle; it seems to have been a lonely childhood. Rebecca sat and listened while she did her embroidery, which he made a point of admiring. I had never suspected him of having the slightest artistic inclination, but he told her that he has always admired creativity, and that it was my mother's musical and artistic ability that first attracted him to her. To my surprise,

Rebecca even talked about her own childhood: how her father adored her and made a fuss of her and called her his 'little princess' and told her that she looked just like her mother – 'a real Irish colleen' with dark curly hair and green eyes. It is like listening to a child telling a fairytale, and none of it seems to fit with the man I knew, who seemed completely indifferent to his daughter and gave her no care or protection at all.

If Father has noticed that we have separate rooms or thinks our relations odd he has shown no sign of it.

17th November 1882

Father left yesterday, but his visit has made a great difference. I was concerned that our new ease would depart with him but last evening, when I got home, Rebecca was sitting on the verandah and smiled as though she was glad to see me. When I emerged after bathing and changing for dinner, she told the bearer he could go, and poured my sherry herself. Over dinner she asked me if anything interesting had happened in court today, and seemed interested in my answer. Later she asked if I had any objection to her making some cushions and place settings for the house. I told her that this is her home and she must do whatever she wishes to make it comfortable. Then I plucked up the courage to ask if she regrets her decision. She did not answer but simply smiled, a smile so enigmatic that I felt like a callow schoolboy faced with the Mona Lisa.

Later we sat on the verandah, each apparently absorbed in our tasks, with the scent of night jasmine heavy in the air. We hardly spoke, but at bedtime, when she rose to go, she hesitated by the door and gave me a look I have often seen her give Roland: a playful smile with a widening of the eyes that seems to invite intimacy. She paused there a moment and, when I did nothing, smiled that smile again and withdrew. I sat, wondering if I should follow her, but then I remembered the thing Father used to say that so infuriated me – 'Softly, softly, catchee monkey, Henry' – and I stayed where I was.

23rd November 1882

The past week has been maddening. I don't know how she does it, but Rebecca has a sort of magnetism that makes it impossible not to be aware of her. I have seen the effect she has when she enters a room: she does not even need to speak, simply to stand there, and every man's head turns towards her, and every woman's lips tighten.

In the evenings, as we sit on the verandah, she sewing and I reading, I feel her presence so acutely that every nerve in my body is alive. I sometimes wonder if she is aware of the effect she is having.

When I got to bed last night, it was impossible to sleep. I was in a torment of desire, imagining her pale smooth skin, those mesmerising eyes, the smell of her hair. I finally fell asleep, only to have the dream again. I woke to find myself clutching someone and shouting, as I often did as a child, but this time it was not Father's strong arms holding me but a woman's. She was kneeling beside my bed, her face close to mine; in the dark I could not make out her features, but I knew her by her perfume. Embarrassed, I tried to sit up, but she pressed me back again. 'Close your eyes.'

I closed them.

She stroked my hair. 'Just rest now.'

I listened to her singing softly, and then I must have drifted off to sleep and when I woke in the morning she was gone.

At breakfast, Rebecca was quiet, as she usually is in the mornings. I know she finds it hard to get up, not helped by the laudanum that she was prescribed to calm her nerves after her father's death. She was so much her usual self that I started to wonder if perhaps I had dreamt her presence in my room. Had it been her? Or had I dreamt of some other woman – my mother perhaps? At last I said, 'I hope I didn't disturb your rest last night?'

She smiled and asked if I often had bad dreams, so I told her something of my childhood nightmares, though not their cause, and she listened with such sympathy that I dared to say, 'I hope *you* are feeling less unhappy now,' and she gave that tantalising smile again.

I have been thinking about it all day, trying to interpret it, and this afternoon Hussain had to ask me something three times before I heard him.

27th November 1882

I saw Roland at the Club today, where I was lunching with Farraday to discuss our next tour, and almost laughed in his face.

Last night Rebecca and I consummated our marriage. I did not want to leave her this morning and all the time I was talking to Farraday I was thinking about her. I was so distracted that he began to rib me and said he could see that I needed a honeymoon. I told him I had used all my leave but he said he could manage with Hussain and gave me the week off. I went home to find her resting and climbed back into bed with her. In daylight it was even more delicious. I feel as though I could spend a lifetime doing nothing but making love to her and never tire of it.

13th January 1883

I wish I knew more about women, or had someone to advise me. All is well when we are alone – Rebecca is loving and tender and I am happier than I ever imagined it possible to be. All through the day I find myself anticipating coming home to her, to that first glimpse of her wide smile as she sees me, and the softness of her body as we embrace. Sitting across from her at the table, I wonder if the servants can see my impatience to get the meal over with so we can be alone. Later, as we sit on the verandah, I savour the anticipation, looking up from my papers to watch her slim fingers pulling the needle through the cloth, imagining how they will feel on my body later. Sometimes she meets my eyes and smiles, and I have to restrain myself from dragging her into the bedroom then and there. When we are alone she seems content; it is other people who are the cause of her unhappiness and sometimes I wish I could consign all the servants, Farraday, Hussain and the rest of the world to hell.

For the first few months after our wedding, we refused all the usual invitations issued to newlyweds, pleading her recent bereavement and subsequent illness, but we cannot continue to do this indefinitely without causing offence. Last week Farraday invited us for dinner and it seemed unwise to refuse for several reasons. I have been aware that there has been some gossip about our marrying so soon after Rebecca's father's death, especially as Roland's courtship of her was well known. Shortly after our marriage, I received an anonymous letter warning me that there was talk that Rebecca was carrying Roland's child. As five months have now passed, it seemed wise for Rebecca to appear in public to scotch this rumour.

At the dinner I could tell that everyone was curious, but the gentlemen were too polite to do more than congratulate me. Rebecca seems to have been less fortunate. When we joined the ladies after dinner, I noticed that her face was white and she was holding herself rigidly, just as she did when alone with me in those first days after our wedding. In the carriage on the way home I asked her what had happened. All she would say was that they had asked her questions designed to humiliate her. When I asked what kinds of questions she would not tell me, but I imagine they must have touched on the rumours I mentioned. When we got home she wept and wept and I could not comfort her. Eventually her ayah told me to go, and leave Rebecca to her.

The two of them are much closer than I had thought, and when Rebecca has one of her headaches – they are sadly frequent and cause her great suffering – Zainab is the only person she can bear to have near her. When I think that her ayah has cared for her from birth it is not really so surprising, but except at these times Rebecca cannot bear to have the woman near her, and is so rude to her that yesterday I felt it necessary to intervene, only for the woman to take her side against me!

10th March 1883

Rebecca is pregnant. The doctor confirmed it yesterday. He has advised me that she will need to be weaned off the laudanum but not until the second trimester, in case it causes difficulties. I am due to go on a fortnight's tour next week but Zainab assures me she will take every care of Rebecca in my absence.

28th March 1883

Poor Rebecca. I was recalled from my tour last week because she has had a miscarriage. It was all over by the time the doctor came. The child was a boy. Rebecca is extremely distressed and the doctor has once more raised her dose of laudanum, which he had been gradually decreasing as it had begun to give her nightmares and stomach trouble. I wondered if it could have had any connection with her miscarriage, but he thinks not, although he deems it better that she stop taking it before risking another pregnancy.

When I went in to see her she was deeply depressed, although her concern seemed to be less about the loss of the baby and more about what others will say of her. I do not understand why it causes her such distress, but assume that to women, whose whole life revolves around home and society, the opinion of others must matter more than to men, who can lose themselves in work or other interests. Yesterday, when she came out on to the verandah for the first time, I noticed she was working on a new embroidery – a pattern of trees with intertwined branches that appear to bear, in place of fruit, what look disturbingly like babies' hands and feet.

13th May 1883

Last night we had dinner at the Hussains'; he has invited us several times and it seemed rude to keep deferring it. Rebecca was reluctant to accept, but I thought that being with Mrs. Hussain, who is an unusually intelligent and thoughtful woman, would put her at her ease. In the event I wish that I had left her at home, for from the moment we arrived it was clear she did not want to be there. The Hussains came out to greet us but when Hussain offered her his hand she looked startled and stepped back without taking it. I think we both put it down to shyness, but when his wife came forward and offered hers Rebecca barely touched it. I think I was not the only one who noticed that afterwards she kept rubbing her fingers with her handkerchief as though to cleanse them, although she had the grace to blush when Hussein asked if she wished to wash her hands.

At dinner she did not say a word. When addressed by either Hussain or his wife, she looked at me as though they were speaking a language she did not understand. It was extremely awkward and I was unsure how to respond. I could hardly apologise for her behaviour, and yet her rudeness was hard to ignore. The conversation became so stilted that the Hussains eventually stopped trying to draw her out and addressed themselves exclusively to me.

On the way home, she withdrew into a corner of the tonga and barely spoke. I was angry and told her that I was ashamed of her behaviour and that she had not only insulted the Hussains, but also exposed me to an embarrassing situation at work. At first she did nothing but cry, but when I demanded an explanation she asked in a tearful and accusing voice what I expected people to think about us if we insisted on dining with natives. I was angry enough to reply that I did not much care what people thought, to which she retorted that it was obvious that I did not care about her either. This was so absurd that I refused to dignify it with a reply and we did not speak for the rest of the journey home. I can hardly believe that just yesterday I thought myself the luckiest man alive.

20th May 1883

Rebecca has been unwell again. It started the day after the Hussains' party, which she spent in bed, weeping. When I asked her what was wrong she said she always knew that I would be disappointed in her and would regret having married her. She was like a small child, sad at being punished. I took her in my arms and kissed her and told her I did not regret anything and that all married couples were bound to have some disagreements, but she would not be consoled. That night she developed a migraine, which lasted for five days, during which she lay in a darkened room with Zainab sitting beside her wiping her temples with cologne.

Now that she is well, it is as though she has forgotten the event ever occurred. I would like to discuss it calmly but I am afraid of upsetting her again. The whole episode has left me with a feeling of unease.

Lila

Aunt Mina died a fortnight ago, just as the weather was getting warm. She caught the influenza in early February. It has carried off thousands, including many who survived the trenches. Some of our patients died of it just as they were getting back on their feet. In the end it was decided to discharge those who could be cared for at home in order to avoid it spreading to them.

In late February the convalescent home in High Elms was finally closed altogether, but by then I had already moved to the Beauchamps' to nurse Aunt Mina. I welcomed the opportunity to take care of her and, over the three months that I nursed her through influenza, pleurisy and finally pneumonia, we did grow to understand each other better.

She died just before dawn as I sat beside her. Mrs. Beauchamp and I had taken it in turns to stay with her as she began to slip away. For two days she had been in a coma but just as the dawn chorus was starting she opened her eyes and smiled – the open smile of a young girl – and then she looked past me and said in a joyful tone, as though a long-awaited visitor had just entered the room, 'Cecily!' I turned my head

267

but of course there was no one there, and when I turned back she had stopped breathing.

I sat beside her in silence, holding her almost weightless hand in mine, and – as often happens after a peaceful death – I felt a lightness in the room, a feeling of release. I got up and opened the window, as we used to do in the hospital; it's an old custom, meant to let the soul out. I don't know if I believe in a soul but it seemed the right thing to do. I pushed the sash right up and put my head out into the cool morning and listened to the birdsong, and when I pulled it back in the room felt empty.

Last Saturday, on a beautiful spring morning, with the larks singing and the blackthorn and gorse blooming in patches of white and yellow on the Downs, we walked to the little Norman village church for the funeral. Mr. Beauchamp and Simon had come down from London for the weekend.

I stood beside Simon as we sang Aunt Mina's favourite hymn, 'O God, Our Help in Ages Past', and it seems as though nothing much has changed in the world, for it could have been written about the last four years.

> The word commands our flesh to dust –
> Return, ye sons of men;
> All nations rose from earth at first,
> And turn to earth again.
>
> Time, like an ever-rolling stream,
> Bears all its sons away;
> They fly, forgotten, as a dream
> Dies at the opening day.

I thought of all the men who were still living in a waking nightmare and glanced at Simon. Tears were rolling down his face. I slipped my hand into his.

Like flowery fields the nations stand,
    Pleased with the morning light;
The flowers beneath the mower's hand
    Lie withering ere 'tis night.

All over the church people were weeping now, not for Aunt Mina, but for the sons and brothers and husbands and lovers they would never see again.

The following day, after morning service, Mr. and Mrs. Beauchamp met me in his study to go through the details of my inheritance. Looking at them, I realised they have aged. I have been so absorbed with Aunt Mina that I have noticed nothing else for months. Mrs. Beauchamp is as elegant as ever, though her hair has faded; she was wearing a narrow damask overdress in pale grey over a plain charcoal-coloured skirt. Mr. Beauchamp's dark hair is streaked with silver, and I noticed a web of lines around his bright squirrelly eyes.

'Your aunt made me her executor and left me with some information that she wanted passed to you after her death,' he said, as he unlocked his desk drawer and took out a package of papers. He hesitated before adding, 'Information about your mother.' My eyes must have widened because he said quickly, 'I understand your aunt told you that your parents had died of the cholera. I'm afraid that wasn't true. I always felt you should have been told the truth, but your aunt wanted to protect you. When you reached twenty-one I urged her to tell you, but she felt it would not be fair when you were so occupied with your war work.'

I shivered and, looking down, saw the hairs on my arms were standing up. 'You're chilly,' Mrs. Beauchamp said, concerned. 'Shall I fetch you a shawl?'

I shook my head. 'What about my mother?' How was it that I had never wondered where she was, had shut her out of my mind so completely?

Mr. Beauchamp went on, 'I'm sorry to say that after your father's death...' He hesitated. 'I don't know how much you know, Lila...'

'I know about Father,' I said. 'Go on.'

He looked relieved. 'Well... it appears your mother never really recovered from the shock. Immediately afterwards she was taken...' He paused.

'She's dead?'

He looked shocked. 'No, no. She was taken to an Army hospital at Deolali... not far from Bombay. It's a place where they hold people who have, er... nervous complaints... until they can be shipped back to England.'

They say her mother's doolally. I remembered overhearing Cook – or was it Ellen? – saying those words.

'Mother's in England?'

He must have mistaken my shock for eagerness because he said, 'No, I'm sorry, Lila. She was never brought here. For some reason she was discharged into the care of a native woman – I have her name here somewhere...' He shuffled through his papers. 'Ah, here it is – Zainab Khan – who undertook to look after her.'

'Zainab? She was my ayah, and Mother's too. But Mother always disliked her.'

'That does seem strange. Possibly it was arranged by your aunt? They live at a hill station called Nasik and their rent and living expenses are paid out of your Father's estate. The medical reports mention catatonia. I understand people with the condition do not suffer, but you probably know more than I about that from your time in hospitals.'

I thought of the catatonic patients I had seen: suspended, as though a wicked fairy had cast a spell on them. But in my mind Mother *was* the wicked fairy.

Mrs. Beauchamp put a hand on my arm. 'We're sorry to give you this news, Lila. It must be a terrible shock.'

'As I said before,' Mr. Beauchamp added, 'I feel you should have been told all this years ago, and certainly when you came of age, but your aunt was of a generation who believed that the less said the better.'

'Did she tell you? What happened... I mean, to Father?'

He hesitated. 'She wasn't sure whether you remembered. If you had forgotten, she didn't want to remind you.'

'How could I forget? He shot himself on his birthday. I saw him... just afterwards, I mean.'

They looked shocked. 'My dear, how dreadful for you,' Mrs. Beauchamp said.

Mr. Beauchamp cleared his throat. 'Lila, are sure you want to go on now? Perhaps this is enough news to absorb for one day.'

'No, I'd rather know it all.'

'Well, I assume you will want to continue with the arrangements made for your mother's care?'

'Yes, it seems best, don't you think?'

'Unless you want to bring her here? Your aunt's house – your house now – would be large enough to – '

'No.'

There was a silence. He said carefully, 'Then might you want to visit her?'

'I think not. Anyway, there wouldn't be much point if she's catatonic, would there?'

They exchanged a glance. 'No, I suppose not. Well, erm... maybe we should discuss the Will,' Mr. Beauchamp said briskly.

'Your aunt has left you everything, as you probably surmised. I have copies of her Will, her bank accounts and investments here. And this for you.' He handed me a thick yellow envelope.

I thought of the notebooks and letters that I had seen on her bureau all those years ago. 'And the other family papers?'

He frowned. 'She didn't mention any other papers. Perhaps she refers to them in that envelope? All she gave me were the papers connected with your inheritance. Any family letters, photographs and so on must still be in the house. I believe most of the furniture was stored away when the house was requisitioned?'

'Yes, it's up in the attic.'

He nodded. 'The house will, of course, require extensive renovation after its usage for the past three years, but, even taking into account the cost of restoring it, there should be enough left to give you an annuity that will meet your needs adequately. And then of course there is your father's capital, although most of the income from that is taken up with provision for your mother as long as she lives.'

'I understand.'

'Of course, if you decided to sell the house and buy something smaller, that would increase your capital and give you a better income. I would not say you are wealthy, but you will certainly be comfortable even if you choose never to work again. In that respect you are more fortunate than many young women.'

He meant of course that, unlike many women, I shall not be forced to earn my own living. Since the war ended there have been repeated reminders in the press that most of us are doomed to remain spinsters and will have to support ourselves. And, perhaps to make up for it, in February 1918 certain women over thirty had finally been given the vote, ostensibly as a reward for our help with the war effort. I thought Mrs. Beauchamp would be triumphant but, as she said sadly, it is hard to rejoice when the cost has been so high.

'But of course Lila will want to work,' she said now. 'You're much too intelligent to sit at home doing nothing. And now you're a woman of means you're free to do as you wish. I know you had hoped to return to India, but might you be better off here? We need doctors too, and Simon is really very fond of you…'

I looked at her, astonished. Could she mean what I thought she did? I thought of the advertisements placed in the paper by women whose husbands or lovers had been killed, offering to make themselves useful by marrying and caring for incapacitated soldiers.

'There's no hurry to decide,' Mr. Beauchamp said when I remained silent. 'You've hardly had time to get your bearings, what with your war work and then nursing your aunt, and High Elms is in no condition to be occupied, even if you had the staff. What Amelia means is that we would be delighted, and so would Simon, if you continued to live with us.'

I was grateful for the offer. Even if it were possible for me to live at High Elms, I could not bear the thought of living there without Aunt Mina. I am surprised by how much I miss her, and regret all the years we wasted when we could have been a comfort to each other.

Mr. Beauchamp waved my thanks aside. 'We've regarded you as part of the family since you were a child. You and Simon and, of course – ' he paused and said in a sombre voice ' – Jagjit.'

'Have you had… is there any news?'

He looked down at his hands, then back at me. 'No, nothing. I'm sorry, Lila, but it's been almost six months since the war ended. All the officers' camps and most of the others have long been emptied and I think we have to accept…'

Out of the corner of my eye I saw Mrs. Beauchamp shake her head.

That afternoon, after Simon departed for London, I went up to my room and opened Aunt Mina's envelope. It contained a letter and a small packet tied with string. The letter was undated but written, I presume, around the same time as her Will.

Dear Lila,

I am sorry that I could not be the kind of friend to you that I would have wished to be, but somehow I have always been backward when it comes to friendship. Cecily had the gift and she was generous enough to share her friends with me, though I always knew I was only a hanger-on. After she left, I failed to engage with the world the way I should have done. Perhaps it was a failure of courage. Even my fiancé, Peter, was inherited from Cecily, but perhaps if he had lived and we had had children things might have been different. But then a family is a hostage to fortune.

We have never talked of the terrible things that happened to our family in India, except once. It may have been a mistake not to have told you before, but I thought when you first came here that it would be better to let you build a new life, free of the past. I know George Beauchamp believed I had no right to keep your history from you, and he may have been right. In any case, you are now of age and an independent woman, and should you wish to know more you will find all the papers connected with that history in the bottom drawer of my writing bureau. I am enclosing the key with this letter.

I should warn you that you may find what you discover hard to bear. You are strong, though; I have known that since the day I met you. It must have seemed to you that I wished to destroy that strength, but the truth is I envied you. You have much of your grandmother in you. She always thought I was the brave one, but she was wrong.

Although I have left you the house, I would not wish you to remain at High Elms and live the kind of solitary life that I have lived. So much has changed in the last few years that I am no longer able to judge what is for the best in this new world. It may have seemed to you that I did not care for your independent spirit, or agree with your choice of friends, but what happened in India has haunted me all my life, and perhaps made me more untrusting and unforgiving than I should have been. However, to the best of my ability, I have always acted in what I felt were your best interests.

I hope that you find more fulfilment and happiness in your life than I have in mine.

Aunt Mina

Henry

7th January 1894

After twelve years of marriage to Rebecca I should have thought nothing would surprise me, but I arrived back last Tuesday to discover that she had broken into the drawer of my desk and made a bonfire of my diaries — all except the one covering my first three years back in India, which, ironically, was in an unlocked drawer with my childhood notebooks. I kept them locked up because, about a year after we married, she read one of the entries I had written about her and became hysterical. It was the first time I had seen her like that, and it showed me just how unstable she was. It had never occurred to me that she would read my private papers.

Zainab broke the news to me and when I asked if nothing had been salvaged — in my experience books do not burn easily — she said she had come on the scene too late to save them and the mali had poured water over them to put out the fire, which naturally would have made the ink run.

I am surprised to discover how much their loss has affected me. They have, after all, served their purpose of helping me to find expression for my thoughts. I had never intended that anyone else should read them — and yet I am angry — so angry that I have been unable to speak to Rebecca about it for fear of what I might say. I wonder if she knew how much they meant to me. I don't imagine it even occurred to her to think about it, because the one thing I have learnt about Rebecca is that she is completely wrapped up in herself. I do not condemn her for it: it is a feature of many people who have suffered greatly that, far from being ennobled by it, they become completely absorbed by their own suffering and are incapable of imagining anyone else's.

And there is no doubt that Rebecca has suffered. Five miscarriages would be enough to overstrain any woman's nerves, even one without her disposition. And that loss, together with her dependence on laudanum, which no effort on my part or that of the various doctors we have had over the years can wean her off, has made her a creature completely ensnared in her own fears. She sees enemies everywhere. For example, she complains that the servants do not like or respect her, but she is so impatient and critical that it is scarcely surprising. I know that she is inexperienced in running a household; Zainab seems to have fulfilled that role in her father's house, presumably having assumed it after Rebecca's mother's death. But the male servants resent being told what to do by a female one, and Hindus by one who is not only a woman but a Muslim.

Rebecca's distrust of me started when she read the diary, burnt now, in which I had expressed concern about her mental stability and wondered whether, on my next long leave, to take her to England to consult one of the new mind doctors. Once she got that idea in her head, no amount of reassurance would convince her I was not taking her there with the intention of confining her in an asylum.

I have gradually come to realise that most of her feelings of persecution exist only in her own mind. It is true that other women do not take to her, but the rumours about our marriage are long behind us and it sometimes seems to me that it is her own secretive behaviour that creates the impression that she is concealing something. Then there is her irrational dislike of Indians, whom she accuses of cunning and dishonesty and all kinds of venality. In fact there is no one she trusts, even the woman who has brought her up from infancy and who is clearly devoted to her; nor I, who have done my best to protect her, mostly from herself.

Over the last dozen years, her conviction that everyone is gossiping about her has grown into a mania, with the result that we have been unable to remain in any place, or I in any post, for more than two or three years. Initially, in a new place, all is well. She takes on a new lease of life and with it her old bloom – at thirty she is more beautiful than ever and still possesses that magnetism that attracts men and alienates their wives. For a few months she basks in the attention and interest; and then she becomes convinced, usually with good reason where the women are concerned, that she is disliked and talked about. Then the fantasies begin: they are persecuting her, asking her impertinent questions designed to expose some disgraceful secret which they imagine she is concealing; the servants are plotting against her and spreading rumours about her. And so it goes on. Eventually there comes a time when she will not leave the house, then her room, finally her bed. The I.C.S. is a small world, and as people are transferred from place to place they carry stories with them – stories that have not done her reputation, or my career, any good.

The pregnancies have always occurred in the period soon after our arrival in a new place, when she is blooming and seductive. I still find her hard to resist, even though I am familiar with her little tricks: the slight upturn of the lips, accompanied by a sudden widening of the eyes and the small undulation of her hips. But it is no longer her power but her weakness that controls me. When I take her in my arms now, it is because I want to prove not my own worthiness but hers – to convince her that she is worth loving. Sometimes I find myself filled more with pity than desire, but I know it would crush what little self-respect she has left if she saw that she had lost her power over me. Her ayah and I have been the two fixed planets orbiting her sun, marking her place in the heavens and keeping her from sinking into the outer darkness.

Re-reading the one surviving diary from our marriage, I am saddened by the difference between what she was then and what she has become, though even then there were signs that all was not well. I once saw a crow with a broken wing dragging itself along the ground while being eaten alive by ants; I put the poor creature out of its misery, and sometimes I almost feel it would be kinder to do the same for her. I have come home five times to news of another miscarriage – strangely they have always happened in my absence – to find her shut away in her room, half-mad and sedated with laudanum. We wean her off it and the cycle starts again. The doctors all say there is no apparent reason for her inability to carry a child to its term, and suspect it may be something to do with her nerves.

These days I feel nothing so much as weariness at the thought of what I will find when I come home.

20th March 1894

Rebecca is pregnant again. I am sick at the thought of another tragedy, another lost baby, another breakdown. I cannot believe I was weak enough to allow myself to be seduced.

It happened about a fortnight after I got back. I was keeping my distance from her, still angry about my diaries, and when she realised I was not going to go to her, as I usually do, she came to me in the night, pale and sad, and wept like a child, until I pitied her and took her in my arms. And then I did not have the heart to reject her advances. Afterwards I was angry with myself and prayed that she would not conceive, but God – if He exists – did not see fit to hear my prayers.

28th March 1894

I am so shaken that I do not know if I can write this. After all these years I would have thought nothing could surprise me, but since seeing the doctor yesterday I feel as though I have woken into a nightmare. He apologised for not informing me before but he has been away in England on a family matter and did not feel it was something he could reveal in a letter. He confessed he was in two minds about telling me at all but did not feel he could let the situation continue and did not want to go to the authorities.

I notice I am delaying writing the words, as though putting them down in ink will make them real. *Rebecca's miscarriages were not an accident* – that is what he told me. My wife has been aborting her babies… has killed five of our children with cold-blooded deliberation.

I did not believe him at first and accused him of maliciously spreading rumours; I even threatened to sue him for defamation of character. I almost began to think Rebecca was right about people persecuting her. I know that he, like most people, has never liked her, but I could tell that he was sorry for me. He told me he had suspected it with the previous miscarriage but this time he found evidence of it. When he showed me the piece of twig that local women apparently use to procure an abortion I was nearly sick. I knew at once who was behind it, for there is only one person close enough to her to have helped her, and without whose knowledge she could not have done it.

I don't know what to do. In her present condition I dare not upset her, and yet I cannot allow her to destroy this child like all the others. Why did I not reject her advances? And yet part of me is angry, angry enough to be glad she is pregnant, and vindictive enough to take pleasure in the fact that I will force her to carry this child to term whether she wants it or not.

29th March 1894

Last night I dreamt that I was in one of those strange gardens she embroiders so exquisitely. It was like the Garden of Eden, except that baby hands and feet were growing from the tree branches in place of fruit, opening and closing their fat little fingers like sea anemones. The plants at my feet had plump pink lips growing in place of flowers, all opening wide and quivering, as though they were screaming. The air was filled with the sound of it: short bursts of high-pitched screaming, stopping and starting like a chorus of crickets. Things were scuttling along the ground by my feet, and when I looked closer I saw that they were eyeballs moving along on their spider-leg lashes. I came to an apple tree. There was the stench of over-ripe fruit in the air and as I approached it the tree came to life and a twiglike arm reached out to me, holding an apple streaked purple, yellow and sickly green. My fingers sank into it and I realised it was rotten. I turned it in my hand and realised it was the back part of a baby's decaying foot and threw it from me in horror. The screaming got louder and louder and the ground began to move under me. I woke to find Rebecca shaking me by the shoulder and calling my name.

I shrank back, then got up and went out on to the verandah to get away from her. The skin on my neck and back was crawling. She followed me and began to stroke my shoulders and I flinched away.

'Go to bed.' I could not even bring myself to say her name.

'You're angry with me,' she said, in that hurt child voice that usually awakens my compassion, but all I felt was rage and disgust. She put her hand out to me and I stepped away.

'Don't touch me!'

She turned away, miserable. I will have to tell her I know, but I feared that if I spoke to her then I would become violent. If I am honest, I intended to punish her, to make her suffer. I know that her greatest fear is of being ostracised, and it is a result she always provokes in the end – a self-fulfilling prophecy. One of the terrible things I have discovered is that there is pleasure in tormenting someone who seems to invite it.

This morning her ayah – that bitch of a woman, Zainab – came to see me. She said in an accusing voice, 'How can you be so cruel to her when she is carrying your child?'

I was so suffused with rage that my teeth were chattering. I got her by the wrist and dragged her into the front garden away from the house and the servants.

'How dare you say that to me? Do you think I don't know what you've been doing, you and your… your… precious girl?'

Her face went white.

'Yes, I know it all. The doctor told me yesterday. Why did you do it? All those babies… my children… murdered!'

She put her hands to her cheeks in pretend shock. 'What are you saying, sahib?'

Her playacting turned my rage to ice. I said coldly, 'The doctor told me what he found. How many times? Were they all done deliberately?'

She did not reply.

I told her she was dismissed, that she must leave my house today and that she would get no pension from me. Nor would she ever see Rebecca again. 'Think yourself lucky that I'm not handing you over to the police. If you were tried for this you would be hanged.'

This afternoon she came to me and broke down. She fell to her knees and clutched my feet and begged me not to send her away. 'She's all I've got. She is my life,' she kept saying.

'And my children were mine,' I retorted, trying to back away, but she followed me on her knees.

'She did not mean to hurt you, sahib. She was afraid...'

'Afraid of what? Tell me why she wanted to murder our children... and why you helped her.'

And then she said something that astonished me. 'They say that you can tell when a baby is born if it has Indian blood. She was afraid the baby would look Indian.'

I stared at her. 'But why on earth should she think...? Do you mean she thinks that I...?'

'No, sahib. Not that.' And then she said something I found almost as hard to credit as the doctor's story – she told me that she is not Rebecca's ayah at all, but her mother!

This is her story. According to her, Ramsay had a preference for little girls and bought her virginity and exclusive rights to her when she was twelve. She was then being trained as a courtesan in Lucknow by a woman to whom her brother had sold her after their parents died. Ramsay fell in love with her and bought her out. He took her as his bibi, but when she became pregnant she insisted on marriage and he agreed, to keep her happy. They lied about her age; she was just fourteen.

'He still loved me then,' she said bitterly.

They lived together as man and wife in Calcutta, where he worked as a manager for a tea company. It was the comment of an Englishwoman that the baby was so fair she could pass for a European that gave him the idea. When he was appointed manager of a new tea plantation in Assam, where no one knew him, he took the opportunity to change his story. He told Zainab that Rebecca, who was then two, would have a better chance in life if she was thought to be white, and that from now on she must pretend to be Rebecca's ayah and say that her mother was dead.

It was a preposterous story. Did she really think I was such an imbecile as to believe it? 'But why should he do such a thing? And why would you accept it?' I demanded.

She shrugged. 'He was tired of me. He always liked young girls. And what choice did I have? He told me that unless I agreed he would send me away and I would never see my daughter again.' Her voice shook as she said it, and suddenly I remembered her panic that night when we had stood in the temple above the tank as Roland and Rebecca walked below. And something else: an image of a pair of sandalled feet near the base of a white pillar illuminated by moonlight. I looked down. Her feet were high-arched, with four long slim toes and one short one, like the feet on a Greek statue. I revisited that feeling of *déjà vu* I had when I first saw Rebecca's feet on the day I proposed to her. How could I not have seen it sooner?

Her story seems to explain much that has puzzled me about their relations. If it is true, then I have been party to a terrible injustice. I have even threatened Zainab, in almost the same words as Ramsay did, that I would separate her forever from her daughter.

But is it really possible that Rebecca is ignorant that the woman is her mother? Zainab assures me that she is; that she herself, afraid of losing her daughter, agreed to do everything she could to make Rebecca forget.

'I told her not to call me Mama and when she didn't stop I would slap her, but still she persisted. One day when she kept on repeating it he shouted at me to pack my bags and go that evening, so I took her to the bathroom and I held her head under the water, and I told her I would stop only when she called me "ayah". But she is stubborn, like him... she was choking and crying but she would not say it... she would not...' Her eyes filled with tears. 'But I continued until she fainted. Afterwards she got a fever and was so ill I thought she would die. The doctor said it was a brain fever, and when she got better she no longer called me mother. And from that day she stopped caring for me, only for her father. But I do not blame her for it. It was he... that sewer... may he spend eternity burning in Jehannum.'

I have no idea what to make of this story. I do not trust her and yet she told it to me with such emotion that, despite myself, I could not help feeling moved. She has begged me to say nothing to Rebecca for fear of provoking another brain fever, for she says Rebecca has had several in her life. 'At school, the other girls tormented her. They were so cruel that she became ill and had to be sent home. And you saw yourself how ill she was when that... that sewer Sutcliffe... abandoned her. I thought she was going to die then too.'

'But I still don't understand,' I said. 'Does she think I care about such things? That I would reject or abandon her? I have never given her the slightest cause to think so!' On the contrary, it has always been she who expressed a dislike of Indians and behaved badly towards them. And yet it all makes sense: her greater ease with men who, blinded by her beauty, ask no awkward questions; her tearful outbursts when other women question her about her people; her fear of the servants, for they are the quickest to spot pretence and affectation. It occurs to me for the first time that our servants may well know what I have been so blind to, which may explain why she has never been able to assert her authority over them, and why Zainab has had to run the house. I know they do not like her either – I have heard them call her a 'churail' – but they fear her. (Ironic that a churail is a witch, the ghost of a woman who has died in childbirth.)

It only occurred to me after our conversation that if the reason her mother gave for Rebecca's actions is true – that she feared her babies might give away the fact that she has Indian blood – it must mean that she knows the truth. Is it possible that she can both know and not know? I have sometimes thought she seems almost like two different people; I still remember how loving she was in the early days of our marriage, and her kindness to Father.

I do not know if Zainab has told her of our conversation, but her chastened behaviour seems to suggest it – or at least suggests that she has been advised to act repentant – for I no longer trust her, trust either of them.

30th March 1894

I spoke to the doctor today and he has advised me to wait for another month until the pregnancy is firmly established before withdrawing her laudanum. We have agreed that in the interim she will need to be watched at all times. I have applied for an immediate leave of absence on compassionate grounds for, repulsive as the thought is, it seems to me the only way to ensure the survival of this child is for me to act as her jailer. As a double surety, I have told Zainab that if Rebecca loses this child I will hand them both over to the police and the doctor will give evidence against them.

2nd April 1894

I realised this morning that I cannot continue to ignore Rebecca. I shall have to make some attempt to get her to confide in me. Although I am angry and disgusted, I also pity her, for − like a snake − she cannot help her nature, which has been twisted by the deceit practised on her since her infancy.

This afternoon I invited her to come and sit on the verandah with me, for I could not bear to be alone with her in her darkened room. She came out and sat, her hands folded in her lap, with the same blank expression she wears when she is in the company of other women, and I suddenly saw that her composure is a mask, and that she is not relaxed at all but holding herself still with every muscle tensed, poised to ward off the attack she is always expecting.

'It must be exhausting to be you,' I said.

She looked at me. In the shadow of the verandah the disparity between her eyes was less marked and once again I marvelled at her beauty, but it no longer moves me. Nor am I any longer taken in by her promise of light and warmth, a promise I know from experience is hollow, as hollow as she is when the show is over and she sinks back into herself: an empty bucket being lowered into a cold, dark well.

She did not reply and I could tell she was going over my words suspiciously, weighing them to assess any threat they might hold.

'I don't want to torment you. I just want to understand,' I said. 'Tell me what you remember about your childhood. The truth.'

She looked down at her hands and began to talk, obediently, like a child doing what it is told. She told me about her childhood, the hill station where she grew up, all the usual stuff she has told Father and me over the years about how close she and her father were, how he doted on her and adored her. I must have made a movement of impatience because she glanced at me and added quickly, 'But that was when I was little.'

'Tell me about later.'

She hesitated and then said, 'I had one friend there – the daughter of one of the women who worked on the tea estate. I called her Ungoo. We played together although Ayah didn't like it – she said I would pick up "jungli" habits – but I used to sneak outside in the afternoon when she was sleeping and meet Ungoo at the edge of the garden.'

Her voice was dreamy. I wondered how much of what she was telling me was the truth and how much a fantasy.

'Our games were quite innocent at first, but then, when we were about nine or ten, Ungoo started doing things that she said were secret – things that I mustn't tell anybody. Things she said men did to women.' She glanced at me as though expecting some reaction but I kept my face blank.

'Go on.'

'Then I would go back before Ayah woke and slip back into bed and pretend I'd been there all the time. And then one afternoon Ayah found us and saw what we were doing.

She was angry and she told Father and he sent me away to boarding school.'

'Tell me about school.'

'I hated it there. The other girls were horrible to me. I didn't know anything about books or fashion or famous people or any of the things they talked about and they made fun of me and called me names, said I was "country-born" and ignorant. They called me a witch because my eyes were different colours. And it got worse and worse. They accused me of doing things I hadn't done – things like stealing their trinkets and putting nasty things in their beds. They even hid some of their things in my box so it looked as though I had stolen them. When they asked about my people and I said that my mother was Irish, they made fun of me. One of them said I was lying. Then they started singing every time I entered a room… they pretended they were just singing to themselves so the teachers wouldn't know, but I knew it was meant for me.'

She sang in a soft breathy voice:

'There's a dear little plant that grows on our isle.
'Twas St Patrick himself that sure set it;
and the sun on his labour with pleasure did smile,
and with dew from his eye often wet it.
It shines thro' the bog, thro' the brake and the mireland,
And he called it the dear little shamrock of Ireland;
That dear little shamrock, the sweet little shamrock,
The dear little, sweet little shamrock of Ireland.'

Her mouth twisted. I watched her, mesmerised. I find it hard to understand now how I could have been so caught in her spell that I did not perceive how mad she is.

289

'It got worse and worse. They told dreadful lies...' Tears gathered on her lower lashes and, unmoved, I watched them tremble there. 'No one would sit next to me at table or in class. They stole my books and hid them or spilt ink on my homework so I got into trouble with the teachers. Then one day someone put broken glass in the face cream of the girl who teased me the most, and it scarred her face. They said that it was me, that someone had seen me with the jar, so the school sent me home. Ayah was angry with me. She didn't believe me – she's always been against me – but I was glad to be home with Daddy. I thought he would be pleased to see me, but he wasn't, and he wouldn't read me stories any more, or even come to my room to say goodnight. He said I was too old for all that and he was ashamed of me. And then I got ill.

'When I was better I went looking for Ungoo... It was the monsoon and I went to the plantation where her mother worked and she was there, planting tea. I didn't realise it was her at first – she was wearing one of those palm leaf shelters they use to keep the rain off – and then she stood up and she had a baby strapped to her back and... it was horrible! The baby had blue eyes!' Her voice broke. 'And then some months later another of the girls had a baby and someone complained to the company... so we came down to the plains and Daddy got a job with the steamboat company.'

The story fits more or less with what Zainab told me, and the tales I've heard about Ramsay, but she recited it so flatly that it seemed like a story she had heard or read rather than experienced. And yet I can see no reason for her to invent it. But there is still no admission that she knows, or suspects, the truth about her own birth. I am tempted to tell her, but it would do no good. She would simply add me to her list of persecutors.

When I told her that I have taken three months' leave to take care of her, she smiled, but her eyes were those of a trapped animal.

14th May 1894

Rebecca has been off the laudanum now for three weeks and is suffering dreadfully. Her skin has turned grey, she sweats and shivers and begs us to give her 'just one drop'. It is pitiful to listen to, but the doctor insists we must not weaken, as if she is still taking it in her sixth month it could cause a premature birth. Zainab stays with her day and night. I believe she would give in, if she dared, for she cannot bear to watch Rebecca suffer. I am concerned about what will happen when I return to work for I have used almost all my long leave and will need to go back at the end of June.

5th June 1894

Today I had a letter from Father to say that Kishan Lal has died. I have not seen either of them for more than a year. Father said he went peacefully. *'I was at his bedside and he remembered you at the end and asked me to give his regards to chotta sahib. I shall feel his absence greatly; he was with me for more than thirty years.'*

Father is eighty-four, too old to live alone without someone he trusts. I have asked him to come to us. He and Rebecca have always got on well, and he will be company for her when I go back to work and also another a pair of eyes for me. I cannot, of course, tell him the truth, but he knows she is highly strung. And he will be a match for her mother for, even at his age, he is a man who commands respect.

19th October 1894

I am a father. Our daughter was born five days ago in the early hours of the morning – a small but healthy baby with a thatch of dark hair.

She was born in the hospital at Patna, as Rebecca developed a fever a few days before her birth and had to be rushed to hospital. The midwife brought her out to me, tightly wrapped in swaddling clothes. I took the stiff little bundle in my arms and looked into her face. Her delicate skin had a yellowish tinge and her eyes were closed; she looked self-contained and peaceful, like a tiny Buddha, perfect and complete in herself.

It should have been the happiest moment of my life but all I could feel was depression at the thought of the world she is being born into: a world in which the prejudices and judgements of others may distort and twist all that potential. I pictured Rebecca as an innocent baby and felt like weeping when I thought what life has done to her. For a moment I wanted to hand the child back, to refuse the responsibility for this precious, fragile life. I wonder if this is how my mother felt as she held me in her arms.

The midwife was watching me. 'She takes after you,' she said, in a meaningful tone, but when I smiled at her she looked away.

I went in to see Rebecca. She was lying with her face to the wall and would not look at me. The midwife tried to place the baby in her arms but she kept them clamped to her body. The doctor beckoned me outside. He was a young man recently come from England. He appeared uncomfortable and, like the midwife, avoided my eyes. 'Your wife seems to be suffering from a delusion that the baby isn't hers,' he said. 'It does sometimes happen that women don't take to motherhood. It may improve with time.'

'Did something happen to upset her?'

He said reluctantly, 'When we delivered the baby we noticed there was a large mark like a bruise on her lower back. The midwife said it was a sign that the child has Asian blood. I remembered reading about it in medical school – it's called a Mongolian blue spot. I'm afraid your wife overheard the conversation and it disturbed her. We assumed...' He hesitated.

'Assumed...?'

'That she would have known.'

I stared at him for a few moments before I realised they thought that I had deceived Rebecca about my origins. I wanted to punch him, but what would it have achieved?

When we got home I put the baby in Father's arms and he looked down at her and smiled and said, 'She has your mother's eyes.'

One part of me was glad, another sorry that she should carry anything of our history. I would like to free her of it all – of that grinding weight that bears down on us and pushes our lives in directions we never dreamt of.

Lila

Yesterday, the doorbell rang as I was coming down to breakfast. I opened the door and the postman handed me a letter. As I took it, I felt that mixture of dread and excitement that I always feel these days when I see my name on a letter. No one writes to me except Barbara. The letter was stamped and postmarked in England and addressed in a hand I didn't recognise. I tore it open. Inside was another envelope, addressed to me in Jagjit's father's hand.

I went so white that the postman made me sit down in the hallway and went round to the kitchen to ask Enid to bring me some water. Hearing her fussing over me, Mrs. Beauchamp came out. 'What is it, my dear? Not bad news, I hope?'

'From his father.' My lips felt as clumsy as they had when I first started speaking again.

'Do you want me to stay with you while you read it?'

I nodded, took a deep breath and tore open the letter.

20th April 1919

Dear daughter,

I am sending this with the son of my friend who is going to England, so I can be sure it will reach you. I am happy to give you good news. Jagjit is alive and is at home with us.

I burst into tears.

Mrs. Beauchamp put her arms around me. 'My dear, I am so sorry.'

I pushed her away. 'He's alive.'

'Alive? But my dear, how wonderful!'

'That *is* good news, Miss,' Enid said beaming. She always liked Jagjit.

'It is real, isn't it? The letter… it's not a dream?'

'No, my dear, it's not a dream.' Mrs. Beauchamp smiled.

'Do you want me to pinch you, miss?'

'I don't think that will be necessary, Enid,' Mrs. Beauchamp said. 'Why don't you take the letter upstairs and read it quietly, Lila? I'll send a telegram to Simon. He'll be so relieved.'

I went upstairs to my room and stood looking out at the slope of the Downs. It seemed right that the bluebells should be in flower – I could see clumps of them along the fence.

Jagjit was in a camp very far in the desert. After the war, they were left without food. He and the other men walked for many days. My son was lucky to be found by some kind British officers in a Jeep who were looking for their men. They kept him in hospital in Aden for two months but he was too sick to tell them his name. He is still very weak and has many bad dreams and is much disturbed in his mind. The doctors say he will get better but he is very much changed. When I met him at Karachi I did not know him.

He tells me the reason our letters did not reach him was because when they left Kut he changed places with an old soldier who was wounded. He gave up his own place in the officers' truck, as only officers were allowed to ride. He thought when they reached Baghdad he would be able to rejoin them, but instead they were forced to march for many hundreds of miles through the desert and the Turkish guards were very cruel. Many men fell down and were left behind to die.

He tells me the British at Kut did not behave well to the Indians. Here too they have broken the promises they made when our sons went to fight in their war. The Rowlatt Act has upset many people, and you must have heard what happened in Amritsar one week ago, when soldiers fired bullets into a crowd of people who had gone there for the Baisakhi festival. There were many women and children in the crowd and some people jumped in a well to escape and were drowned. Some of them were from our village.

Jagjit says he no longer wishes to work for the British. Instead he wants to use his knowledge of the law to help our people who have been put in prison by your government. He asks me to tell you that he will not return to England, and that it is not safe for you to come here.

Daughter, I am sorry to tell you this news, but Jagjit is all I have left. You know that his brother Baljit was killed in France, and his mother also died in January without knowing that he was alive. Only Baljit's wife and small boy are with me, and when I am gone there will be no one to care for them. I am an old man now and I want my son to settle down at home and marry a girl from our community. I am sure your family would also prefer you to marry a good English boy. I hope you will understand.

Jagjit sends good wishes to your aunty and his friend Simon's family and thanks you all for your many kindnesses to him.

Respectfully, Purushottam Singh

I stood holding the letter, reading and rereading it, my joy turning to bewilderment. How could he send me such a message? I thought of all the letters I written to him over the years, without ever getting a reply, even after I had been told he was probably dead. Did I mean nothing to him?

I picked up Aunt Mina's packet and ran out of the room and down the stairs, passing Mrs. Beauchamp at the bottom. She turned as I rushed past. 'I was just coming up. Is everything all right?'

I tried to speak, but the fist-sized lump in my throat blocked the words.

'Lila?'

I pushed the letter into her hand and fled past her out of the door and round to the back. At the fence I caught my skirt on the brambles as I scrambled through the gap. I wrenched at it, and felt satisfaction as I heard the material rip.

Back at High Elms, I walked past the cavernous downstairs rooms, neither home nor hospital now. The cream oil paint that covered the wallpaper was marked where electric wires had been ripped down, and with the scrapes of the beds and wheelchairs of those who had suffered and died there. I went up to my old room, which I had been allowed to keep when I was nursing there, and lay down on my bed. Muddled thoughts went through my head – thoughts of Father and India, of all the doubts and fears of the last few years. I saw that I had, without realising it, swung between two possible futures: Jagjit alive and myself married to him, or Jagjit dead and myself alone and grieving. I had never envisaged the possibility of Jagjit being alive and myself alone. Why did I never count?

Grief turned to self-pity and resentment and I fanned the flames. I would not cry. I was tired of not knowing, of always being in the dark. It was time to find out.

I shook the key out of Aunt Mina's packet and went up to the attic.

Henry

Father died in October, shortly after Lila's fourth birthday. Thinking of him has prompted me to start keeping a journal again, even if only temporarily. I have missed writing down my thoughts but have had little time for reflection, what with the demands of caring for Rebecca, an ageing father and a baby, as well as a new career.

I resigned from the I.C.S. shortly after Lila's birth. The world of the 'Heaven-Born', as it is satirically referred to, is an exclusive and snobbish one, and Rebecca's nervous state, together with rumours that I had 'a touch of the tar brush', made us pariahs. Clubs refused to admit me on transparent pretexts and we were not invited anywhere, which made my position as a civil servant untenable. A magistrate needs to be respected, and if Indians know his peers do not respect him one can hardly expect them to do so.

It was Gavin McLean, my old friend from school, who encouraged me to apply for the Political Service. They were looking for people to conduct a survey to establish the boundary of the Durand Line that had been agreed between us and the Amir of Afghanistan, and the fact that I had spoken

Hindustani since childhood gave me an advantage. Gavin of course, being half-Chinese, and a superb linguist, can pass for a Gurkha, Tibetan or Central Asian when occasion demands.

I was initially concerned about leaving the baby with Rebecca, for she continued, and continues to this day, to insist that Lila is not her baby but was substituted in the hospital. No amount of reasoning has been able to alter this conviction. I even named the baby 'Lilian' after Rebecca's supposedly Irish mother, in the hope that this might placate her, but it has made no difference. Zainab and the servants immediately shortened it to 'Lila', a name I have always liked, and 'Lila' she has become to everyone but Rebecca, who rarely refers to her at all. I deeply regret that she will grow up, as I did, without the love of a mother, but Zainab dotes on her and lavishes on her all the love she has been unable to offer her own daughter. Right from the first, she took jealous possession of the baby, and as soon as she was fed her wet nurse was dismissed to the compound, and dismissed altogether as soon as Lila was weaned.

My greatest shame is that I have been complicit in the pretence that my daughter's grandmother is a servant – a deception that she will surely one day reproach me with. But Zainab herself will never agree to tell Rebecca the truth, believing that being forced to accept it would make her worse. My argument – that it is not truth but lies and deception that feed suspicions and irrational fears – cuts no ice with her, but I cannot deny that she understands Rebecca better than I do.

Despite Zainab's care, I was concerned at the long absences, sometimes of several months, that my new career has entailed, but Father assured me he would take care of the household and for the most part it was a success. Rebecca respected and loved him and he was kind to her, while Lila adored being jogged up and down on his knee, playing at 'horsies', while using his beard as the reins. I knew he could not live forever – at eighty-eight he had reached a good age – but his death has hit me hard, for my admiration for him grew with every year. I always left the household in his charge with confidence, even when in the last year his wits began to wander and he imagined that I was his brother James and that Rebecca was Cecily. I believe there was a genuine affection between him and Rebecca. He had suffered from depression and guilt for so many years that I was grateful to her for providing him with some comfort and peace in his last years.

After his death she suffered another of those 'brain fevers', and once again her head has been shorn. When I went in to see her after it was done, I was so moved I could scarcely speak. She looked as she did on the day I proposed to her, when she seemed to me the embodiment of everything a man could desire in a woman.

2nd January 1899

I have been in two minds what to do, unsure whether, without Father's supervision, I can safely undertake the extended travel my work requires. Zainab assures me that all will be well. I have discussed with her the possibility of returning to England and seeking treatment for Rebecca, but she is against it. She is convinced it will reinforce Rebecca's conviction that I intend to have her confined in an asylum. And Zainab's own life would be even lonelier than it is here for, although the other servants dislike her, in England there would be no one who even speaks her language.

I must admit it is a relief to remain here, for I love my work. The freedom of travel, the beauty of the mountains, and mingling with the fierce proud tribesmen of the Northwest Frontier is fulfilling in a way the I.C.S. never was. All that matters in the Political Service is how well one does one's job, and I have been fortunate in having Gavin as my friend and mentor. He is the cleverest man I ever met, and well respected in the service despite his mixed origins.

The game we play is a risky one, more like being a soldier – my original ambition – than a civil servant, though it requires more guile. Lord Curzon said earlier this year that the territories that lie between India and Russia are 'pieces on a chessboard being played out for dominion of the world'. There is a real pleasure in using one's wits and living on the edge of danger, but now that Father is gone I wonder if it is a game I should be playing. Like him, I no longer believe in our right to be here, and, if something were to happen to me, what would become of Lila, left in Rebecca's care?

I have been thinking for some time of making Aunt Mina her legal guardian in case of my death. I do not think this would present any great difficulty, for Rebecca has never shown the slightest interest in Lila, and I have on occasion suspected that she may even have tried to harm her. There have been a couple of injuries that happened in my absence that Zainab explained away as accidents, though I have noticed that she now takes care to keep Lila away from her mother.

I have had another offer of help, too. Just before Christmas I bumped into Roland Sutcliffe here in Peshawar. His regiment is here at the request of the Amir to check the raids being made by the Waziris along the Frontier. We have not seen each other since I moved from Bhagalpur soon after our marriage, though we have exchanged the odd letter from time to time.

I invited him to tea and he came and was a great success with Lila, who took to him immediately. Her presence helped to ease the tension, for Rebecca froze him out, despite all his efforts at gaiety and charm. He is a captain now, but still unmarried and, judging by his conversation when I meet him alone, not much changed. He has been over twice since then and each time Rebecca has thawed a little and Lila has greeted him like an old friend. I suspect part of his appeal is that he too has a beard and allows her to climb on his knee and pull it, as Father did. He has offered to continue to visit in my absence and get a message to me if I am needed.

I shall miss Lila when I go back to work. Over the last couple of months we have spent a lot of time together, riding into the country, often taking a picnic with us and staying out all day. And, each time I return home to be greeted with that dazzling smile that Father said she gets from my mother, I thank God again for that doctor who told me a truth it must have been unpleasant to disclose, and by doing so saved her life. For her existence has more than made up for every other disappointment in my life.

27th March 1907

It is eight years since I made the last entry in this journal. My life has been too busy to allow it. My work entails writing lengthy reports and since Father's death I have tried to spend all my spare time with Lila. In recent years those dreams and depressions that used to plague me have recurred less frequently, but my recent discovery about Rebecca has revived them.

Last week, when Gavin and I arrived back from a mission, we were intercepted by a messenger who had been sent to watch for our return. He warned us that the room we rent in the bazaar to change in and out of our disguises was being watched, so we decided to go straight home. I waited till the chowkidar had gone for his tea and then slipped in the gate. In the hall, I noticed Roland's blue and gold striped puggree on the stand, but there was no sign of him on the verandah or in the drawing room. As I turned towards my room, I heard laughter coming from Rebecca's bedroom. I wish now that I had gone in and confronted them, but I was aware of the need to change out of my disguise before the servants saw me.

I went to my room and changed quickly, scrubbing the dye off my face and hands as best I could before going back into the drawing room. I entered the corridor just as Roland emerged from Rebecca's room, still straightening his uniform jacket. He looked startled to see me, but recovered quickly and said he had been paying a sick call on Rebecca, who was in bed with one of her headaches. I should have smashed my fist into his face – I am stronger now than I used to be and well trained in hand-to-hand fighting – but maybe the years of pretending to be someone I am not has become a habit, for instead I stood there making polite conversation until he took his leave.

Zainab, of course, must know. Nothing happens in this house without her knowledge, but I learnt long ago that, except when it comes to Lila's welfare, her first allegiance is always to Rebecca. I have said nothing to Rebecca herself, because I know it would achieve nothing, but I wonder how long this has been going on. Was it right from the beginning? Did he agree to watch her for me, knowing all the time that he intended to seduce her? Has she held a candle for him all those years? Was even the short time when we seemed to be happy a lie?

I cannot blame her for taking from him what I was no longer prepared to give, for I have not spent a night with her since Lila's birth, despite knowing that her whole sense of herself depends on her ability to attract desire. Perhaps it was cruel of me to marry her and then deprive her of the only thing that gives her a sense of worth; I thought of myself as her rescuer but all I seem to have done is transfer her to a prison with stronger bars.

What really hurts is Roland's betrayal – that he should have pretended once again to be my friend, offered to care for Rebecca and my child, and then taken advantage of my trust and hospitality. And yet I have always known what he is like, known that he has no respect for marriage, and that deceit and secrecy just add spice to his adventuring.

29th March 1907

I have been feeling very low since I discovered what a fool I have been. The knowledge that everyone in the house – all the servants and, of course, Zainab – must have known what was going on and were sniggering behind my back has been humiliating, and for the first time I have some sense of what Rebecca must have suffered all these years. You would think that might have made me more patient, but yesterday when she came to me with some trivial complaint about Zainab as she so often does, and begged me to dismiss her, I lost my temper and told her that I was sick of her lies and pretence and if she felt people were untrustworthy it was because she herself was incapable of honesty.

I suggested that she stitch into one of her precious embroideries the motto 'The Truth Shall Make You Free', then told her it was time that she faced the truth, however unpleasant, that Zainab is her mother. I was just passing on to Roland when she began to scream at me and call me a liar, accusing me of being in league with her enemies, and then she became hysterical and threw herself on the floor and had a fit, with her teeth chattering and her limbs jerking.

Zainab came and took her away and dosed her with laudanum. She said nothing to me but I truly believe that if she could poison me and get away with it she would do it without a second thought. Fortunately Lila was out on her pony, although she has witnessed plenty of her mother's hysterical outbursts over the years.

30th March 1907

Last night Rebecca came to my room while I was sleeping. I woke, already aroused, to find her in bed beside me, using all her seductive wiles, and for a moment I was tempted to succumb – it has been a long time since I have been with a woman – but then the thought struck me that she must use the same tricks with Roland and I pushed her off.

She became hysterical again and screamed at me that she hated me, and tried to scratch my face with her nails. She was screaming so loudly that Zainab came. Between us we got her back to her room where Zainab quieted her, I suspect with more laudanum.

I went into Lila's room to see if she had woken. She was sitting up in bed and I sat down beside her and said, 'Don't worry, darling. Mother has one of her headaches.' She nodded, though I could tell she didn't believe me. She is twelve now and too old to swallow these excuses. I realise it is time to get her away from here. I have telegraphed Aunt Mina to ask if she will have her. I am loath to send her away, remembering how I hated it myself, but I am afraid of what witnessing these scenes will do to her.

I read to her for a while, then she played with my lucky Sussex stone and asked me to tell her again how I had got it. I told her my mother put it round my neck when I was born but I have never told her more – it is too sad a story for a child. I thought again of Father, trying to protect me, and how I resented him for sending me away. I will miss her dreadfully, but I know she will be safer in England. In any case, it is only a matter of time before I shall have to return myself.

It seems that Zainab was right about Rebecca, as she always is. Since I told her the truth about her mother she has been paler than ever, and as still as if she is turning to marble. I fear I have pushed her too far and that I must now seek treatment for her. They tell me there are doctors in London who have produced remarkable cures for hysteria, and they may even be able to wean her off the laudanum. But the thought of breaking the news to her and, if I am honest, the thought of returning to England and finding an ordinary job in some city office, both fill me with dread.

9th July 1907

Gavin McLean is dead. Colonel Anderson summoned me today and told me that he was stabbed in the bazaar last night. He asked me if I had any idea how he might have been betrayed. Something in the way he asked suggested that he suspected it had something to do with me. I said no, and we went through the names of all the Indians and Gurkhas who work with us, but there was no obvious suspect.

When I got home I went to my study and discovered that the drawer in which I keep the duplicate copies of my reports has been broken into. It must have taken considerable force and been done before my return, for I have not had occasion to open it since I got back.

I summoned all the servants and questioned them. At first they denied any knowledge, but eventually Afzal Khan admitted that some men had visited the house while I was out riding. I asked why he had not mentioned them to me. He said that Zainab has forbidden the servants to gossip about Memsahib's visitors. Of course they must all know about Roland and, through their grapevine, so must the whole cantonment. There must also have been talk about our estrangement and the fact that Rebecca has not emerged from her room for the last three months, but remains locked away, taking all her meals there and seeing no one except Zainab.

I sent them away – all except Zainab – and demanded she tell me who these visitors were. It took the usual threats of taking Rebecca to England and leaving her behind to break her down, but I am past caring about decency. If Gavin is dead because of them, they have done more damage than anything I can do to either of them.

It turns out that Rebecca has not just been taking the prescribed laudanum, which the doctor monitors, but has been buying opium on the side. The men who came have been supplying her for some time, and it seems to me likely that at least one is in the pay of the Russians or Chinese and has used her as a way of getting into the house.

I went straight back to Colonel Anderson, told him what had happened, minimising Rebecca's part in it, and offered my resignation, which he accepted. He advised me that I may be in danger myself and that it is perhaps time for me to return to England. In any case, he says the Great Game is nearly finished since we are now facing greater threats in

Europe from Germany's growing military might. A meeting has been arranged next month to work out the terms of the alliance between us and Russia, and it looks as though we will now agree to leave Tibet to China. Colonel Anderson was kind enough to add that I should not blame myself, and that Gavin's death may not have been connected with his work but have been an attempt at robbery, but of course neither of us believed it. Pathans never forgive a slight or a betrayal, and over the years both Gavin and I have lied and deceived to get information.

As I was leaving, Anderson stopped me and said, 'I think you should know that your wife is planning a special birthday party for your fiftieth birthday and has invited Jane and me.' Jane is his pregnant daughter, who is staying with him while her husband is away. 'She said it was to be a surprise, but I suspect you have had enough surprises to last you for some time.'

12th July 1907

There seems no choice now but to return to England, for I have nothing to keep me here. I have decided not to take Zainab with us. It may be cruel but I cannot forgive her part in this and Rebecca will better off without her. England will give her a fresh start. No one will know her history there and perhaps once away from her mother's influence and from Roland there may even be a chance for us to reach some sort of understanding. Aunt Mina has replied, agreeing to take Lila, and I have arranged for her to go ahead of us as I do not wish her to witness the scenes that will no doubt ensue when I break the news to the two of them. Poor Lila – how I wish I had sent her out of this madhouse to England when she was born.

I shall be fifty in a couple of days and all I can think of is what a mess I have made of my life. I thought I was saving Rebecca, but Roland always understood her better than I did. And, if not for my poor judgement, Gavin would still be alive. There were so many things that I should have seen. I understand now the poetic justice in Oedipus putting out his eyes to punish himself for his metaphorical blindness. If it were not for Lila, who has brought so much joy to my life, I could wish that I had died with my mother in the bibighar.

Lila

It is dawn when I finish reading my father's diaries and grandmother's letters. My eyes are gritty from lack of sleep. Outside my window I hear a blackbird singing and the rooks cawing in the tops of the elms.

I leave the house and walk through the back garden to the fence, passing the bush where I used to bury the packed lunches Cook gave me before going up on to the Downs. I scramble up the hillside, my boots sliding on the muddy path. It takes me some time to find my childhood hideout. It is still there, only much smaller than I remember. I stoop and push my way through the scratchy gnarled twigs until I am safely inside, then I sit on the damp ground and howl, as I used to do when I first came here. I howl for Father, for the sadness of his belief that his love was not enough, for poor Uncle Gavin, for my grandmother and grandfather, for Aunt Mina, and even for Mother, but most of all for myself. And for the first time I feel it: the weight of the past bearing down on us, and see how, struggle as we might, we stand no chance of breaking our fetters, of making our own lives. And now I understand the real meaning of that saying, *He punishes the children and their children for the sins of the parents to the third and fourth generation.*

It is mid-morning when, exhausted by my tears, I finally make my way back to the house. I wash my mud-streaked face and then sit down in front of the mirror. I look at my tangled hair and swollen eyes.

Two lines run through my head:

> Beware! the root is wrapped about
> Your mother's heart, your father's bones

They are from 'The House of Eld' and I understand them now. We carry our parents inside us, their blood in our veins, their voices in our heads. And from Mother, who I thought had given me nothing, a 'touch of the tar brush': my own personal fetter. If people knew, would they spit at me and call me names? If not to my face, then behind my back? Is this the shame that Mother felt when the girls at school tormented her? I understand now why it was easier for her to deny the truth, but I also see that that denial magnified the shame and fuelled her moods, her depressions, her headaches, and the belief that people were always talking about her and mocking her.

A phrase comes to my mind – *there is a want of grit about them* – and I see Simon snatching my book away before reading out, in a mocking voice, that passage about half-castes to taunt Jagjit and me. Mother certainly wanted grit. And wasn't there something about the mixing of races bringing out the worst features of both? Is that why Mother was like she was? Or was it just the effect of living for so many years fearing the contempt of others for something she could not help?

But why am I thinking like this? After all, no one need ever know the truth. What would be the point of telling them? And, as I think that, I catch my reflection in the mirror and for a moment Mother is looking back at me, and her eyes are saying, 'See, you are more like me than you know,' and I feel the root tangling round my heart.

Up in the attic again, I hunt around among the shrouded shapes, raising clouds of dust. I found Aunt Mina's desk fairly easily yesterday, covered with dustsheets, in a corner with the other furniture. But I have no idea where to look for the carpet bag. It is nearly two o'clock and I am faint with hunger before I find it, stuffed into a trunk with Father's name stencilled on it in white paint. It must have been shipped to Aunt Mina from India, I suppose, after his death. Inside are some of his books and bronzes, including the statue of Shiva dancing the world into being in his ring of flames. Once again I see that dancing shadow, growing and shrinking on the wall behind Father's desk, and taste again that metallic taste and feel Mother's nails cutting into my shoulders as she smiled.

I throw a cloth over it and continue to excavate. In a corner of the trunk my fingers encounter something soft and furry, like stiff velvet or carpet pile, and a memory comes – wiping cobwebs off my fingers. As I pull the carpet bag out, a cloud of dust comes with it. I turn my head, trying not to breathe it in. Can this really be the bag into which my grandmother placed my father as a baby?

I release the brass catch and pull out a screwed-up bundle of yellowed cloth. I can see only the reverse, covered in a chaotic criss-cross of overlapping stitches in different colours, with knots and loose ends.

Back in my bedroom I open the tablecloth and lay it out on my bed. The deep border consists of a repeating Tree of Life pattern covered with fruit and flowers. Only, when I look closer, I see that what I initially took for bunches of fruit are

312

small fat hands and feet; the tulip-shaped flowers are really plump pink lips with protruding tongues; the daisy-shaped ones are eyeballs, caught in a net of red veins, and surrounded by long looping eyelashes.

I raise my eyes to the centre of the cloth, which would have been revealed when the serving dishes and platters were cleared away. In the centre, the motto 'THE TRUTH SHALL MAKE YOU FREE' is repeated four times to form a circle. A swagged garland of pear-shaped sacs hangs from it, each containing a mangled foetus.

The remaining space between that and the border is filled with what at first glance look like the temple carvings in a book that Simon once found in my great-grandfather's study. It was inscribed: *For H. Partridge, with best wishes from A. Langdon, Christmas 1856.* After one glance I refused to look again; Jagjit took it from Simon's hand and put it back on the shelf, coolly remarking that they were sacred carvings representing the uniting of the male and female principles.

When I look closely at the couples on the tablecloth, I see that the male figures vary: some are fat, some thin, some dark-skinned, some light, some bearded, some turbaned. But the woman is always the same: she has black curly hair and odd eyes – one green and one blue. In some of the couplings she is small – child-sized – compared to the red-haired man with whom she is doing things that no child should be doing. In others she is a woman. One man appears again and again: tall, blond and blue-eyed, sometimes wearing, and sometimes holding in one hand, a blue and gold striped puggree, and flourishing a riding whip. Even Mother's embroidery is not fine enough to make the man's face recognisable but I recognise the hat, whose presence on the hall stand always told me that Uncle Roland was visiting.

I wonder which bit was in front of Father. And then I see it – the woman is kneeling before a tall man with white hair and bright blue eyes. He wears a uniform jacket with colonel's epaulettes, but no trousers; a thin red line of puckered backstitch runs from the corner of his eye to his mouth.

Saliva spurts into my mouth. I remember Father's frozen face as he raised his eyes from the tablecloth to Mother's. Did he believe it? I can barely remember my grandfather, but I know he would never knowingly have betrayed Father. Did she make it up or did she take advantage of his confusion, his hope, that finally, finally, Cecily loved him as he wanted to be loved – as we all want to be loved? And, if so, did she do it out of pity, or for revenge, or because she was desperate to be loved herself?

I roll the cloth up and stuff it back into the bag. When I lift the bag off the bed I see that it has left a sprinkling of fine brown powder on my bedcover.

'You didn't have enough wood on it,' Simon says.

It is afternoon. I am in the garden and he is looking over the fence from the path that runs along the bottom of the hill.

'What are you doing here? I thought you were in London.'

'Mother telegraphed me twice. Once to say that Jagjit was alive but you were upset. Then again this morning – she was worried when you didn't come home last night. She showed me the letter. I've brought food.'

We stand watching the smouldering remains of the small bonfire. The flames have calmed me, burnt away the images, and now I feel cleansed standing in the open air. Today it is warm and muggy, with high silver-grey clouds drifting in a blue sky.

314

'What were you burning anyway? Cloth?' He pokes at the charred material with his stick, uncovering the blackened metal clasp of the carpet bag.

'Just some old things I don't need any more.'

He nods. 'Want to walk?'

I join him on the path and we make our way up to the top of the dyke. My eyes and nose feel hot and swollen with weeping, but my mind is empty. I am cried out. I am also hungry, and realise I haven't eaten for over twenty-four hours.

We sit down and Simon hands me a sandwich. 'I'm sorry about Jagjit. But he does have reason to be bitter. Townshend appears to have had it in for the Indians from the beginning, accusing them of malingering and blaming them for all his failures, although their officers say they fought bravely. And now this business in Amritsar that his father mentions... They're trying to hush it up; they've even blocked the post from Punjab to stop word getting out here.'

'What happened? Do you know?'

'Apparently there was some sort of political meeting to protest about the Rowlatt Act. Political meetings are banned and it looks like General Dyer panicked and opened fire on a crowd of unarmed civilians in an enclosed space from which there was no escape. Hundreds were killed, including women and children... They're calling it a massacre and the nationalists are up in arms. It's hardly surprising that Jagjit is angry.'

'I still don't understand why he signed up. Why either of you did...'

He grimaces. 'The truth is that it was his idea... I wouldn't have had the courage. I only did it because I thought we'd be together. I stupidly assumed if we signed up at the same time they'd put us in the same regiment, even the same company.

315

And when they refused him it was too late; they'd already accepted me for the Reserves. Maybe I could have changed my mind but I didn't want him to think me a coward. It was stupid, but the strange thing is, horrible as it was, I miss it.'

'What is it that you miss?'

'The men, strangely. Their camaraderie… It was all so beastly and yet they were always cheerful: whistling, ribbing each other. And their gallows humour that somehow made light of even the worst moments. They have a gift for happiness. I envied them because they didn't seem to have the expectation that life should be good to them. They're not brought up, as we are, to feel that they need to stand out in some way, to be different, which is just another way of saying to be alone. They're happy to be ordinary – just to be alive is enough, and in each other's company. They don't feel they have to change the world. And here I am, alive, and knowing I'm lucky to be, and yet life seems so empty, so flat… There's absolutely nothing to look forward to, because what could possibly matter after that?'

He turns his head away, but not before I see that his eyes are brimming with tears. As mine fill in sympathy, I realise that I have lived with that feeling ever since Father died. Since then I have had no one, nothing of my own. Jagjit was the only person I trusted, the only one who seemed to care for me above everyone else, the only person with whom I felt I belonged.

I picture the empty years stretching ahead of us and I think of the people all over the world who have lost someone, and all the pain that has been, and is, and is to come, and it feels as though my heart is cracking and then I start to shake and I can't stop. Simon turns to look at me and I try to hold myself together but I can't.

'Lila, what is it?'

I try to speak but my lips are quivering and strange blaring noises are issuing from my mouth. I turn away but he pulls me towards him and holds me tight against his chest, his arms hard around me. 'It's all right,' he says. 'It's all right.' He strokes my hair and talks to me and then there is nothing but the darkness and the shadowy god dancing and the whole world shaking and blood fountaining and I know it is the end, the Kali Yuga, and I am glad.

When I come to, I am lying in Simon's lap. I look up at him, confused.

He smiles down at me. 'Just rest. You're all right now. It's shock. I've seen it happen time and again.'

I sit up and he hands me his handkerchief. I feel drained. We sit looking out over the fields and church spires and small villages, a quiet landscape that gives no sign of the sadness and suffering that lies behind the façade of every house.

'Why is life so bloody, Simon? What's the point of it all?'

He shrugs. 'You're asking the wrong person. Jagjit was always the one with the answers. We used to talk all the time... about life and what it meant, especially when we were travelling in Europe. We'd lie awake the whole night sometimes, just talking. He seemed so wise; I really thought he knew everything.'

'Why did you stop writing to each other?'

He hesitates. 'He turned out not to be as understanding as I thought.'

I wait, sensing he is balanced on the edge of telling me something. His eyes shift away and back and I see he has made the decision. He says slowly, 'You know the day we saw him off...?'

I nod, remembering him helping to take Jagjit's cases down to his cabin and the awkward atmosphere when they came back.

He turns to look at me. 'Did you ever know how jealous I was of you?'

'But why? I thought I was in the way, a nuisance... because he was your friend and you wanted him to yourself.'

His eyes hold mine. 'It was more than that, Lila.'

For a moment I don't understand what he means and then I do. I stare as my mind goes back, reliving and reinterpreting all the times we spent together.

He smiles. 'I loved him. Does that shock you?'

'No. I didn't... it never... How stupid of me!' I remember Jagjit complaining that Simon never left him alone, about his possessiveness, and suddenly I'm worried for Simon. 'Did he know?'

'Not till that day.' He smiles at my concerned expression. 'Don't worry, I didn't go down on my knees and declare my passion, but I might just as well have done for the reaction I got. He'd sat down at the table to write out his address in India for me. I was standing beside him and I wanted so much to touch him – more than I've wanted anything in my life – just to put my hand on his shoulder. It would have been a natural thing to do but I didn't dare. I didn't intend to say anything either, but when he stood up and handed the paper to me he said, "Now you'll have Lila all to yourself," and I realised that *he* was jealous. And I ... I just blurted out, "It's not *Lila* I'm in love with." And he laughed and said, "Who, then?" and... my face must have told the story, because his changed...' He pauses and swallows. 'And I knew I'd made the most awful mistake. I mean, he was perfectly polite – that was what was so terrible – his sudden politeness, as though we were strangers who'd just been introduced. He put a good face on it, but that was the last I heard from him.'

'Why didn't *you* write? I remember now. He did ask you to write to him.'

'Why do you think? I felt humiliated. I didn't want him to think I was pursuing him.' He's silent for a moment. 'It was a shock, because of all the people I've known he was the least inclined to condemn anyone.'

'I have Indian blood, you know.' The words are out before I have time to think.

He raises his eyebrows. 'That's a sudden change of subject.'

'I've just found out. I wasn't sure I'd dare to tell anyone. My mother, apparently... Are you shocked?'

He considers for a moment. 'I don't think so, but then I haven't had time to get used to it. You're still you.'

'And if you'd just met me?'

'And knew? Would I have a preconception about you? Probably. It's how we are. What about you? Are you shocked?'

'Um... not really. Well, maybe a little. More surprised... but again, if we'd just met...'

We smile at each other. This is the most relaxed I've ever seen him, the most relaxed I've ever felt with him, or anyone since Father died. Even with Jagjit, I always wanted him to like me, so I was never fully myself. I look out at the great open plain below us; for the first time in a long time I feel as if I can breathe.

'Simon, if you could go back to how you were before the war, would you?'

There is a long silence while I watch the clouds blowing towards us over the patchwork of fields below. It is still where we are, but up there the wind must be fierce, pulling the clouds into different shapes before shredding them. I watch an elephant change into a roaring lion and then an old bearded man, his mouth agape as though bellowing curses or prophesies. I hear that vibration again, for the first time in a long time. The syllables reverberate through my mind. I know what they are now.

He says quietly, 'If I could turn back the clock and save all those men, take the whole world back to before the war, of course I would. But go back myself? Do you know, I don't think I would. I like myself better now.'

'I do too... like you better now, I mean. But also me. I was so wrapped up in myself before. Poor Aunt Mina. Father wished he had given me to her to bring up. He thinks... thought... I would have had a better life.'

He looks at me. 'But then you wouldn't be you. You wouldn't be so understanding. I wouldn't be able to tell you things I can't tell anyone else.'

After a while I say, 'But we're still both in the same boat.'

'With a shameful secret, you mean?'

'No. Well, yes, but with Jagjit, I meant. He doesn't want either of us.' And as I say it my eyes fill with tears again.

'Oh, come on, Lila. You know he wants you. He always has.'

I give a small snort. 'He has a queer way of showing it.'

'He's afraid.'

'Of what?'

'That he's forgotten how to love? That he doesn't deserve love? That it will be snatched away from him?'

I know how that feels. 'Tell me what to do, Simon.'

'Do you love him?'

I look at him.

'Then what are you really afraid of?'

I open my mouth but no words come. I'm afraid of so many things. I have always thought I was brave, self-reliant, but I see now that I am just a coward... that all my life I have withdrawn from people, shut them out, told myself I didn't need them. I think of Aunt Mina, of the losses and rejections that made her withdraw into her own Fort of Despair, of Mother, frozen in her fear, and realise that I am not so different. Since Father died I have made myself an island.

He touches my arm. 'What were you planning to do before you got his letter?'

'I don't know. I'd decided to go back to India... I've always felt it was my home. Your mother encouraged me to apply for a place at the King Edward Medical College in Lahore. They would have me, but I don't know if I want it now.'

'Why not?'

'Same reason as you... it'll look as if I'm pursuing him.'

'So you're going to sacrifice everything to your pride? Or is it fear?'

I think of Mother again, fear turning her to stone. 'Simon, what would you do if you were me?'

His eyes are the same shade of silver-grey as the clouds behind him, and for a moment I feel as though I am looking through the empty eyeholes of a mask and the sky is speaking to me.

'The only thing there ever is to do. Choose, and accept the consequences.'

And so I do. I choose to go home.

Acknowledgements

To my two generous friends, both of whom read several drafts of this book and gave me unconditional encouragement and support at either end of the project: Kevin Parry, for knowing what this book was about before I knew it myself, and for reminding me when I forgot, and Firdaus Gandavia, for insightful suggestions and encouragement when I was ready to give up.

Also to Peter Abbs, James Burt, Jamie Crawford, Celia Hunt, Chandra Masoliver, Bill Parslow, Dorothy Max Prior, Indra Sinha and anyone else who read one or more drafts, especially Dylan D'Arch for valuable military tips, and India Stoughton for being my biggest fan.

To Maggie Phillips of Ed Victor, without whose encouragement and reminders I would never have finished the first draft, and to Candida Lacey, Vicky Blunden, Linda McQueen, Dawn Sackett and all the other staff at Myriad, for being a joy to work with and for their total commitment to making this book as good as we could make it.

Finally, to David, India and Jared Stoughton for their love, support and tolerance of my abstraction during the years it took to write this novel.

Sources

The events in this book are all based on real historical events and many of the background characters are real, although the main characters and their personal histories are invented. However, I have sometimes borrowed incidents or snippets of dialogue or description from contemporaneous accounts to add veracity.

On p.20 the lines quoted are from the *Bhagavad Gita*, translated by Juan Mascaró with introduction by Simon Brodbeck, Penguin Classics 1962, 2003; translation copyright © Juan Mascaró, 1962; introduction copyright © Simon Brodbeck, 2003.

The text on pp.42–3 is excerpted from the article 'Encounter at Kurusetra' by Ravindra Svarupa Dasa in *Back to Godhead* magazine Vol.19.1, 1984, copyright Bhaktivedanta Book Trust International, www.krishna.com. Used with permission.

On p.82 and 164 the lines quoted are inspired by a poem by Mir Taqi Mir, loosely translated by Indra Sinha.

On pp.110 and 311 the passages of the book Simon reads aloud are taken from *Candles in the Wind* by Maud Diver, Wm Blackwood & Sons, 1909, pp.45–6.

On pp.31, 181 and 311 the story referred to or quoted from is 'The House of Eld', from *Fables* by Robert Louis Stevenson, Association for Scottish Literary Studies Scottish Literature, University of Glasgow, *www.asls.org.uk*.

My research sources are too numerous to mention but the main ones are as follows.

For the Indian Mutiny, *Our Bones are Scattered: The Cawnpore Massacres and the Indian Mutiny of 1857* by Andrew Ward, John Murray, London 1996, tells the story of the entire mutiny in an admirably lucid and accessible way.

The events at Cawnpore as described by Cecily and Arthur Langdon are based on accounts in: *The Story of Cawnpore* by Mowbray Thomson, Richard Bentley, London 1859; *Cawnpore* by G.O. Trevelyan, Macmillan, London 1865; *The Tale of the Great Mutiny* by W.H. Fitchett, Smith, Elder & Co, London 1901; and *Annals of the Indian Rebellion 1857–1858*, compiled by N.A. Chick, Sanders, Cones, Calcutta 1859.

Cecily's voice and some of the anecdotes she relates were inspired by *Tigers, Durbars and Kings: Fanny Eden's Indian Journals 1837–1838*, John Murray, London 1988, and *Traveller's India, An Anthology*, Oxford University Press, Oxford 1979.

Information about the local women's suffrage movement came from newspapers and articles in the Special Collections at Brighton library.

Information about the Indian Army in the First World War came from *A Matter of Honour: An Account of the Indian Army its Officers and Men*, by Phillip Mason, Jonathan Cape, London 1974, which was one of the surprisingly few books I found about the First World War in which the contribution of the two million Indian soldiers is explored or even mentioned. In a surprising number of books about the war, the word 'Indian' does not even appear in the index.

The description of the Indian Hospital at Brighton is based on: *Dr. Brighton's Indian Patients – December 1914 to January 1916*, by Joyce Collins, Brighton Books Publishing, Brighton 1997; and *Blighty Brighton: Photographs and Memories of Brighton in the First World War*, QueenSpark Books, Brighton 1991.

Books useful in researching the Mesopotamian campaign in the First World War were: *Kut: Death of an Army* by Ronald Millar, Secker and Warburg, London 1969; and *The Siege* by Russell Braddon, Jonathan Cape, London 1969.

And finally, my thanks to the Imperial War Museum, the Army Museum, Chelsea, and Colindale Newspaper Library, whose staff were extremely helpful during my research in the days before some of these resources were available online.

And of course Wikipedia has been useful for quickly double-checking dates and facts from more reliable sources.